TAURUS

UNSTABLE GRAVES

BETTY GUENETTE

Renaissance
Diverse Canadian Voices

This is a work of fiction. Any similarity to any events, institutions, or persons, living or dead, is purely coincidental and unintentional. UNSTABLE GRAVES © 2024 by Betty Guenette. All rights reserved. No part of this book may be used or reproduced in any manner whatsoever without written permission except in the case of brief quotations in critical articles and reviews. For more information or to request permission to reproduce content, contact Renaissance Press.

The author expressly prohibits any entity from using this publication for purposes of training artificial intelligence (AI) technologies to generate text, including without limitation technologies capable of generating works in the same style or genre as this publication. The author reserves all rights to license uses of this work for generative AI training and development of machine learning language models.
No part of this book or its cover art was generated by artificial intelligence.

First edition 2024

Cover design by Nathan Fréchette and Joy interior design by Nathan Fréchette. Edited by Molly Desson and Shawn Brixi. Legal deposit, Library and Archives Canada, May 2024.
Paperback ISBN: 9781990086717
Ebook ISBN: 9781990086779

Renaissance Press - pressesrenaissancepress.ca

Renaissance acknowledges that it is hosted on the traditional, unceded land of the Anishinabek, the Kanien'kehá:ka, and the Omàmìwininìwag. We acknowledge the privileges and comforts that colonialism has granted us and vow to use this privilege to disrupt colonialism by lifting up the voices of marginalized humans who continue to suffer the ongoing effects of ongoing colonialism.

Printed in Gatineau by
Imprimerie Gauvin - Depuis 1892
gauvin.ca
We acknowledge the support of the Canada Council for the Arts.

Conseil des Arts du Canada   **Canada Council for the Arts**

To my steadfast **Taurus** friends and family members:

My youngest son, Paul Guenette,
an overly tall, high-school French teacher.

Also, to my social son-in-law, Rick Gibbs,
and our friendly in-law and retired teacher, Lise Bradley.

They all carry the pleasant gene characteristic that maintains
their reliable 'status quo' image, plus showing off their constant
loyal and caring personality so typical of the earthy Taurus sign.

*We don't inherit the **earth** from our ancestors;
we borrow it from our children."*

Indigenous proverb

1

"You're not serious, Mr. Fraser? You want me to check out something in the bush?" Erin Rine, a Registered Nurse in the community, glanced up from the elderly man's leg stump she bandaged and fixed her dark, blue eyes incredulously on him. "Do I look that foolish?"

"Of course, you don't." The old man stared at the nurse, then turned to gesture at the large, grey dog sitting at rigid attention in front of the cabin door. "My dog races to the woods and barks loud enough to wake the dead—now that's a gruesome thought." He turned his head back to gaze at her as if clearing away unpleasant pathways his mind solemnly travelled. He shook his head and waved a hand. "Never mind that. Chum fussed last night during the storm. I let him out once the downpour stopped. Now he keeps coming back, pacing between my chair and the door, nudging me to follow him, but I can only manage to get to the hilltop."

"That's his problem," Erin said, "or yours. The bear population increased this year with the spring hunt cancellation. I am not going into a forested area by myself."

The man shook his balding head in agitation. "I can navigate over to the rise with my walker, but the heavier spring rains made the ground too muddy along the river. I won't be able to work this contraption in the muck. I can watch out for you from the top of the hill."

BETTY GUENETTE

"Right. And what'll you do? Throw your walker down at an angry bear?" Erin shook her head in exasperation. "You'll fall over, and I'll be the appetizer."

The man's beard wiggled in annoyance. "You think I'm that decrepit, Nurse? I've maneuvered this walker for weeks. I need to get around outside and check my pelts in the sheds."

"I'm sorry, no." Erin taped the bandage and stood. "A bear attacked me when I was a young girl." She lifted the bang of red hair off her forehead. "This scar's my souvenir. The family dog saved me from being mauled, maybe killed. I'm terrified of bears."

"Hey, I'm a hunter and a crack shot. I can keep you in the rifle's sight. Besides, you'll have Chum to protect you. He's used to wild animals."

"Oh, no, been there already. Bear versus dog or person—no contest. Try to get a relative to check. Better yet, call 911 for help."

Erin's cell phone rang.

It was Marge Booth, secretary at the Home Care Nursing office, calling. "Erin, you need to boot your tall bod over to visit Mr. Turner next. He accidentally pulled out his catheter last night and his wife's fussing. She says he bled a little, but now he can't pass much urine."

"No problem, Marge. Tell them I'll get there soon." Her nursing job was switched to commute to a different outlying district, north of Sudbury in the Hanmer and Capreol area. Once reliant on the INCO mining company, her Ontario hometown, Sudbury, boasted a population of over 155,000 people and encompassed wide, forested areas amid rivers and more than 330 lakes. The building of the largest smokestack in the world turned the ugly rock landscape, rendered bare from toxic sulphur fumes, into a re-

2

greening program that enabled people to now boast about their attractive city. She sighed, thinking about the full day's workload ahead, then turned on hearing the dog whimpering again behind her.

Seeing her look toward him, the grey dog clawed at the door and whined, then swivelled his head back to check on her. She stared at the shepherd mix gazing at her with big, soulful eyes. He tilted his head as if to ask: *what's taking you so long?* Was she really allowing herself to be guilt-ridden by a dog?

"Nurse, you've got high rubber boots and a raincoat. What if someone's hurt—or dying?"

She pleaded now, realizing her defences were crumbling. "Can't you call family, or don't you have any friends?"

"No, I only have Chum."

Erin looked down at the man's leg. The doctor amputated it below the knee when the bullet wound became badly infected. Was she going to find trivial excuses to get out of this situation? "What if you fall and shoot me like you shot off your leg?"

The man's grey beard worked up and down. "I did *not* shoot myself. My dumb neighbour tripped over his own hunting boots. The bloody idiot forgot to put the rifle's safety back on."

"Can't you call him to check out the woods with Chum?"

"The bugger took off on holidays." Harbouring a mutinous look, the old man pursed his lips. "But I don't want to see the damn fool anyway."

She sighed, slumping her shoulders, finally nodding in agreement. Wouldn't you think, at thirty years old, she'd have developed some smarts? "No promises on going far, but I'll take a quick look." She pulled out a plastic bag and taped it around the man's bandaged leg to keep it dry. Then she helped him shrug into his jacket before donning her raincoat and boots.

He leaned against the counter, plopped a cap on his head, and positioned the walker. Then he checked his rifle and held the weapon out to her. "Safety's on, but still carry the barrel pointed down." At her hesitation and look of distaste, he pointed to the end of the barrel. "That's the shooting end there."

Erin scowled and took the unwieldy weapon. "I think I knew that much," she mumbled. When she opened the door, Chum jumped, barked, and charged through the opening, banging against her legs and almost knocking her down. The dog raced up the hill and stopped for a few minutes to check on their progress before winding his way down the muddy slope.

The trapper judged each placement of the walker's legs, avoiding rocks and holes. She figured he wouldn't want the nurse hauling him up if he toppled over after bragging about his prowess. She paced alongside him with the rifle's sights eyeballing the ground, balancing its awkward weight by holding tight with both hands.

The man glanced sideways at her. "We'll go by those two big maple trees. I'll lean against one and—well, there are lower branches I can grab onto if I run into a problem."

Erin's eyes opened wider. "You mean in case you fall. Now you're thinking this isn't such a good idea?"

"I won't fall. I'm guarding against what could happen—but nothing will."

Arriving at the hilltop, Erin shifted the gun to one hand against her side, reached over and pressed the poles of the man's walker deeper into the mud for a better grip.

4

UNSTABLE GRAVES

"Good thing you didn't get a walker with wheels." She glared at him, taking in a full account of the situation. "Mr. Fraser, how can you balance yourself on one leg, hold onto the walker, and—assuming you need two hands—shoot this gun thing?"

"It's a rifle: a .308," he sputtered. "I'm short. I can lean my elbows on top of the bars."

She handed over the rifle with a sigh and watched while he fiddled with the scope, leaned his arms on the walker, and eyeballed the distance.

He peered up at her through thick, bushy eyebrows. "If I do fall, well, I've often hunted game lying flat on my belly. Don't worry. You'll be safe enough." The man wiggled around and pointed to where Chum paced, waiting and watching. "There's a creek going into the Vermillion River right past that large group of pine trees. Follow him."

Erin turned and looked at the thick evergreen foliage far below. The buds and new leaves showed on maples and birches, and their soggy, woodsy scent wafted toward her on the damp breeze. The dog barked twice and headed toward the dense pine grove.

"With my bad luck I'll find an irate mother bear and trapped cub. Oh!" She yelped and jumped when Chum let out a bloodcurdling howl. "Darn, I may be an Aries sign and not think before plunging into stuff headfirst, but even I know this is dumb."

She looked at the trapper's resolute face and took a deep breath. Chum waited. Erin prayed the elderly man proved vigilant at spotting and shooting bears. She needed to focus on boot placement here. One missed step, and she'd slide into oozing mud. She tramped around mushy areas, treading on rocky spots to keep upright, but kept glancing back to check that the trapper's gun safely covered her. She grabbed at an overhead branch of a fir tree, shivering when droplets of water cascaded into her jacket hood to dribble icily down her back.

The man said an area opened up near the roadway branching off from Highway 69 North. A creek beside the road flowed into the Vermillion River. Chum howled again before he padded to the edge of the pine woods to stop and look back.

"Hang on, dog, I'm following you, whether I want to or not... and I don't." She reached the bottom and noted patches of water through the trees. "Wait for me, Chum."

The dog barked and ran into the pine glade. Erin glanced back up the hill at the trapper, then waved to indicate her passage into the denser bushes. She pulled the jackknife out of her pouch for protection. Her martial arts training would prove useless in this muck, so not going to be kicking any bear. Geez, did she think she'd be able to stab one of those animals? She moaned. If she got that close to a bear, she'd be ripped apart by its massive claws.

She heard the dog scrambling ahead, then water splashing, so she edged forward. "Chum, come here." He whined but stayed out of sight inside the grove of trees.

When she parted the branches to check on the dog, Erin gagged, tasting the bile rising in her throat. She grabbed a branch above her head to maintain her shaky balance. "Oh, God!" The dog had crossed the creek and now dug in the river's soft, wet sand next to what appeared to be a human hand. Another hand beside the first reached from the muddy ground, the fingers tilting toward where she stood frozen.

Erin scrunched her eyes shut, thoughts whirling, envisioning the hands as a matched set. She shook her head to clear the hideous sight. Opening her eyes, she stared once more at the unchanging scene. The earlier rain likely washed the hands clean,

UNSTABLE GRAVES

their whiteness contrasting against the scarlet red nail polish and a ring with a green gemstone. That hand, bent at the wrist, seemed to point in her direction in accusation. Erin's body started to twitch all over, but numbness spun through her head, freezing her thoughts. Chum whined, startling Erin, who swivelled and scanned the bushy area. To the far right, she glimpsed a narrow country road devoid of traffic. The suffocating silence pressed down on her. She shuddered and gulped in the humid air scented with sodden foliage. Erin sighed with relief when she heard Mr. Fraser's strained voice calling out for her and the dog.

She faced the horrific scene again, her eyes fixated on the fingers, not wanting to believe what she saw. The dog's frantic circling around the hands roused her. "Chum," she called, her voice shaking. "Come on... let's go back... she's beyond our help."

With another glance and final sniff at the burial site, the dog whined and padded toward her, then lagged behind, grumbling in his throat while she scrambled back up the hill.

The elderly man silently watched her climb warily up the precarious hill. He lowered his rifle, grasping the walker with one hand while he straightened from his forward-bent position. Both his voice and beard quivered. "What... what did you find, Nurse?"

She stuttered. "There's likely a body... well, I only glimpsed hands... and one partial arm. She's been buried in the mud... near the roadway. Your dog was trying to dig her out." Erin flexed her shoulders, gingerly took hold of the rifle, and helped him reposition the walker. "We need to get you inside where it's warm and notify the police."

She tramped alongside him as he shuffled and hopped his way down, aiming each thrust of the walker with precision. Chum stalked behind, but kept halting to look back and let a deep rumble out of his throat.

The trapper bumped through the doorway, then turned and folded his body into the worn lounge chair. His hand trembled when he patted the dog's head. "Must have happened last night. You said '*she.*' You think it's the body of a woman buried there, likely killed?"

"Looks feminine, from the hands sticking out of the mud." She shivered again and placed the gun on the floor, tight against the wall. "Can I make hot tea or coffee for you?"

"No, thanks." He picked up the phone to dial 911. "I'd like a slug of whiskey, but I better wait for the police. Don't want them thinking I'm an old drunk having hallucinations."

Her cell phone rang. Marge again. "Erin, Mrs. Turner called back. She says her husband's belly is swelling. She sounds more upset."

"I'm going right now, but I'll need to return here, Marge. There's a problem."

"Oh well, as long as you found your patient alive, this time."

Erin gave no response to this.

Marge gasped. "I'm kidding. Erin, what happened?"

"My patient's alive and well, Marge. I'll call you back later." She clicked off her phone. "Mr. Fraser, are you okay to stay by yourself for a while? You can inform the police about finding the body till I get back from my other sick patient. I shouldn't be long. I'll bring Chum some doggie treats out of my car when I return. He deserves it."

"Sure, Nurse. Chum can lead them to the grave. Be easier for them to take the body out by the far roadway, though." He nodded. "Probably how she got there. Impossible to drive in from this side, and I would have heard a car. I wonder... who is she?"

On her drive out, Erin hoped when she returned that she'd meet a different inspector in charge of this investigation. Last month, the lead detective, whom she briefly dated after, criticized her for leaving a murder scene. Initially, she considered that death a natural one, but the following deaths in the case involved her landing in a dangerous position. No question about this being a murder case. That poor woman—or young girl? She shuddered, shook her head, and squared her shoulders when she arrived at her next patient's house. This time, she was not involved in a murder. The discovery of the body belonged to a dog. Didn't that sound like a brilliant excuse?

Mrs. Turner watched at the window. She pulled open the door to hurry the nurse into the bedroom, only giving Erin time to shed her wet coat and muddy boots.

Mr. Turner tossed around in bed, moaning. "Oh, I can't pee at all, Nurse."

While she set up her supplies, Mrs. Turner chattered non-stop about the confusion after her husband's bladder tube was pulled out.

Erin checked him over, lightly tapping her fingers over the swollen, taut abdomen. "Did you bleed a lot when the catheter came out, Mr. Turner?"

"Only a little. I had a vicious nightmare and jumped right out of the bed. Oh, my belly hurts. The tube caught on the rail." He

UNSTABLE GRAVES

rolled onto his back again. "The pain woke me up fast. The catheter got yanked out with the bulb still inflated."

Erin poured the cleaning solution into her tray and donned sterile gloves. She talked to the man while performing the procedure. "If there are blood clots blocking the passageway, I may not be able to reinsert one." She introduced a sterile catheter into the man's penis but met resistance further up the canal. Then she used a syringe to flush saline and freed numerous clots. She still couldn't advance the tube into the bladder. The man twitched and bit down on his lip, trying to remain stoic during the procedure.

"I have a smaller catheter with a curved tip that should work." She restarted, twisted and wiggled the catheter up until she got past the obstruction. "Usually, the prostate causes the problem, but yours was removed. Probably swelling or more clots in the passage." She threaded the catheter further in until reddish urine mixed with blood clots flowed out.

"Good news, Mr. Turner, the tube's back in. You'll need a doctor's appointment to get checked over." The canister half-filled before settling down to a steady trickle. She flushed copious amounts of saline through the tube until the returns cleared. "You're back in business."

"I'm a hundred percent better already. Thanks, Nurse." He lay quiet. "I felt so much pressure in my gut that I expected my bladder to burst right through my belly."

"Nurse Erin, right?" Mrs. Turner asked while Erin packed up her equipment. "I've made tea to wind down. My, my, what a production. Have a cup with us before you go?"

Erin washed her hands, nodded, and sat beside her patient's bed. She accepted the hot, black brew, blew on it, and sipped appreciatively. They didn't know how much she needed the reviving drink after her earlier discovery. She could spare a few minutes, but a niggling chill playing snakes and ladders along her spine caused her to tremble.

"You're cold, Nurse. Would you like more hot tea?"

"No, thank you. I must be going." Erin took a last swallow before she stood and checked her patient again. "The waterworks are functioning, Mr. Turner. Now, do take care and make sure you see your doctor soon. I'll send in a formal report."

Arriving back at Mr. Fraser's, Erin groaned on seeing the tall, attractive man standing outside the cabin, looking like he was waiting for someone. She took a deep breath, got out of her car and strode over. "Inspector Luke Landry, I presume?" she quipped in a light voice.

"Erin Rine, I feared the culprit must be you again." His voice sounded exasperated. "When the trapper said his caregiver was a tall, redheaded nurse new to the Hanmer and Capreol district, I got a flash of *déja vu*. You have a deplorable habit of finding bodies and leaving the crime scenes."

"I needed to visit a sick client." She inhaled. "He couldn't wait much longer."

"The old nursing excuse again. What seemed so important this time, Miss Rine?"

Erin fumed and gave an impudent response. "My patient suffered with a swollen bladder and was unable to urinate. After many tries, I managed to twist a catheter up his blocked penis and drained out the clotted blood and urine." She contained her smirk when he twitched, likely controlling a shudder.

"You needn't use such graphic details," Luke said.

"You asked me what was 'so important' for me to do."

"Well, I'm sorry I asked that leading type of question."

"I'm not under your investigators' microscopes this time, Inspector Landry. I wouldn't know the dead woman."

"How are you sure the buried person's a woman?" He shot the question at her.

"There you go again, suspecting everyone." Erin's temper flared anew. She took a moment to breathe and counted to ten before looking back at him to answer. "I'm assuming it's a woman's body because of the slender hands, red nail polish and flashy, green stone ring."

He nodded. "Well, now that you're back, try and settle down the trapper. I'm not getting much information. He's fussing since he insisted that you check out the woods."

"I hope he feels guilty. I tried to ignore his pestering, but he wouldn't let up." She walked toward the cabin. "The dog's behaviour forced the issue. I thought someone was hurt."

"Someone was—hurt." The Inspector followed her to the cabin. "That dog helped until we tried to excavate the body from her grave. He kept digging with us. One of my officers, Adam Brady, brought him back here to the cottage."

"I remember Adam from your unit," she said, relaxing with this easier conversation. "He's that tall boy who trains a German shepherd. He'd be great on your canine force."

"I can manage my own unit, thank you, Miss Rine. Adam has lots to learn before he can specialize." He stopped. "As you tend to quote Astrology, Adam's a Taurus like my lawyer friend, Mark Richards. My Aquarian sign seems to agree with them."

"Then you should have a good month since May belongs mainly to the Taurus sign." She bit back a retort that her fire sign would soon ignite him. There was no sense in revisiting their prior sexual attraction. She resisted letting that temptation go too far, by luck more than planning. Besides, he acted formal and aloof now, so why think of the past? Miss Rine, indeed. "Taurus is an

UNSTABLE GRAVES

earth sign, a very nice personality, and pleasantly comfortable," she added. "I must check on the man's bandages in case they loosened with all his hopping around."

"Have walker, will travel. He's some bushwhacker." He followed her into the cottage and spoke to the trapper. "Do you have a license for your gun, Mr. Fraser?"

"Of course, Inspector, for two rifles and two shotguns. I run a legitimate business here, acting as a guide for hunters and fishermen coming north. I trap as well." The man looked down at his leg stump. "I lost part of my left leg from the bullet, and when I'm fitted with my prosthesis, I'll be restricted. But I can drive my truck and quad through the bush using the right foot."

"It's been off-season, though," Luke said. "When your shooting accident occurred, were you both out hunting with rifles?"

"We weren't really hunting." The trapper took a deep breath. "The idiot fellow said he was fed up with winter. He wanted to go rustle up rabbits or nuisance crows. Beaver is always fair game along the river. They have a bad habit of damming and blocking the streams. After all this messy business, he took off for a couple of weeks to sunny Arizona. Good riddance!"

Erin rechecked the intact bandage and stroked the anxious dog's head, feeding him some of the promised treats she brought back. "He swore to shoot a bear if it charged me."

"I'd need not kill the animal. A warning shot's usually enough." The trapper cringed on seeing Erin's eyes reproving him. "Well, bears are unpredictable, and they try to avoid human contact. There are more of them foraging around after their long hibernation. I'm cautious."

"We sighted bear markings, but nothing moving around," Luke said. "You're quite isolated here. Does the Vermillion River turn at the end, closer to the road?" At the trapper's nod, he continued. "You didn't hear any cars last night?"

"In that storm? No way to drive down my mucky slope or through the marsh below. The frequent rains make the ground treacherous. No problem by the highway, though."

"Isn't there a retirement home and some townhouses right across the river?" Luke asked.

The trapper glanced up. "You know the area, inspector?"

"I've visited a friend's grandmother who lives in Rivercrest Manor. You see flashes of the water from your place here, but can they see the water from their side?"

"No way, if you're thinking someone could see anything last night." The trapper shook his head. "From the top of my hill, I can only see their odd trail and the hill that descends to the river. I can't see the lower shoreline through the trees. The river forks the other way, and it's quite marshy near the road." He shrugged. "Chum started fussing when the night got darker and the rain started. Nobody would have been around, except the murderer."

"I'm scheduled to see a patient in the apartment building beside that Manor." Erin checked her watch. "I'd like to go unless you have other questions, Inspector?"

"None at present, but I know where to find you, Miss Rine."

"Um, Inspector?" She pulled at her hair, a nervous reaction from childhood. "My name won't hit the papers, right? My boss hates negative publicity."

"I can understand your clients' fear if their visiting nurse keeps finding people dead and murdered on her rounds." He gave her a grim smile. "I'm sure we can keep your involvement quiet, for now."

She pursed her lips, glaring at him. "I have no such involvement this time, Inspector. Lay the blame on the dog and file me as a Good Samaritan."

Erin called on the elderly woman who lived in an apartment next door to Rivercrest Manor. Before going in, she looked around, noting dense foliage at the side while the darkness seemed to extend into the rear areas. The forest scenery masked the trails. Mr. Fraser said the river looped around the opposite side of the road and flowed into many small lakes.

"I told my daughter that I would not move next door." Her patient, Mrs. Billings, nattered away her bitter thoughts. "She thinks I need someone to look after me because I fell. Everyone falls, but if you're elderly and fall, they think you should be placed."

"Family members tend to worry. Your leg looks better, Mrs. Billings. The X-rays showed a hairline fracture, but you punctured a deep hole through the skin. The wound's healing." Erin stood up after changing the dressing. "Do you use the walker, or are you on crutches now?"

"Sometimes use the crutches, a bit hard on the armpits. Jeepers, I also have two canes. I use them all, depending on my strength or mood. If I'm tired, I use the walker." She gazed out the large back window. "In a couple of weeks, I'll be able to walk the short trails back there. Oh, that nice elderly man from the Manor's stocking up the bird feeder."

Erin donned her jacket. "I'll be back in a few days to recheck the wound."

UNSTABLE GRAVES

"Um, what did you say?" Mrs. Billings stretched her neck to see better out the window. "Oh, dear, there's a bear heading to the feeder." Her voice rose on a shrill note. "That man's still out there. He doesn't see the bear coming up behind him."

"What?" Erin darted to the window, looked, then turned and tore out of the apartment. She flew down the stairs to race out the front door. Pulling her keys out of her pouch, she used the remote to unlock the car door and reached in to grab the can of bear spray. When she ran toward the Manor's driveway, a man stepped out of his car at the gate. She veered toward him, grabbed his arm and pulled him along, panting as she explained the elderly man's plight.

Erin glanced sideways at the man with her. "Mark, I didn't recognize you. I wish your policeman friend, Inspector Landry, was with you. He'd have a gun." At the trail's entrance, they watched the older man strolling back while the bear clawed and gobbled the seeds out of the feeder. They stopped and gulped in air, waiting for him to come near and walk a safe distance from the wild animal. "Don't yell, or we'll give him a heart attack."

Mark recognized the elderly man from the Manor, held out his hand in greeting, and then took his arm. "Hello, Mr. Creswell, look behind you."

The man turned, gasped, and swayed. Erin and Mark each held an arm and ferried him back inside the Manor. He was shaking when they sat him down. "I can't believe I was that close to a bear. Do you think it would have attacked me?"

"That's possible. Depends on its hunger level," Mark replied. "We'll need to talk to the supervisor. She can warn the other residents."

Erin told them that Mrs. Billings, next door, spotted his predicament from her window.

"I've seen her outside, and then I heard she fell while walking the trail. She hasn't been active lately." The elderly man rubbed his hand across his face. "I'll thank her when I'm not so upset."

Mark grinned when they walked out. "What did you plan to do, Erin, when we reached the man and the bear?"

"What? Plan? Oh, wow—I don't know, Mark. I couldn't leave him unprotected. I did grab the can of bear spray." She shook her head. "I ran toward a bear, me? I didn't even take out my jackknife." She frowned at her folly and waved goodbye to Mark, who started to unload a few bags of groceries. She climbed the stairs back to her patient's apartment and picked up her nursing bag, staying a few minutes to explain that Mr. Creswell only seemed shaken.

"Guess they'll take away the bird feeders now till wintertime," the woman said. "I suppose, at our age, we should know better."

When Erin returned, Mark stood by the car waiting for her. "I've told my grandmother of your exploits. Do you have time to meet her? She gets lonely."

Erin checked her wristwatch and nodded. "Only for a short while."

Mark led her to the elevator. "Gran is on the third floor. I like her living here since they have 24-hour coverage. The Manor's not an active care facility, so they keep their independence."

Mark introduced her after they entered the apartment. "Erin Rine, meet my only blood relative in Canada. This is my grandmother, Gladys Richards."

"I suffer from arthritis, so I will remain seated." The tallish, white-haired woman rocked in her chair. "Come and sit near me, please. You're the nurse that interested Luke last month."

Erin laughed. "Mrs. Richards, the fact that he assumed I murdered my patient qualified me as an interest. I believe Luke would suspect his own mother."

Mark grimaced. "How true. You haven't seen him lately?"

"Well—uh, I did meet him again this morning. It's not a secret. I just prefer not being mentioned in connection with police business, especially murder." She glanced at Mark and his grandmother. "My client's dog spotted a mostly buried body across the river. I don't really know anything more about it. Luke did show up, acting his usual officious self."

"That news will soon leak. It must be a murder. And so close to my place." Gladys tapped a finger against her mouth. "I wonder if it's someone from around here."

"Well, I don't know anything else about her."

Mark tensed, his lawyer instincts activating. "How do you know it was a woman?"

Erin sighed at her slip. "I don't really know. I just guessed it after seeing the slender hands."

Gladys nodded. "I'm sure she's right, Mark." She glanced from Mark back to Erin. "So, you met Luke again today. The lad has a good heart, but he doesn't let any emotion show. Repressed upbringing, you know. His parents were too strict, and they worried about how everyone viewed them. Keeping up a stoic front was their way."

Mark nodded in agreement. "I visited their house a few times during our law school years in Ottawa. It was like spending time in the frozen food section at the supermarket."

"Mark brings Luke to visit me sometimes. I get lonesome since my son and his wife, Mark's parents, retired to Florida." Mrs.

Richards sighed. "Luke doesn't bend, poor boy. I think of him hovering at a bright window, like those forlorn moths."

Erin smiled. "You sound prophetic, like my elderly neighbour, Celine Lauzon. Do you believe in spiritualism or ESP?"

"I like to keep an open mind. Many things in life we can't explain. My late husband was a minister and a good man, not into accepting what he considered abnormal attitudes. I believe in good and evil; God and the devil; the past, present, and future; and all their overlapping concepts." She looked at Mark. "The younger generation have trouble believing in what they can't see, hear, or touch unless they're spaced out on drugs. I believe time warps exist. Some people are more receptive to them than others."

"I'd love to introduce Celine to you. She reads horoscopes and is interested in zodiac signs but isn't fanatic about it. She keeps quiet about what she perceives, sometimes mutters ambiguous thoughts." Erin laughed. "Most of the time, her words don't make sense, even to her."

"I would like to meet the lady. She sounds uniquely intriguing. Our residence has hired a new woman manager who promises more congenial activities. She wants to have gatherings to promote hobbies for stimulation and forging new interests." She smiled. "We can play cards together, though not on Sunday, my late husband would say. He considered it gambling."

As Erin left, she mentioned she'd try to drop by again on her rounds.

"That would be a treat to have more visitors. Please call me Gladys." Her eyes twinkled. "And you can keep me informed about Luke and this interesting investigation."

5

With all the extra activity, Erin skipped lunch. She munched on a nutty nutrition bar and drank a bottled water while driving between her patients' visits. Before heading back to town, she checked the folded, paper map in her car. Some lines wove past Mr. Fraser's, though no streets were marked anywhere out that way. They must have been logging roads or driveways to farther cottages around both towns, Hanmer and Capreol. The map showed numerous small lakes while the river meandered circuitously. She'd have to ask the trapper about the area. "Am I trying to interfere in this murder? No, I'm only curious," she muttered, believing her words.

Erin lived with her bachelor brother, Bill, in their small family home that he purchased after their parents' deaths from strokes a few months apart. Erin was a late, menopausal surprise, and Bill was ten years older. Her other siblings, another brother and two sisters, were all aged five years apart and were older than Bill but lived elsewhere. This living arrangement with Bill was temporary until she decided where to go next.

She worked odd part-time jobs after graduation, then nursed in England for a few years, with full-time posts being too scarce in Canada. She returned home when the job market improved. Bill, a loner by nature, managed and worked steady afternoons at a computer centre. They didn't see each other often. He called her a mega jinx, swearing she was a dangerous person and that she harboured disruptive forces that often erupted into catastrophes.

She told him that most of her troubles were minor except the recent murders.

"Juno, Rhea," she called. The dogs hurried out to greet her. "Bill must have taken you jogging. You're both too quiet." Juno was a friendly chocolate lab, whose size illustrated the lab's love of food. The little cavalier spaniel, Rhea, a stubborn darling, tipped her head sideways, looking up at her.

"Some guard dogs you two are." She scratched them behind their ears, laughing when they rolled over, showing their bellies for more rubbing. She handed them each a doggie biscuit before showering and changing into sweats.

As she finished her heated leftover stir-fry and toasted bagel, the phone rang.

"Erin, this is Celine, *ici*. I have lots of the worry about you. Is the tea on?"

"The water's boiling already." Erin smiled on hearing her elderly neighbour's voice, littered with her French nuances. "Can you walk over with your leg as is?"

"With the cast off, I can fly. I am the light *personne. Mais,* I will carry a cane," Celine laughed. "I am coming over to *visite.*"

When she arrived, the elderly woman sat down and wagged the light cane at Erin. "I suffered the bad vibes about you *aujourd'hui*. Did you get into the *problèmes encore*?"

Erin poured their tea and sat down with a resigned expression. "You didn't peer into your crystal ball to see what trouble I landed in this time?"

"Do not talk silly. I have no ball. You look *très belle, Chèrie."* She frowned. "Lately, you have the look bleak. I think you met an attractive man, *non*?"

UNSTABLE GRAVES

"Really? Now you've thrown me off." Erin took a sip of tea and pursed her lips. "Anyway, remember how I changed locations to avoid memories of the murders last month? Well, I managed to land in another mess. Today, I found a partially buried body."

"Body? It should all be buried. Oh, *pardon*, you do not mean in the graveyard."

"No, it was near my patient's property. His dog fussed all night, and the man begged me to check the woods. I found two hands sticking out of the mud."

"*C'est ca*! You met Luke again." At Erin's dismayed look, Celine smiled. "That is why you shine, or glow, I think is the word, *correct*? Does he suspect you for this murder, *encore*?"

"No, he does not. He acted his most proper, officious self."

"Oh, the cold shoulder. He gives you that. *Méchant* Luke."

"About the body, Celine. Well, there were only two hands showing, but they looked eerie: like they were rising out of the ground, one pointing at me." She shuddered. "They appeared to be a woman's hands, with red nail polish. One finger wore a ring, looked like an emerald stone."

"Emerald, *oui*. The green gem is the precious birthstone for this month of May." The older woman closed her eyes. "The emerald stands for youth, fertility, and good luck."

Erin grimaced. "I don't know about the first two points, but I think she ran out of the third point: luck. All I know is that she didn't bury herself in that muck."

"*Probablement* a crime of the *amour*. *Mais*, you do know something else. The emerald ring may be a birthstone for May, and in astrology, *possible* the earth sign of Taurus, the strong bull. Did the hands look young to you?"

BETTY GUENETTE

Erin squinted at the thought. "Young? Yes, I suppose, but not the hands of a child. That would be sad." Erin tried to shrug away the unpleasant memory. "Well, enough of that gruesome topic. Tell me how your physiotherapy's going. You look smaller now with the cast off."

"The ankle, it is stiff. The bad physio girl bent the leg all over the places. *Mais,* I will soon forecast the weather with the aches and pains."

"I'll tell Bill. He's already leery about your fortune-telling expertise."

"William, he will regret *encore* being your brother with more bodies popping up."

"Geez, popping up? And I only found one body this time."

"So far. *Pauvre* William. He refuses to dwell on anything *extraordinaire.* The *personnes* today are *très* busy to sit and think. It is not *magie* to use the brain cells."

Erin laughed. "I won't repeat that to Bill. He's a lost cause regarding your insight or anything he sees as weird."

"Weird? *Merci* for that *comment.*" Celine twitched, screwed up her face, shut her eyes and chanted in a deeper, chilling voice.

> *"Emeralds abound*
> *Throughout the play,*
> *So, watch those actors*
> *In the fray."*

"Oh, Celine. I never understand your words until it's too late."

"C'est bien. Moi aussi, je ne comprends pas."

After Celine went home, Erin needed exercise even if the dogs didn't. They loved playing and going on excursions. Say the word "walk" or pick up the leashes, and they bounced around. Hearing the snap of the metal clips, the dogs jumped up, raring to go.

She liked having free evenings at the house while Bill managed the afternoon shift. But she knew she was becoming too comfortable and should get her own place. After straining his nerves with her bad vibes circling his house, Bill brought a discarded horseshoe from the racetrack and hung the iron token over his entry door, the open end facing upwards to catch the lucky flakes cascading down.

"I'll make the darn thing fall on your head," Erin told him after saying that some people hung the shoe downwards to let the luck fall onto them.

"No way. Have to catch the blessings first. Our Irish mother and English father agreed this was correct. I'm hoping this charm will keep our neighbourhood witch away." He scowled and muttered, "Maybe I should hang up a cross."

She didn't give credence to Bill's comments about her being a harbinger of bad luck. She only experienced accidents like getting locked in castles or stuck in elevators until the murders last month. Bill always exaggerated tales about her ominous character.

Erin pulled out of her memories to look at the two dogs. "Hey girls, a short walk, though you're no protection." Meandering along her usual route, she glanced at Sudbury's tall smokestack in the distance, noting the wind direction sending the pollution away from the city.

On her brisk pace home, she jerked the dogs to the far edge of the sidewalk when a truck skidded to the side of the road ahead of them. Juno's growl turned to welcome barks when a big German shepherd vaulted out of the truck, and a man unfolded his lean, lengthy frame out its door. Both her dogs tugged against the chains and barked in their hectic concerto, twirling around and around.

"Hi, Erin. I'm Adam Brady, from the police force. Remember me—the tall one? I recognized the dogs first, then spotted you jogging along with them." His large dog sat at attention and regarded her two silently while they sniffed around him and rumbled noises in their throats. "Major will sit quietly and not upset them."

"You're out of uniform, so I couldn't place you right away. I wasn't aware that you knew the dogs. You must have visited our place when the officers interviewed my brother last month." She kept pulling the leashes tighter. "The two belong to him and are totally untrained, but they're pushovers for a kind word or treat. Are you involved in the new murder investigation, or shouldn't I ask?"

"I wound up a burglary case today. I'm sure Inspector Landry will let me help with the investigation now that I'm done. Good boy, Major." He patted his quiet dog.

Rhea, small but bossy, kept sniffing around the new dog. Juno became bored and sat at attention along with the German

UNSTABLE GRAVES

shepherd. Major kept a steady eye on the two dogs assessing him. Erin pulled harder on the leashes, but the smaller dog tangled them up with all her squirming. The two larger dogs watched her antics with tolerant expressions.

Adam bent down and separated the leashes. "I like Major to interact with other dogs. If we see you again, I'll stop by and let them get reacquainted—if you don't mind?"

"We'd love to see you anytime, Adam. Your office investigated my life thoroughly last month. I can bug you with questions about this murder without remorse." She laughed. "You must have a birthday soon. Luke said you're a Taurus."

"I'm nearer the end of the month, on the twentieth.

"I'll ask my neighbour to read your characteristics—she's too erratic to tell fortunes. You remember she's sort of psychic?"

"Well, most of us laugh at that ESP nonsense." Adam shrugged his shoulders. "I'll be nice, though, and not embarrass the woman."

"I'm sure you would be polite. Celine can tell you traits about your sun sign. People born under Taurus are good workers, stubborn, and don't like change, but that's the extent of my knowledge. Most people like having fortune tellers predict their future."

"Not if it's bad scenes. That scares people," Adam said. "And I don't believe in woo-woo stuff and predictions."

"She helped me figure out that last case. Anyway, her wisdom pointed me in the right direction, finally. It's all in fun, usually." She paused and said, "Well, I must be going." Erin tapped his arm, strode a few paces, then called back over her shoulder. "Make sure you check in and bring Major."

Poor Adam. She wondered why he looked so sad. He gazed at her like someone had stolen his last piece of candy. Major gave a short bark and pawed against his master's leg. Adam started, stared down at his dog and smoothed a hand through his hair. "Okay, Major, time for us to go home too."

7

Luke studied the homicide notes and Coroner's reports. The woman was youngish with marked bruising around the neck, indicating strangulation with a thin rope. The notes read, "Clothing intact: worn jean jacket, hipster cut-off jeans, short tank top, underwear undisturbed. Laced boots. No purse or extra items in pockets."

He thought the tattoos would help. One was a red and blue hummingbird hovering over greenery above the right ankle. The other showed a trickle of green ivy across her backside below the waistline. He pictured the hipster jeans would have exposed the peak of the ivy tattoo.

Luke looked up as his computer and data processing officer came in. "No ID on the victim yet, Ralph?"

"Nothing." The officer, Ralph Tyson, frowned, looking down at his papers. "Good teeth, but no dental files found. We did broadcast bits of info to check out recent missing persons. But we only got some crank calls that checked nil."

Beth Janus, an older female officer, sauntered in with a cheeky grin. "Hi, Boss. We have a full dossier on your nurse, Erin Rine, from last month—saves a lot of checking there."

He ignored the jibe. He needed to after realizing the sexual draw Erin always evoked in his dampened senses. He managed to shelve the attraction, but the flames were only banked. "Tell me what info you got on Mr. Fraser."

Beth smirked. "He's exactly what he says. Henry Fraser:

seventy years old, always worked the bush and trapping lines, a miner for many years, but retired early at fifty-five." She glanced at her clipboard notes. "He worked enough years underground and preferred the outdoor life. Not hard up for cash: augments his pension as a guide and trapper. Never married, so no family, but always keeps a dog. Good health up to the shooting accident. The docs amputated the lower-left leg when a severe infection set in."

"This shooting incident, were there no discrepancies or further questions?"

"The man who shot him, James Mortimer, is away on holidays, but the police report is conclusive. They both agreed Mortimer tripped, and his gun went off. Apparently, he'd taken the safety off to shoot at movement in the bushes. Out of hunting season, he assumed it was a bear." Beth chewed on her pencil as she checked her notes. "Mr. Fraser was angry but didn't want to press charges. Laughed bitterly and said that suing a client or a friend wouldn't look good for his hunting business. Mortimer got a slap on the wrist and fined for carelessness with a firearm."

"The dumping ground they used is too secluded for witnesses if the murderer buried her in the mud via the other side of the road as the trapper suspects. We need to identify her and work from that end by checking out her family and friends."

A ping sounded in the next room. "There's my fax." Ralph left to return shortly. "Now, this sounds promising. Central got a query from two young women who live together. They're worried because their roommate, a third one, hasn't come home. Occasionally, she'll stay out one night, but never for this long. When they heard the bulletin about the woman's body, they got scared. This Jewel Martin woman fits the description for age, sex, and body size." He handed the paper to Luke. "Look at the address."

Luke whistled. "That's close to the Manor, across the river from the trapper's place. Maybe we'll get a break for a change." He drummed his fingers on the desk. "I'll stop at the morgue to see if the body's ready for viewing and leave my truck there. Beth, follow in the squad car, pick me up, and we'll drive out to interview them. We may require an ID confirmation, and the two roommates will be more comfortable with an older woman present."

Beth placed both hands on her slim hips. "Older woman, you say? You'd better not be hinting that I'm matronly, Boss."

Luke, wise enough to just smile, didn't entangle himself by attempting a response.

Carrying her nurse's kit, Erin strolled into a new apartment block on her client list. It was a chic-looking place, though not offensively opulent. When she entered the foyer and rang the bell for Ellen Demille, the tenant buzzed her in. With this being a first visit, Erin sat down and proceeded to fill out the medical history forms.

Erin questioned the woman. "I only know about your breast surgery resulting from an infected ring piercing. I'm to do packing around the nipple area. Can you tell me anything else?"

"I can tell you loads about my side issues, but I don't think you'd want to hear most of it." The attractive brunette's pencilled eyebrows rose as she sat in the chair and unbuttoned her blouse. "I am worried about the implants, though."

"What did the doctor say? I'm sure they discussed removing them due to the infection." Erin cringed. "My goodness, the pierced spot went right through the nipple?"

"Sure did. Almost lost my strategic point, and that would've been a huge disaster. I took off the dressing for you but not the packing. I didn't want to get germs in that blasted hole." She drawled her words, watching Erin's reaction. "I kept two hoops on both nipples, but the doctors removed the infected ones. Those openings were bright red and swelled up too much for me to attempt pulling them out. I took out the ones on the left that looked fine in case this breast disease was catching." She tilted her head, smiling. "I needed the extra attraction for my career,

UNSTABLE GRAVES

you know."

Erin looked at her and smiled back, not surprised by the blatant admission but by the woman's apparent comfort in telling these facts to a stranger. "Guess it's not my place to question why, but are you a stripper?"

"No, I'm too lazy for all that sweaty exercise and climbing up and around some damn slippery pole, likely fall off the damn thing. I prefer to lay on my back, gaze at ceilings, and enjoy myself. I work as a fashionable evening date for an exclusive escort service, and I'm also a selective daytime hooker on my own time. You can call me by my working name, Eliza."

Erin shook her head. "The life of a prostitute is dangerous, and women are too vulnerable. You must have heard about the young female killed by the shore of the Vermillion River. They're looking for anyone reported missing or a relative to identify the body."

"Well, I'm not out on the streets, or at least I'm not a lady of the night. I'm refined, like in the movie *Pretty Woman.* I like rich, upper-class men. They pay extremely well."

"You enhanced the breasts for the job and have all these piercings. No tattoos?"

"No, I think that's cheesy and permanent. The piercing is painful enough. I like pleasurable pursuits. I'm cultured, you know, and I have a university degree. I kept the belly ring and earlobes, of course, and the nose and tongue." She tapped the tiny diamond stud on the side of her nose and stuck out her tongue. "This is my marble."

Erin sighed. "I hate giving unwelcomed advice or sermons, but the nose and tongue are in major germ areas and are a huge risk for more infections with those extra openings."

The woman shrugged. "Win some, lose some. Course, I almost

lost the nipple."

Erin withdrew the soiled packing and stared at the dual openings. "It's healing, but you will have a faint puckering, though it shouldn't affect the overall appearance."

Erin chuckled and cleaned the area. "When I worked in England, one of our plastic surgeons misplaced a lady's nipple during her breast reduction surgery. It was such a scramble to find that tiny point. The nipple tissue got stuck on the inside of a sheet, and there was some tense fumbling for minutes before they found it. They reattached it in a hurry."

Eliza coughed, laughed, then grimaced. "What a court case that would have been: an exposé and pictures aired showing a holey breast."

Erin's smile reached her eyes, showing her liking for the pleasant, candid woman. "You'll be back in business soon. At least your work's done mostly in the dark."

"Don't kid yourself. Think of lunchtime quickies and pre-dinner appetizers. And plenty of men like to see what they're paying for."

Erin laughed and probed with the packing and dressing. "At least you work for a living and are in demand."

The woman grinned. "One of my clients must have got a little too amorous with the nipple ring. And it was such a lovely heart-shaped one."

Erin enjoyed talking with the brazen woman; but she didn't comment on that remark. What could she say? The woman wanted to shock her, but she'd seen plenty in her nursing days.

"Okay, Eliza, all done. I'll check back on you in a few days." Erin got up to leave, then stopped, unable to resist making a mischievous retort. "You do know between us 'ladies,' we represent the two oldest professions in the world."

UNSTABLE GRAVES

Eliza countered, tongue-in-cheek, "They do say, in the olden days, our trades often crossed paths and represented the lowest of all vocations."

Erin grinned, gave Eliza a thumbs up, and left.

The two young women who called the police station about their roommate were Kelly Santon and Melanie Frampton. Kelly was short and thin, a dark blonde with highlights, and a bouffant hairstyle. The small, partly Asian woman, Melanie, sported long, straight black hair clamped in back by an ornamental brooch. She chewed her fingernails.

Luke introduced himself and Beth to the young women. "We're here to investigate the call about your missing roommate and need to ask some pertinent questions." He sat at the kitchen table and motioned Beth and the others to sit in the other chairs. "Now, first: would Jewel have gone to stay with relatives?"

"No. She has nobody except a lowlife cousin who doesn't work and mooches money," Kelly said. "Her elderly aunt died and left Jewel a small annuity. She leased one of those bug cars. It's in the parking lot. I checked." The woman rubbed her eyes with a tissue. "She hasn't stayed away this long before. We heard that bulletin about the murdered woman."

"Where does Jewel work?"

"During the day, she's part-time at a downtown call center. On Saturday evenings, she works as a teller at the harness racetrack."

Beth took notes while observing the two women.

"You said she never stayed away such a long time before?" Luke confirmed.

"Never. Often one night, but not two. She should have called us by now or been back."

UNSTABLE GRAVES

"Did Jewel have scars or marks that could help identify her?"

"No scars, but she has two tattoos." Kelly's voice trembled. "One of a tiny bird on her leg, and she has another of ivy across her lower back."

Luke sighed and spoke quietly. "In case this woman is Jewel, do you have a picture?"

Kelly jumped up, her hands scrambling through a drawer to find pictures of their friend.

"I may keep these for a while." He checked the photos. "I'm very sorry. You should prepare yourselves for bad news. With the tattoos, the body does seem to be that of your roommate. I'll need a family member to check the body for identification."

"Oh, no!" Kelly choked out and wailed. "She's been my best friend forever." She took a few deep breaths. "How did she die?"

Luke hesitated and spoke softly. "It looks like she was strangled." Both flinched, and Melanie's hand went to her throat. Luke didn't want to mention the muddy burial yet. "Where does the cousin live? We need to contact him."

"Lester the loser? No fixed place, and he doesn't hang around. We'll have to do it."

Melanie gasped. "I can't... do that... Kelly." She started to shake and rock back and forth in her chair. "I only moved here a couple of months ago," she said, looking at Beth. The frightened brunette clasped her hands around her knees. "I'm attending University on a scholarship program to obtain my nursing degree."

Beth pulled her chair closer to Melanie and wrapped an arm around the quivering woman.

Luke looked at Kelly. "Have you lived out here a long time?"

"Jewel and I lived here for a couple of years, taking a few courses and working part-time. We were able to sublet fairly cheaply to Melanie. I work at the liquor store."

"You don't know how to get hold of this cousin, Lester?"

"Lester Lisson. No way would he murder her. He always showed up for money, and she was pretty lenient with him. She always gave him some cash. The trust fund from her relative was mainly to help with her education. She took bird courses to qualify. She's not real smart, always easily fooled by people, especially men."

"Any romantic leads?" Beth asked.

"Well, she dated a few boyfriends, but no one special."

"But Kelly... lately, she got serious about someone. She got that emerald looking ring, an early present for her birthday." Melanie twitched and stuttered. "She was proud of it. It's the birthstone for May, you know..."

Kelly broke into the conversation. "She never lasted with anyone special, though. She was a clingy type: got too serious, too fast. She scared them off."

Luke noted how the young woman now used the past tense for her friend.

"Jewel bragged about a macho guy and told all those lawyer jokes." Melanie shivered. "I believe her date was married. She's not usually that secretive about current lovers."

"You're guessing, Mel. The police want concrete evidence."

"That's okay," Luke said. "We get lots of extra information. Sometimes, there's a glimmer of potential evidence. How old was your friend?"

"She's turning twenty-eight," Kelly pursed her lips, "same as me."

"Why would she keep her dating a secret?" Beth asked.

"Probably because the guy was married, and she knew we'd

give her a hard time," Kelly blurted. "She clammed up. Always went for the wrong types and believed all their promises."

Beth rose and asked which room belonged to Jewel. Melanie showed her, watching and fidgeting while the policewoman opened drawers and closets. The room was neat but plain.

Melanie rubbed both hands over her arms. "We don't keep a lot of stuff. When you move around, it's a nuisance to haul everything. And we need to get a stronger padlock on our apartment door. We're right on ground level."

Beth didn't tell her that the pull-up windows also made for easy entry.

While the two women checked Jewel's bedroom, Luke glanced through a small photo album. He selected a couple of pictures, of which one, Kelly said, was a rare picture of Lester.

"I would like you both to come to the coroner's lab with us. We need to get a positive identification. We'll leave Melanie waiting in the car if you're up to checking the body, Kelly."

"Yes. If it's Jewel, I owe her that much. We were both alone and gravitated to each other. She was too trusting, needy, and wouldn't listen once she set her mind to something."

"We didn't find another purse," Beth added, coming out of the bedroom. "Did she usually carry this big one?"

"No, she used a clutch that fit in her jacket pocket. It had her info and money."

Luke paused. "Bring her purse, Beth; check the contents while we drive in."

He drove. Kelly perched beside him, stiff as a plank, while Melanie whimpered and slumped in the back with Beth.

Kelly took a couple of shaky breaths, hunched over and spoke in spurts. "Lester, her cousin, is a small-time crook. He hasn't done jail time yet—or been caught, as far as I know. Tends to keep a low profile and brags about how much smarter he is than the cops. We can't leave anything around that he can pocket and exchange for money."

"Do you remember when he last visited?"

"Three or four days ago, looking for the usual handout. We fed him, and Jewel spared him a couple of twenties. Melanie and I hid our purses."

"You mean he came over the night before she went missing?"

Melanie shuddered. "Yes, he joked about her having a heavy night with an expensive date. He offered to go along as protection for a fee."

Kelly shook her head. "Jewel told him to stay away. He stole another old jalopy that day and threatened to follow her and the date. What if he did, and now he's missing too?"

Melanie squealed. "Oh, Kelly, don't say things like that."

Beth rummaged through the purse. She drew out a lawyer's card. "You mentioned an aunt's inheritance money. Is that why Jewel kept this lawyer's card?"

"Maybe that's who she got involved with," Melanie whispered.

"That trust fund was years ago," Kelly said. "There was nothing left."

At the morgue, Kelly followed Luke, hanging onto Beth's arm. Melanie stayed behind in the back seat of the car, stiff and gazing forward blankly. They heard her hiccup or sob when they left her locked in. Kelly shivered on entering the colder section of the labs and took shallow breaths once their nostrils were hit with the lingering odours of preservation chemicals. When the coroner's assistant pulled back the sheet to reveal the damaged, bloated face and bruised, swollen neck, Kelly gulped and swallowed. She turned away and nodded at Luke's questioning look. "It's Jewel." She turned around, almost tripping in haste, fleeing through the door with Beth hurrying to keep pace with her. On the way out, she stopped and asked hoarsely, "Why is Jewel's face swollen and discoloured?"

Beth answered, "The autopsy shows that someone strangled her, Kelly, and she's been dead a few days. We'll need your help to catch the person responsible for her murder."

Luke caught up with them, ensuring Beth would take the women back to their flat before finding his truck.

Beth handed him the lawyer's card before she got in the police car with the women. "This law firm is located in the Stark building, Boss. I think you'll recognize one of the names."

Luke stared. The business card belonged to the firm of his best friend, Mark Richards and his partner, Craig Gibson.

10

Erin tried to keep her mind off the murder case and focus on her workday. She checked on an older logging man who broke three ribs when the tree he cut fell the wrong way, almost landing on top of him. The ribs would mend without intervention, but an open wound on his upper torso became badly infected. She cleansed and repacked the gaping hole to allow for proper healing and drainage through the vacuum pack.

"You took your pain medication when I called, Mr. Slater?"

"Yes, Nurse. I'm not that brave—now it only hurts when you poke the gauze inside that big hole or when I take deep breaths."

"You need to keep up with the deep breathing and use that spirometer. The effort makes you fully expand your lungs. You don't want to get pneumonia."

"I use the breather a lot. I can almost hear and feel those broken ribs rubbing together. Cripes, they grind against each other so hard they must send sparks flying."

Wrapping the final bandage around, Erin grinned at his comments.

The man chuckled, too, then hitched forward and grabbed at his side. "Oh, don't make me laugh, Nurse. That really hurts."

"Doesn't the person on the ground get hurt by a falling tree, not the one strapped on and sawing through the trunk."

"I don't want to talk about that damn accident." His face took on a rebellious look. "Good thing I wasn't alone this time, or I'd still be out there, broken and dying on the ground."

UNSTABLE GRAVES

Next, she checked on a young man who almost died from an aneurysm leaking inside his brain. An escalating headache and projectile vomiting propelled him to the emergency department, where he lost consciousness shortly after arrival.

"The emergency docs told me that if I'd waited much longer, Nurse, I would have died. And I'm still forgetting things."

"Well, Jake, your chart says you'll always have short-term memory lapses, but you're ambulatory—you can move around. Your pulse and blood pressure are back to normal."

"Good thing my job's a no-brainer. I clean offices at night. The head doc told me I should take a retraining course through government funding." He shrugged. "Even if I don't get a good job, the learning will help my brain work better."

His roommate laughed. "What brain, Jake? You already forgot they took yours out."

"Asshole," Jake countered. "At least now I have an excuse to be stupid. What's yours?"

"I don't need one." His friend, Ernie, rubbed his bald head. "You wanted a reason to get your head shaved to look pretty like me."

Erin quit counting all the pierced rings and stopped trying to decipher the tattoos on his friend. She wondered how many were hidden on his body, not that she cared enough to ask or look. Back in the car, she turned on the radio and caught the latest news. No name yet for the murdered victim, or the police weren't releasing the info. Her brother, Bill, wouldn't suspect that she found this body. He always claimed that she and trouble ran on parallel planes. The news only mentioned that a trapper's dog led the police to the burial site.

Finishing the afternoon by running IV antibiotics, she called her secretary friend, Marge Booth, to have her meet for coffee and a chat at Timmy's beside the office.

The older secretary from their nurses' office got coffee and a large, honey-drizzled doughnut, then plunked herself down on the chair across from Erin. "I'm off my diet again, as you can see. I have a healthy stew simmering in the crock pot for supper. Both kids have music practice after school and return home on the late bus." Marge looked at Erin's worried expression. "Now, what's your problem?"

"How do you know I have a problem?" Erin asked in an innocent voice.

"We don't usually get together during the week, especially at supper time."

Erin grimaced. "I wanted to talk to you about yesterday. They discovered that murder victim on my route. I'm worried about our unpleasant boss finding out."

"I heard a trapper's dog found that buried body in the woods. Why would you be concerned about Mrs. Hildeforce's reaction?"

"Remember when you called and you said I had a problem? Well, Mr. Fraser insisted that I check in the bush with his anxious dog, Chum. The man wouldn't let up and kept begging me to look. He has an amputated leg, so he couldn't go. I finally gave in and searched the wooded area with Chum. I thought someone was hurt and maybe dying."

Marge's eyeballs almost bulged out as she leaned forward. "You found that body? The body I heard about on the radio that they're asking for help in identifying. Oh, shit." Marge opened and closed her mouth a couple of times. "I'm speechless. Shit and double shit!"

Erin related the events of the day, glossing over Luke's

46

involvement. It was already bad enough that Celine's eyes gleamed with matchmaking fever.

Marge stared, body immobile but leaning forward, mouth hanging open. When Erin finished talking, Marge took a deep breath, bit off a chunk of doughnut, and slumped in her chair. She chewed for a minute and then blurted out. "See the crap you land in when you listen to a dog."

Erin smiled. "Thanks, Marge. I needed to hear your usual skewed viewpoint."

11

When Erin arrived home, she found a note on the counter from her brother.

"Hey, Calamity Jane," the note read. "Heard they found a half-buried body in the north area where my bad luck sister now works. If this isn't your body, then you're likely digging for bones now." No signature.

She wished she heard some news about the murdered woman. When she checked on the trapper tomorrow, he could tell her something about the ensuing investigation. But the police wouldn't release information to him because they found the body on his property. She did laundry and light housework, took the dogs for a quick walk, and then called Celine to invite herself over.

When she arrived, Celine's calico cat wound around her legs, purring pleasantly. The black tom didn't twitch, staring at her, eyes unblinking. Sitting down, Erin drank some of the offered hot green tea, warming her hands on the mug. "Celine, remember I talked about Luke's lawyer friend, Mark? I think you'd like his grandmother, Gladys Richards. She's a bit stiff, more formal-like, but keeps an open mind about paranormal stuff. She believes there's a lot more we don't know or fathom in our world, and she'd never belittle your quirky ways."

"Quirky? *Quelle* kind of word is that? William says I have the screws loose in my head. Do you think he means that the visions float in and out through the empty spaces?"

UNSTABLE GRAVES

"I can't imagine how you or Bill think. Sometime, if you're visiting your sister in Hanmer while I'm working, I'll introduce you. Most older people love company, especially when they're less mobile. I think you'd be good for her."

Celine raised her eyebrows and didn't question or comment. She took another drink and put down the cup.

"*Maintenant*, I must tell you my news. My twin sister's granddaughter: she trains for a veterinarian. Janelle always loved the animals. She will *reste avec moi* for the late spring placement at an animal hospital here. The clinics are often on demand, and she needs to be available for emergencies. She is *petite*, not the pushover, though."

"A strong personality is good for a woman."

"Janelle is a Gemini. *Mais*, she has the soft side too. Never stand in front of her when the sparks fly. I will enjoy the company."

"Nice if she's able to befriend your dark Salem. Sybil's a doll and loves everyone." She pet the sweet, purring cat. The stoic black tom, ambivalent about being ignored, swished his tail and stalked away. "Does Janelle have pets?"

"*Pas maintenant,* but they always kept cats and dogs when growing up." Celine stopped talking and gazed off into a far corner, a look frozen upon her face.

Erin turned, aiming her eyes at the same spot. "What are you staring at?"

Celine turned her shadowed eyes back to her and spoke in a ghostly voice.

"Dogs... too many dogs are here,
One gets hurt... one has no fear."

"Too many dogs, did you see them? Which dog gets hurt?"

49

Erin leaned forward. "Bill's two, Mr. Fraser's dog, Chum, or Adam's German Shepherd, Major. Which one?"

"I did not *regarde* a special animal, *mais* I heard my words."

"We have cats right here. Why should you be having visions of dogs?"

"*Pas de visions, Cherie.* I got an impression, and the words burst out by themselves. This scenario, *c'est pas bien.*"

"There's that understatement from you again."

"Erin, this month belongs to the Taurus-born, and I sense that we will be meeting with more of them soon. Those *personnes*, they do not like to give up what they own. They are pleasant and *très* protective of family, but can become overly possessive at times of people and things. Their mantra is simple: "*I have.*" Be careful. Never try to take anything away from them."

12

Luke drove back to the scene where Erin had discovered the body and wandered near the wet shoreline after sending his officers, Adam Brady and Trevor Ronzi, to check out the other departments in the Stark building. He would handle the lawyers. Back in the truck, he reversed and crossed the bridge again to check the apartment block. He skirted around back to eyeball the wooded areas and trails before crossing to visit Mrs. Richards at The Manor.

"Well, hello, Luke. I have a feeling this is not a social call."

"No, Mrs. Richards." Luke sat across from her on the couch. "I'm sure you've heard of the murder in the area. A young woman, identified now as Jewel Martin, lived across from you in the red brick apartment house with a couple of other young women."

"I can't get around much with my arthritis. However, my rocker faces the street. I watched them erect that building. My caregiver said they installed all kinds of security systems, and her boyfriend worked with the construction team. He laughed because he said they added an entry door through the basement laundry room for deliveries but put no alarm there."

"That doesn't surprise me. I have a couple of pictures the roommate gave me." Luke pulled out the photos. "Have you ever seen this woman?"

Gladys stared at the picture. "Maybe. She's one of the two blonde women, probably the one who goes out clutching a man's arm, usually after the others have left. Looks around and acts too secretive." She shook her head. "Hard to say. There's a small Asian woman living there, too."

"Have you ever seen this man around?" He handed her Lester's picture.

"Can't say I recognize him. Most of the renters are middle-aged or elderly. I tend to notice the three women more. Such youth and vitality." She sighed. "The men often wear a cap, and my flat is higher up, so I don't get a good look at their faces. You were over there. I detected your walk more than your features when the police car arrived. Check with Mark if he spotted them during one of his visits."

"Does Mark visit more often now that his parents are living permanently in Florida? I will need to question him."

Gladys Richards smiled. "Yes, Mark watches out for me. Yesterday, he came out, and I met that young nurse, the one you dated last month. Erin is lovely."

Luke's hand jerked up as he stared back at the woman. "I did see her a few times, yes. Why did you have to see a nurse? Are you having more health problems?"

"Oh, no, other than this darn arthritis and a lot of boredom. Erin was checking up on a patient at the apartments next door when a bear approached our bird feeders. One of the elderly male residents, Mr. Cresswell, was walking back, and he didn't see the animal behind him. She ran out to warn the man and grabbed Mark's arm when he got out of his car."

"They approached the bear? Erin and Mark?"

"Well, Erin grabbed a can of bear spray from her car, and they didn't get too close. Mr. Cresswell was already on his way back up the trail."

UNSTABLE GRAVES

Luke looked thoughtful. "They should cut back the brush and quit feeding the birds."

"The administration has warned everyone and taken those precautions. We only have a few small trails and sitting areas, and then the woods close in. I heard there's some overgrown trails back along the river on the other side." She smiled at him. "Erin told me about following the trapper's dog and finding the body."

Luke's eyebrows lifted. "But she wanted her involvement kept secret?" He shrugged. "I guess she mentioned that the dog found the victim at the shoreline on this side of the river, down behind the building."

"Near the roadway, right, for access? It's sad for the woman, and for Erin too." She sighed and then smiled. "So nice of Mark to bring Erin up and introduce her. She does seem to get into predicaments through no fault of her own."

"Somehow, she gets involved in these murder cases. Last month, one of my officers wanted to investigate her more thoroughly and tried to convince us she was the likely culprit. I needed to keep an eye on her."

"Poor Luke." Gladys shook her head and reached over to pat his hand. "What hardship that must have been for you."

13

Erin stopped to check on a toddler who underwent surgery for a broken arm. The Children's Aid Society, involved in the case, asked for caregivers to keep an eye on the child's welfare. The young mother claimed the girl fell off a coffee table, and nothing seemed to contradict that. The mother's boyfriend worked at a pizza parlour, and they lived on an assisted income.

Erin checked the colour and pulse at the child's wrist. The cast covered the break near the elbow. The toddler jerked her arm away and whimpered.

"What's your name, little one?"

The child stared back solemnly, pushing her body against her mother's.

"Her name is Annabelle. Say hello to the nurse, Anna," the mother coaxed. The toddler turned and hid her face in her mother's sweater.

"Does she seem to be in a lot of pain?"

"She does," the woman answered. "I give her infant Tylenol every six hours or so. I take care of my little girl." She paused and looked away. "All babies can fall."

"Especially when they're learning to walk and like to climb. Is Annabelle active?"

"Yes, I think she's normal." The mother sounded resentful of the intrusive questions.

Erin believed the mother cared for the child, but she didn't meet the boyfriend. There was nothing of importance to report.

UNSTABLE GRAVES

Later, Erin drove down Capreol's streets. The population had declined, with businesses closing after railroad jobs thinned. Others moved to Sudbury, hating the long work commute. She listened to the radio and heard the police were looking for a small, thin man named Lester Lisson connected with the murder case.

Why was the man involved? Was he a suspect or a witness? Maybe he'd hidden in the bush where the victim was dropped. No, too uncomfortable. Black fly and mosquito season was here, and even the torrential rains wouldn't drown them. The bloodsuckers loved wet climates. The attacking swarms even drove deer and moose onto roads, forcing drivers to watch for them. Nature wasn't kind.

Erin made a quick stop to say hello to Gladys again and heard the latest bit of news on Luke's investigations. On her way out, Erin gazed at the building across the road. Did she expect to see "murderer" written above the door? No blondes appeared, nor seedy men. Next, she stopped at a diner and, smelling the aroma of hot red pepper soup, ordered a bowl to go with her sandwich, savouring the smell of parmesan cheese the waitress shook atop the thick soup. She declined the offered pepper: enough spice already. She wouldn't feel the wind chill after spooning this up. She glanced about, seeing only a few people sitting at assorted tables. She didn't recognize anyone. On her way out, an elderly man entered, smiled, and touched her arm.

"Aren't you the nurse who saved me from the bear?"

Erin laughed. "You're from the Manor. And you didn't need saving after all. Mark and I meant well. I'm sorry, I forget your name."

"Tom Cresswell, no matter." He grinned like a mischievous boy and whispered. "Sometimes, I slip away for a greasy meal of hamburgers and gravy with lots of fries. I can smell the thick aroma from the Manor."

She shook her head. "You think they're trying to keep you too healthy at the Manor?"

"Well, don't tell on me. I don't do it often." He pondered a moment. "You know, I warned away a young blonde woman this morning. I told her not to hang around the area because of that roaming bear. She said she was walking to meet someone."

"Did you see if anyone followed her?"

"No, but then I did see a skinny bum: a small, shabby man— you know—peering around the place. Hope she wasn't waiting for him."

"What did the man look like? Any special features?"

"I spotted a silver earring on one ear under his cap. Well, I didn't see the other ear." He raised his eyebrows. "I don't take to this notion of men wearing women's jewelry."

"If you see him again, please tell Mrs. Richards right away. Her nephew and his detective friend are looking for someone shady who matches that description."

"Will do. All this talking has made me hungrier. Thanks again." He licked his lips and scurried into the diner.

Erin rushed to see Gladys again. "I can't stay. But I want you to know that I talked to Mr. Cresswell. I might be stretching my imagination, but he may have seen that Lester guy loitering around. The police are televising his picture. I told Mr. Cresswell to tell you if the fellow showed up again since he could be the guy they're looking for. Then you could call Luke to catch him."

The woman shook her head. "Luke has gone to question Mark to see if he saw the young women when he visited me. If the information helps solve this horrendous crime, I will do my duty.

UNSTABLE GRAVES

Is Mr. Cresswell okay after his bear fright?"

"Well, he's sure acting chipper this morning. I met him at the corner diner sneaking in for a greasy lunch. Don't tell on him."

"We all know about his weekly escapades. The staff let him think he's fooling us. He needs some drama in his life." She sighed. "I'm thinking in our aging, lonely lives, we all do."

14

Luke drove back to town, parked, and entered the lawyers' office for Gibson and Richards. Ralph, his computer expert, beeped him from the office to inform him that Trevor called in with new information. One of the firm's young male security guards had watched the girl, saying he thought she was cute. Of course, he didn't know which office she visited. He only observed her waiting at the elevator.

Upstairs, Luke entered the lawyers' office and smiled at the older secretary. "Hi, Lois. I have questions about a young woman: I need to know if she visited these offices." He showed her the picture. Lois shook her head, saying she didn't recognize her. He asked her to check through their files for a Jewel Martin. She nodded when he asked to see Mark, and he strolled into the lawyer's office.

Luke handed him the smiling photo. "Hi, Mark. I'm investigating a murder. Do you recognize this woman?"

Mark held the picture up. "Possibly—no, I don't think so. Where does she work?"

"A teller out at the racetrack Saturday nights and occasionally at the call centre." Luke slid the morgue photo to him.

"Haven't gone out there since opening night at the casino." Mark winced. "Geez, Luke, I don't have your affinity for corpses. Hope you don't show that picture to the parents."

"No parents, only a missing male cousin. Jewel Martin lived with a couple of roommates in the apartment building across from your grandmother's."

"Oh, well, I may have seen her there. I go out to see my grandmother a couple of times every week. I've seen a couple of young blondes enter and exit, but I've never talked to them."

"Someone says the victim entered your office building."

"I didn't work for her. Maybe she visited an office on another floor." He looked up. "Was she in the temporary typist pool? Um, why the strange look?"

"She kept your business card in her purse, and her friends think she dated a married man, probably a lawyer." Luke sighed. "The lad on security duty said she waited at the elevator."

"This is a big building. There are realtors and stores on the second floor. She may have visited one of those."

"She had your company's card, Mark. I'll need to see Craig Gibson as well."

"Well, Casanova next door would jump any available woman, but he's not a murderer. He likes to gamble at the harness racetrack and check out the scenery. He wouldn't get involved in any shady business that could upset his rich wife."

"Do you recall seeing the victim at the track?"

"I haven't been to the races. Like I said, Luke, I did go to the casino on opening night.

"The victim was involved with a tall, dark man. Was that you?"

"Hell, you fit that description, same as me and numerous others." Mark glowered. "Cut the bullshit. I'm Mark, your friend, remember?"

"I think I know you, but a murderer doesn't wear a transparent mask. Anyone is capable of retaliation when threatened with exposure. Your wife is a brunette, but I remember you always corralled the best-looking blondes in law school."

59

Mark gawked at him, his body stiffening. He stood up and forced out a reply. "I can't believe I'm hearing this crap. I think this conversation is over—Officer Landry."

15

Luke shrugged at his friend's rebuff, believing it part of his job to be vigilant and suspect everyone, then left to talk with the secretary. Lois was the elder Richards' secretary before Mark's parents retired and moved to Florida. "Are you never going to retire, Lois?"

"I'm only in my late 50's, Luke. I like to work, and I'm comfortable in my job." She pointed to the working desk. "I didn't find that name you gave me in our computer files. She wasn't one of our clients."

"How many people are employed in this office?"

"Well, we rent the entire third floor. There's one receptionist, Lise Cameron, for the two offices, and both lawyers have their own private secretary. I handle Mark's affairs, and Craig's secretary is Cathy Wallace. The offices also share Annie, a young girl doing a co-op school placement. She's new." Lois shrugged. "Annie's the gofer girl and runs errands to and from the courthouse."

"I suppose you won't gossip about your employer?"

She gave him a haughty look. "You know me well enough. I mind my own business and don't worry about their personal lives."

"I may have to challenge you on that. I'm investigating a murder case, and this office seems to have a connection with the victim."

Luke left and spoke with the other two women in reception,

handing them the nicer picture of the murder victim. "Have either of you seen her?"

"Nope, don't think so." They shook their heads indifferently and handed back the photo.

He visited the next office. An attractive brunette smiled at him. He showed his ID card and asked to speak with Craig Gibson.

"Certainly, Inspector." She pressed the intercom and told her boss the police wanted to talk with him. "Do you need a specific file?"

"Not right now. I'll have questions for you later."

After entering Gibson's office, Luke sat and assessed the man across the desk. His features were more effeminate than rugged, in his opinion. Women probably found his "pretty" looks appealing. The man sat silent, waiting.

"Mr. Gibson, I'm investigating the murder of a young woman who may have sought your services, either for business or personal reasons." He handed over Jewel's fairer picture. "You probably heard about this investigation on the news."

The man gazed at the photo and hesitated before looking up. "I deal with many cases," he said, looking again at Luke's ID card, "Inspector Landry. If I did work for her, I don't remember. Why are you questioning me?"

"Your business card was in the woman's purse."

"I imagine lots of people have our card. She may have planned on seeing a lawyer for some transaction. What's her name?"

"Jewel Martin." Luke eased back in his chair. "She worked at the call centre and the betting booth at the racetrack."

"Well, I'm at the track most race nights and take interest in a few horses, but the betting lines move fast. How did she die?"

Luke tossed the morgue photo on the desk. "The autopsy

UNSTABLE GRAVES

report says strangulation, then burial in a muddy grave."

The man's colour turned green and then ashen. His hand trembled when he shoved the picture back across the desk. "I certainly can't recognize her now."

"I see you realize the seriousness of our inquiries, Mr. Gibson. I'll also check with your secretary to see if she has any memos on file."

"Cripes, don't show her that gruesome picture. That'll give anyone nightmares."

Luke stared at the man's hand. "That ring you're wearing with the green stone at the centre: is it an emerald?"

"Why yes. The emerald is my birthstone for May."

"Are you a Taurus, Mr. Gibson?"

"Are these silly questions leading anywhere, Inspector?"

Luke got up. "The victim was also a Taurus sign. She wore a green stone ring resembling an emerald a man likely bought for her. And she visited someone in this building."

The man stared blankly with no expression and no further comment.

Luke left to speak to Craig's secretary. "Ms. Wallace? We're investigating a murder case. I'd like to know if you've ever seen this woman, Jewel Martin."

Cathy took the pleasant photo and scrutinized it. "She was the victim we heard about on the radio?" At his nod, she continued, "Don't think she visited here. I'll check for the name in my files." She peered at the photo again. "Too bad, she's not memorable looking at all. Pretty enough, though not a standout for a guy to want to take a second glance." She handed the picture back to him with a questioning look. "Why are you checking on us? Was there a court case involved?"

"This office card was in her purse, and the security guard saw her downstairs."

"Well, let me look." Cathy scanned through numerous cases. "Nobody with that name listed here, Inspector. You could ask Lois Anders next door. She may have her in their system."

"I've already checked over there. Neither Mark nor Lois recognized her."

"Well, she may have planned to see someone or changed her mind and never got around to booking an appointment with either lawyer."

He got nothing from further questioning; however, he knew people at the racetrack who surely had the answers he needed.

16

The gaunt man pulled the visor of his hat farther down his forehead and slipped along the path behind the Manor. Lester Lisson knew his smarts outshone the police. He muttered and cursed his cousin's death. "How fucking stupid of her! That damn Jewel. Didn't I tell her to bring me along for protection? Of course, I wanted a little payment. I'd have kept her alive. The dumb woman thought she was too smart. Now her money and handouts stop, and I need to get a new cash backup plan." Pilfering without being spotted eventually turned into a crapshoot. No matter how good he was, he knew his luck would run out.

He crossed the road and snuck to the apartment door after the cops left to talk to Kelly. Melanie, the dummy, hung back and alternated between rubbing her eyes and chewing her fingernails. He had been stunned to hear about Jewel's murder, her body found strangled and buried in mud. How gross was that? Kelly knew more and said she'd tell him later, giving him her cell number. The police came back with more questions, saying they wanted to find him.

"Good luck with that, dumbass coppers."

He hotwired another old car to get around and dirtied the license plates. After talking with Kelly last night, he arranged to meet her again today across the road on that secluded bush trail. The apartment block was too busy. It was a short conversation after that old man from the Manor stared at him and watched him move behind the building. Kelly hurried away after giving him more information.

When Lester backtracked and reached the shadowy lane at the Manor where he'd parked behind bushes, he lit a cigarette, inhaled, jumped in the car, and drove back to town. With the continuing cold and wet weather, he could always wear gloves without being conspicuous. No cops would tag him for these escapades, either the car theft or the break-ins. No fingerprints. He kept one step ahead of the law. He muttered further, "Not a problem avoiding cops. I know all the tricks. I have the brains, all right." As usual, he took precautions and travelled the quieter back roads, following the speed limits but not driving too slow, wanting to avoid routine checks.

Kelly found something new. She listened in on the phone extension while Jewel believed she slept. Lester knew he needed to get the dumb woman's co-operation. She said Jewel went to meet this man at a deserted place—how stupid was that? No way he would go to an isolated spot to get mugged or killed. After all, he had the smarts. Last time he didn't find money lying around their place to nick. That new woman probably dipped into the cash and blamed him.

He would've liked to put the touch on this lawyer boyfriend of Jewel's, but he guessed Kelly would try to get ahead of him. Earlier, he snapped a photo of Jewel with a man. What if he was the guy who killed her? What a crock of shit that would be! Kelly knew more than she said, likely hearing the guy's name during the phone call. Lester would've offered to drive her to a meeting place or follow her for protection, but she'd say no like Jewel did. Another fool. Damn silly women. No sense at all.

UNSTABLE GRAVES

In a few days, he would have to ditch the car. "Never keep one long enough to get caught" was his motto. It was surprising how little he walked. He was good. Right now, he would take a drive-by near that lawyer's office. Kelly said the police found their business card in Jewel's purse. At least she knew how to pick them. The guy must have money to burn. Lester sneered and took a deep drag of his cigarette. He needed to figure out how to separate a few wads of the lawyer's mega bucks for himself. No reason he should be left short of money when the guy killed his one legit source of income and his only relative. I'll fix Mr. Fancy Lawyer all right, wait and see. I'm gonna bleed the sucker."

17

Celine phoned Erin before she left for work that morning. "Can you pick me up after your *travail* today? I will spend the afternoon out there to *visite* my twin sister. Cecily got a new blood pressure machine. She would like you to check and see if the readings are accurate?"

"Sure, I will. If you're not in a hurry to get back, we can stop and see Gladys Richards, Mark's grandmother. I stopped in yesterday. I'll call her. She's worried about her grandson. Luke is being insufferable again. He's questioning Mark as a suspect."

"But he is not going to let the *ami* detour his investigation."

"You mean deter."

"I know what I said is *correcte*. Luke goes around and around the *problème*."

After completing her shift, Erin picked up her elderly friend, who enjoyed a short visit with her twin sister. The woman's blood pressure was only a little elevated. Erin showed her how to work and feel comfortable using the machine and told her to jot down her readings for the next visit to the doctor. She then drove to the Manor with Celine and facilitated greetings between the two women. With the pleasantries dispersed, she seated Celine comfortably in the armchair. "Mrs. Richards, can I use your kitchen to make us some tea?"

"Yes, but call me Gladys. Oh, Erin, there are biscuits on the kitchen counter, too."

UNSTABLE GRAVES

"*Appelez-moi*, Celine. I never met your grandson, *mais* I have met Luke."

"Darn Luke. Mark called me, upset because of the adverse way his best friend questioned him. I'm annoyed. That lad grew up in such a cold environment. Like Erin said, Luke would suspect his own mother and search for proof of her guilt."

"*C'est correct!* I met him when Erin *est tombé* into those murders last month, and he suspected her. She is an Aries, *très* volatile. There existed much of the sparks between them."

Erin put the kettle on to boil water and hovered near the door in case of a lull in their conversation. She worried they might need her support to further their acquaintance.

Gladys gained a bemused expression. "Erin said that you study horoscopes and have an exaggerated ESP. Can you guess what astrology sign I was born under?"

Celine smiled. "*Pas vite,* not right away. Sometimes, a person resembles another of similar characteristics, or you react differently to similar signs. My senses tell me you are not an earth or water sign. Let me guess when I *pars*."

Gladys sighed. "I'm worried that Mark may have innocently met the murdered woman at some time or place." Gladys pointed out the window toward the large apartment building. "This Jewel woman lived right across the road with two others in that apartment block. Mark's wife, Sue, drove east to visit her parents. She doesn't know Luke's questioning him about this murder. She's expecting in September and doesn't need this stress." Gladys lowered her voice. "I've seen one of those women leaving their apartment with different men. I think she ran around a lot and likely had low morals." She pursed her lips. "I bet this murder involves fornication."

BETTY GUENETTE

"Oh," Celine giggled. "That word is the same in our French language. We pronounce it in the rich, sultry tones, *for-ni-ca-tion.*

"Depend on the French to embellish suggestive language with their open culture."

Gladys leaned forward. "Our English ways are colder and rigid—not near as much fun."

When the kettle clicked off, Erin tiptoed back to the counter with her hand over her mouth. Then, she dabbed at her eyes, whispering. "They're precious."

The elderly ladies sat straight and quiet when Erin brought in the pot and went back for biscuits. She missed some of their conversation, apparently an important part based on what she heard on her return.

Gladys cleared her throat. "Erin, I've told Celine about Craig, Mark's business partner. She also thinks that Craig is the lawyer who hung around that poor woman. I'm truly certain Mark's not involved. Craig's wife runs a fancy shop. It's quite posh, and she's a total snob. She seems to ignore Craig's shenanigans."

"Maybe the acts of adulteries are not right in her *visage.* Erin, you and I will go to this boutique to see if Craig has the jealous wife.

"What? We can't ask her intrusive questions, not point blank to her face."

"Point? You mean stick the knife in? *Non,* that will not be *possible.* You remember I wanted to buy the pewter eggcups?"

"Funny, I don't remember that at all," Erin sat with the women.

Gladys put down her cup. "I recall now. His wife's name is Sheila Gibson, and her shop is called *The Final Touch.*"

"That is *macabre.*" Celine blinked and spoke in a trancelike voice.

UNSTABLE GRAVES

"A final shot into the sand
Makes fall to all of those who stand."

"Here we go around the mulberry bush again." Erin held open her hands. "Thanks for the ominous info. See how nebulous her warnings are, Gladys?"

Celine ignored the jibe. "We will need your youth and energy, *Cherie. Mais,* in the background, we will help you solve the murder."

"You mean you want me to do the legwork. That stuff I can handle. What weird ideas have you two planned?"

Gladys took a deep breath. "For Mark, I will stop at nothing. Craig is known to be a lady's man. Now, Erin, if you..."

"Oh-oh, wait a minute." Erin held up a finger to point at the two women. "I'll not pamper that guy's ego by talking to him."

"*Bien.* You need to do more than *parler.* The come-on, I think they call it, *n'est-ce pas?*"

"Why set me up for trouble, Celine? I'd land in hot water faster than you can blink."

The two women simply ignored her and went back to their planning. Erin sat silent, arms crossed, fuming.

Celine spoke up. "I cannot imagine if this man has the low opinion for *les femmes* or the high esteem for himself."

"Both, I would say." Gladys pursed her lips. "I often wonder what brain cells these guys have left when they get older and lose their sex drive."

"In France, the *femmes* drink anisette liquor for the *amour.* The women at my club say lots of old men take the wonder drug Viagra and try the aphrodisiac herbs. I watched the ads on TV. Like, 'enhance the power, get her racy.'"

Gladys clamped a hand over her twitching lips.

Erin smiled, too. "I'm not batting my eyes at this Craig fellow. Besides, you said the guy's married. I know you don't believe in fooling around."

"*Mais*, this is for a good cause. You can snuggle and ask the *questions*."

"Hey, hold on now. You ladies will give me a fast and loose reputation."

"We won't worry about that right now," Gladys added.

Gladys seemed proper, but Erin caught the undercurrent of humour mixed with steel in the woman's voice before she continued speaking.

"I've seen two different men with one of the blondes. One's a lady's man, but wore a brimmed hat. I wouldn't be able to identify him. He'd put his arms around her and would squeeze her bu— behind." Gladys shrugged. "I should behave myself as I was a minister's wife. Working on this mystery is more fun than saying my prayers." She pressed a hand over her mouth and stared at the ceiling. "Did I say that? Sorry, Lord."

"We will not tell on you," Celine whispered.

Gladys took another sip of tea and dabbed her lips. "Now, this lecher ran his hand along her arm suggestively—and in public, too. Likely the guy wallowed in fantasies."

"What about the other man you spotted?" Erin asked.

"A lowlife, scrawny, unkempt type. He was twitchy, not touchy. Wore one of those caps with the visor low over his eyes. In fact, she pretended she wasn't with him. How obvious was that? He's gaunt but likely strong and wiry. I can imagine him burying someone."

Celine shut her eyes and chanted in low tones.

"To avoid the shifting sands of time,

UNSTABLE GRAVES

The trees are there to make you climb."

"If it's an earthquake, I don't think climbing trees will help at all." Erin reflected for a moment. "Again, it's gibberish to me. You know, Gladys, her prophecies make sense later, but we never understand them early enough to be useful."

Celine used her cane to get up, planning to leave.

Gladys stood also. "I find this whole visit quite intriguing. You must come again soon, Celine. We will discuss how Erin can act as our eyes and ears. Then we can decipher the clues and help Mark prove his innocence."

Erin scowled at Gladys. "You're as bad as that Mr. Cresswell. You're looking for stimulation and diversion. This is a murder case, not a game."

Gladys waved a hand. "I am interested. My poor eyes get tired if I read too much, and this gives me lots of spare time to sit and think. I relish a good mystery story."

Erin stood near Celine in case she needed help getting around. Celine made her way to the door with her cane and held up a finger. "About your sign, Gladys: *pas de* fire either. That only leaves the air. I am a Libra, but *pas vous*. I cannot *decider* between Gemini or Aquarius."

Gladys nodded. "You are good. I am a Gemini."

18

Erin drove Celine back to town, and they ended up at the door of the fashionable boutique, *The Final Touch*.

"*Maintenant,* Erin. Let me act here like a little confused French lady."

"You seem like a little confused French lady, but scatterbrained is more accurate."

Celine shushed her as they entered the small, lavish shop. "*Bonjour, Madame.* I have long *desirez* the pewter egg cups."

The tall, dark-haired woman behind the counter smiled and assessed them with her calculating eyes. "I have a few such items that might interest you."

Erin glanced about, handling a few antique-style wine glasses, all too ornate and heavy for everyday use. Her ideal pleasure was reading a mystery novel with a glass of red wine in a vanilla-scented bath. It was bad enough when she dropped a heavier book in the water while soaking for hours in the whirlpool tub, never mind spilling this heavy glass. She'd look like the body in a bloodbath.

Celine said she didn't care for the eggcups, stating they were too opulent for her. She twittered away and stared at the woman's hands. "That is a *belle* antique emerald ring. The stone is mystical and can protect against the evil spells. Your husband must have the grand *amour* for you to buy such a present *magnifique*."

"We're both born in May. His emerald ring is in a more modern style."

UNSTABLE GRAVES

"Then you are both *probablement* the sign of the Taurus?" At the woman's nod, Celine continued jabbering, "That earth sign is supposed to be stubborn like the bull it stands for, *mais* the two together make a good couple. I am an air sign, Libra—October—you know. *Aujourd'hui,* I should check for the opals for October—*oui,* the pierced earrings."

The woman led them over to a locked cabinet. "If you see anything you like, let me know." She glanced again at Erin, assessing her. "Haven't I met you somewhere recently?"

"Only if you've fallen sick. I'm a registered nurse. I work in the Hanmer and Capreol area."

The woman lowered her eyelids before looking at Erin again. "Were you the nurse who found that body out past Mr. Fraser's cottage?"

"*Oui, pauvre* Erin. She has all the bad luck," Celine answered.

"I'm surprised you found out I was involved," Erin said. "It's not common knowledge."

"I have connections to Mr. Fraser. I called him to check on how he was doing. He told me about all the investigation near his property."

Celine's eyes took on a detective's glow. "You know the trapper, *bien*?"

"Of course, I know him. I grew up out there at a nearby lodge. It rents out as a seasonal inn now." She frowned. "I'm Sheila Gibson."

"I'm Erin Rine. This is my neighbour, Celine Lauzon."

"I am French." Celine simpered. "Do you have *les enfants, Madame*?"

"No, I don't," came her clipped reply.

BETTY GUENETTE

Celine kept chattering, "Well, being a Taurus, *c'est bon*. As long as you have the main person in your life, you need no others." She screwed up her face and tapped her finger against her lips. "*Mais* the sign, it is supposed to symbolize the procreation."

The woman turned away from Celine and frowned at Erin. "I think I've seen you somewhere, Miss Rine. Maybe at the racetrack? Do you know my husband, Craig Gibson? He's there quite frequently: tall, good-looking lawyer, wears dark suits."

Erin felt a flash of recognition with the description and name. It was not a pleasurable feeling. She remembered him almost drooling over the sexier women. "Oh, I think I have seen him from a distance. My brother has two racers at the stables, and I'm usually out there on Saturdays. I've not been introduced to your husband."

"Most people remember my Erin. She stands erect *avec* her taller brother."

Sheila studied Erin. "Well, I'm five-feet-eight-inches tall and look about the same as you. I think it's an impressive height for a woman."

Celine coughed. "*Tout le monde* at the track were questioned because that young person who was killed, she *travaillait* out there."

"Did she? Well, I wouldn't know. I bet in the casino, not at the racetrack."

Celine bought a pair of opal studs, chatting away. Sheila stayed silent, glaring at Erin, who wasn't looking back. However, Celine, acting befuddled, noticed.

After leaving the store, the older woman spoke first, "This Sheila, she says she did not know the dead *personne*. Then she

UNSTABLE GRAVES

said she only *visite* the slots and not the racetrack. She must have known the woman worked there at the track."

"She's certainly a cold fish. Such hard, glacial eyes."

"A controlled *personne.* Some Taurus ones can be greedy and stingy towards others. The prices in her store were *très cher.*" Celine nodded. "Did you see the daggers in her icy stares toward you? I bet she thinks you have designs on her *homme.*"

"That lecherous man's a creep, and she must have suspicions and misgivings about him." Erin grimaced. "I'm surprised she puts up with his gross behaviour. It's probably the competition she doesn't tolerate."

Celine gazed at her thoughtfully. "If you are suggesting she did the murder, then you must be extra careful. Never stand alone on a cliff with that *femme dangereuse.*"

19

Luke instructed Ralph to have the officers obtain the two lawyers' fingerprints. "Anybody else you think we should check out?"

"We already have the prints of the roommates and also Miss Rine's from last month. How about we get the trapper's prints?"

Luke nodded, agreeing. "Good idea. I'm wondering about the secretaries and maybe Craig's wife. Wait and see about Mrs. Gibson. Might get nasty. We'll follow through if some evidence surfaces suggesting her as a suspect."

"I wonder if the wife got wind of the affair and acted rashly out of anger. Often, the disgruntled spouse takes out both the husband and girlfriend." Ralph began leaving. "We've also put a trace on Mark Richards' wife to make sure she is out east."

"Murder seems like rather a drastic action for a woman to take. It takes someone strong to carry and bury a body. I'll see Sheila Gibson next."

Ralph added, "I know Trevor checked the lawyers' building's entryways. The lawyers' floor is temperature-controlled. None of the windows open, and the exterior doors and windows are set on alarms. The bank has unbreakable windows on the main floor. We checked shots from the building's video cameras, but the victim didn't show up clearly in any. There were a couple of vague shots, but nothing helpful."

UNSTABLE GRAVES

Beth entered. "Boss, how about we dig deeper on the lawyers' office workers? It's possible she visited someone: a lover that worked there."

"They're all women workers except for the guard downstairs. He thinks Jewel went to the third floor, though the officers did check the other levels. No one claims to have seen her in the main-floor bank or the second-floor hardware store."

Ralph shook his head. "So, she disappeared into the elevator, never to be seen again. Almost like she never stepped out."

"The guard said it was closing time, and lots of workers had gone." Luke frowned. "He doesn't remember specific people or times. His rounds take him all over the building."

Beth spoke. "What if Jewel didn't plan to look for the boyfriend but went there to threaten someone else involved, maybe through blackmail?"

"How do you figure that?" Luke asked.

"Well, I don't yet. It seems too easy that Mark and Craig are our only suspects. We don't have enough information."

Ralph nodded. "They taught us at the police academy to always look for the X factor."

"Well, we're trying to find Lester Lisson," Luke said. "He would certainly add to the equation. As to motive, he's an unlikely murderer, but he's likely holding back information."

"Planning on blackmail, you think?" Ralph asked.

"Or he's dead, and we haven't dug him up."

Beth looked thoughtful. "What about Mark's secretary? You said she was older. Would she be jealous of a younger woman?"

Luke smiled. "I know Lois. She's worked there for years as secretary to Mark's father. She's almost sixty and has a tiny frame."

"Well, she might have protective instincts for the son, her boss."

"I can see her holding back information but not directly lying about her involvement." Luke shook his head. "She'd not act outside her starchy, upright character."

"Well, what about the other office employees? Anything strange about them?"

"Nothing jumps out, Beth. The receptionist and gofer girl seem totally disinterested in the situation. The other secretary seems efficient. How about you talk to the women there? You're good at picking up clues and innuendoes I miss. You always get a different handle on things."

"I'll go over there this afternoon. Somebody must be lying or hoarding information."

20

By noon on a relaxing Saturday, Erin had tidied the kitchen and waited, wondering if Bill would mention the murder. He busied himself making coffee before sitting at the kitchen table with the morning paper. After a few minutes of reading, he swivelled his head and fixed a stare at her.

"How on earth did you manage to find a buried body? That's a new one for you."

"What? They weren't supposed to find out or write anything about my involvement."

"Says here that a trapper's dog led the man's nurse to a partially buried body of a young woman." He grunted. "With you around, I'm always surprised I don't wake up dead."

"Geez, Bill, don't be daft. You can't wake up if you're dead."

"Can never know with you or our soothsayer next door. I could easily end up dead and floating above your heads." He grinned. "As a ghost, I'd be light as a feather and less of a giant."

"You're only six-foot-six. There are plenty of people bigger than you, even if you're fit and muscular."

"Fit sounds better than fat. Are they investigating you for this murder?"

"Why would they bother to check up on me? I didn't know the woman."

"You didn't know the one you found last month, and then you kept tripping over more bodies."

"Three is hardly tripping over a lot more."

BETTY GUENETTE

"Three corpses—now four—that's more than most people find in a lifetime."

"Well, I didn't find bodies in England when I worked there."

"As a nurse in a hospital, you probably got your quota with sick people dying." He shook the paper. "Anyway, are you coming out to the track this afternoon?"

"I'll go later. I'm planning to pick up Marge. She likes the new casino, so we may play slots. But I find it boring pushing a button over and over, so I'll come and watch the races."

Bill closed the newspaper and lapsed into his habitual silence while drinking his coffee.

A knock on their door started the dogs into a joyful barking crescendo.

Erin opened it to see Luke. "Darn. What did I do now, Inspector?"

He bent to pat the excited dogs. "Do you have a guilty conscience, Erin? Glad I caught you, and Bill, too. I'm making inquiries about the murdered woman, and I think you both were aware of her. Name of Jewel Martin."

"Sorry, the name doesn't ring my bells, but come in."

Bill turned to greet the visitor. "I don't recognize the name either, Luke, but I don't associate with dead bodies like my sister."

With Luke's confused expression, Erin told him Bill liked to make inside jokes. She motioned him to sit down and poured him a cup from Bill's coffee machine.

Luke settled, tasted his drink, then spoke. "I've got a couple of pictures to show you. This woman lived with two roommates in that new housing complex near Capreol." He handed them the fairer picture of Jewel. "Her only relative listed is a male cousin

82

we're trying to locate. I have his picture. Apparently, he only showed up when he was broke and needed a handout, and she often helped him. We think a lawyer boyfriend is involved, one she met at the racetrack."

Erin frowned, staring at the picture. "You know, I have seen her somewhere."

"Me too," Bill said, looking at the picture. "Did she work in the barns or casino?"

"You're close. She's one of the tellers at the wicket where you place your bets."

"Now I remember, but you don't stay to chat with them. The lines move along too quickly." Bill looked thoughtful and sighed. "You mentioned a lawyer? Was she involved with pretty boy Craig Gibson at the track?"

Luke nodded. "I think so. Well, he denies knowing her, and we're checking into it. Someone bought her an emerald ring with a fake stone, and her roommates think it was a birthday present. She kept quiet about it, and she would be twenty-eight years old next week. The ring may have been a gift from her killer."

"That date makes her a Taurus," Erin said. "Not surprising with the emerald-like ring."

Bill snorted at that comment, then spoke up. "How was she killed?"

"Strangulation with a fine rope—some fibres apparent—so not a specialty rope." He hesitated and then showed them the morgue picture.

"Oh, that's terrible," Erin shuddered and blinked.

"Well, Craig uses his cute mug to lure women into bed." Bill's face maintained a stony quality. "He's too weak to be a murderer, though. And his wife either doesn't care about his affairs or is too preoccupied with her own business to notice. She owns a fancy shop on the outskirts of Sudbury. Seems to do alright from what I hear."

"I've shopped there," Erin said. "What a cold, hard woman. And I've seen Craig at the track ogling other women.

"Get Erin to question him, Luke. She can doll herself up when she wants. Craig would be kept busy trying to keep his tongue from hanging out. He'd spit out the information."

"Thanks, Billy-boy, I love you too."

Bill held up his hand. "On second thought, with her bad luck, the guy would choke to death on his tongue, and she'd be under investigation again."

"I'm going to choke you!" Erin exclaimed. "What makes you so chatty all of a sudden?"

"He's a horse gambler I don't like. Mean bugger. He almost ruined a couple of good horses by getting in thick with betting along with some bad trainers and drivers."

"You mean he acts cruel to the animals?"

"Not enough to charge him." Bill squinted. "And I don't think he'd have the guts to murder anyone. But he's devious and a shady lawyer, I'll bet."

Erin turned away. "Luke, would you like to visit Celine?"

Bill snorted again. "You're probably safe. It's too early in the day for the witch to cast her spells."

"Play nice, dear brother. Her grandniece will be staying with her on placement before going back to veterinary college in the fall. We can let her practise on your dogs."

"Can witchiness be hereditary?" Bill raised his eyes to stare at the ceiling. "Two whackos next door starting a coven would be too much for this sane man."

84

UNSTABLE GRAVES

Luke, once quietly listening and sipping at his coffee, laughed at the siblings' bickering. He swallowed the last of his coffee. "Remember Bill, Celine's vision made me trail Erin when the murderer set the mountain on fire."

"She didn't need to predict the future to know that Calamity Jane was in danger. Trouble is her middle name."

"Luke, ignore him," Erin said after phoning next door, then walked to the entry. "Anne and Jane are my other two names, and he pokes fun at them. He thinks I'm bad luck."

Before the door shut after them, she heard Bill mutter, "I don't think. I know."

21

Celine smiled at the attractive detective. "*Bien*, Luke. How is my favourite Aquarian doing? We missed your company."

"Our department's been busy. Contrary to Bill's belief, I don't consider Erin involved in this murder case. I stopped to talk to Bill about people at the racetrack since he's in a position to hear gossip."

"*C'est correct*. Bill does not talk much *mais* hears more." She smiled mischievously. "You have made yourself scarce. I suspect Erin will find bodies to meet you *encore*."

Erin wanted to kick her under the table but worried about the woman's aged bones, especially after her broken leg just healed. "Luke's in charge of this new murder investigation, Celine. You should tell him about emerald signs. I know the emerald stone is supposedly protective. The gemstone on Jewel's ring wasn't real."

Celine twitched, stared blankly at the wall, shut her eyes, and spoke in a haunting voice.

> *"The emerald is green*
> *Like the grasses and trees*
> *But beware of the earth,*
> *For mud brown it will be."*

"See, Luke. She doesn't make sense. Everyone knows grass is green and earth is brown."

"She could mean earth signs," he replied. "You said the victim was a Taurus."

Celine shrugged. "I often do not mean anything. *Mais, c'est possible.*"

"Well, do you have concrete ideas for me this time?" Luke asked.

"Concrete? You mean the solid facts, not the airy thoughts, *n'est-ce-pas? Moi?*" She gave him a coy look. "I am just a little old lady pretending to be psychic, and you know that is not the *preuve admissible.*"

"You aren't aware of the people involved either. I'm sure Erin informs you about our lack of progress on the case."

"We made a *visite* to Craig Gibson's wife at her store the other day. A nasty *femme,* but the Taurus person is born under the *féminine* planet of Venus. That planet stands for love, beauty, and warmth."

"No warmth in that woman," Erin said and shivered. "Colder than an iceberg."

Luke glared at them both. "You two had nothing to do and wanted to visit the shop out of curiosity, or were you meddling in my murder case again?"

Erin stiffened. "We promised Gladys Richards we'd help with the case since you are harassing her grandson. I remember your inflexible attitude toward me during last month's murder case."

Luke bristled. "And did you find anything of importance I should know about, or are you withholding information?"

Celine patted his hand. "I like Gladys, *mais* please do not get annoyed. Listen to me: check out that woman, Sheila Gibson. She is a Taurus and wears a *magnifique* emerald ring."

"So, Madame, because the victim wore one, you think I should question all Taurus people wearing emerald rings?"

"*Bien, non?* Since this Sheila grew up next to the trapper's cottage, she knows the man and the area *très bien.*"

BETTY GUENETTE

He fixed a stare at Celine and then glowered at them both. "I wasn't aware of that fact. Is this knowledge courtesy of your crystal ball?"

"*Mais,* I tell you, *encore,* I have no ball. We found out because, well, we asked her the right *question,* an accidental one."

"I have a question." Erin bit her lip. "Why were her hands reaching upwards in that pose? She wasn't buried alive and trying to dig herself out, was she?"

"No. We suspect the body was rolled into a ravine in the dark. She probably got wedged on a log there, and then the murderer shovelled dirt on top. With the rain and the dog digging, the hands showed first, being the highest point on the body."

22

Later that afternoon, Adam stopped by to visit Erin. He looked surprised to see another woman outside with her and the dogs. The small woman was attempting to train both dogs to sit and stay. Spotting Adam, the two dogs jumped up and raced to greet him, gluing their noses to his legs as they caught other canine scents on his pants.

Erin smiled. "Adam, how nice to see you, and in uniform too."

The young woman looked up at him and grinned. "*Bonjour.* Are we in trouble, officer? The dogs have their tags, and Auntie Celine hasn't dreamt about any more murders."

Adam drew himself up to his full height. "I'm checking for the inspector to see if Erin knows anything else that could help us with the case."

"How delicious. Is she suspected of digging up the body?"

He frowned at the flippancy and spoke curtly. "The body wasn't dug up; it was buried—well, partially. I can't discuss police business."

Erin introduced Adam to Janelle, her neighbour's grandniece. "Janelle's assigned here in the vet's clinic this month. She's on a fieldwork placement."

Janelle called the dogs back and told them to sit, holding the leashes tighter. Juno wiggled around, and Rhea strayed back to pace circles around Adam, sniffing at his shoes.

"You need a strong and firm voice if you're going to make them listen. My dog, Major, learns fast, but I'm always strict with him. He's a German shepherd."

Janelle tilted her head back, glancing up at Adam. "These dogs have no finesse, and I'm trying to educate them—you look as tall as Bill."

Adam stood straighter, looking down at her. "He's taller. You think that only 'cause you're short. You probably can't tell the difference."

"Whatever. Well, I have work to do, even though others can take time off from their job." Janelle swung away, handed the dogs' leashes over to Erin, and retreated next door.

Adam looked bewildered. He watched Janelle leave, then turned around to Erin with questioning eyes.

"She has swinging moods, Adam. It's the Gemini traits showing up."

"I was driving by," Adam said. "It's near the end of my shift, and I wanted to check on things. Um, did your neighbour have fantastic ideas about the murder?"

"No, but I don't understand what she says till things happen. It doesn't help much. But, at times, she does lead me to the solution in a skewed way."

"That vet trainee, Janelle: she seems brittle. You'd say that her sign doesn't get along with mine?"

"You're on the cusp of Taurus, close to Gemini. I would think so. I'll ask Celine."

Adam took off his cap and ran his hand through his dark blonde hair. "That would be a bit forward. She seemed antagonistic."

"Visit us again and bring Major. Show him off to her. She's a different person with animals. She's found her calling."

"If you don't mind." Adam beamed. "I'd love to visit with my dog on my weekend off."

Erin phoned Marge when she re-entered the house. "Do you think Mrs. Hildeforce suspects my involvement in this murder case?"

"I wouldn't be surprised at all. She can put the pieces together knowing a caregiver found the body when Fraser is on your client list. She's acting like bugs have crawled right up her arse, and I am being polite."

"Glad of your restraint, Marge. I'd hate to hear you let it all hang out. Listen, Bill has to spend the day at the track to work with the horses. Do you want to come with me this evening? You can gamble at the casino between races."

"Oh, I like that idea. Larry's such a couch potato. I'd love to get out." Marge laughed. "Hey, ask Celine if it's my lucky day at the slots."

Saturday night, Marge climbed into Erin's station wagon. "I can't believe I'm going out without my husband or kids to have fun."

"Geez, don't go wild on me and start prowling like a cougar."

"I'm a Leo, the lion, remember. You'll hear me growl if I lose too much money."

"Come watch the first race. If our trotter wins his race, we can get our picture taken with him in the winner's circle."

"Stand next to a frisky, sweaty horse? Don't be silly. No thanks. I'll watch the first race with you, then I'm casinoing."

The first race was full and fast-paced with lots of driver manoeuvres, bottlenecks, and difficult escapes but no injuries.

"Come on, River Lad! Go, boy!" Erin yelled. The race bogged down at the end with numerous breaks in their trotting rhythm. River Lad rode straight and got boxed in halfway down the course. "Well, he got second place. Not bad. Bill's other horse, Chelsea Sky, is resting from an accident, but he'll soon work him out. Now, a round at the slots and then I'll leave you there," Erin said.

"First off, I'm getting a pop and hot dog, Erin, and don't tell me the meat's made from pig's intestines or other gross parts. I know you don't eat the stuff."

"That's a fallacy about wieners. Too much fat in them for me to indulge and not feel guilty anyway." After a few rounds of popping coins in a slot, Erin waved bye to her friend.

Before she left home, Erin applied makeup and dressed in a snug sweater under her jacket. Here, she unzipped her jacket, glanced about, took a deep breath, and then skulked over and eased onto a stool at the spectators' bar beside Craig Gibson.

He glanced at her, eyes narrowed, and took another swig of beer. His gaze slid over her body, leering before leaning against her shoulder and offering to buy her a drink. She cringed and willed herself to accept the casual social contact. When he whispered in her ear, his voice thick and drooling with anticipation, she feared he meant to poke his tongue in her ear. She twisted away and coughed to disguise a gagging reflex. This sort of investigative work was thoroughly unpleasant.

He draped his arm casually around her waist and spoke in a low, husky voice. "You're that sexy Erin, Bill's sister. I'm Craig. We can quit this noisy place, go for a short ride, park somewhere, and make lovey-dovey."

Erin wiggled farther to the opposite side of her barstool and told him she wasn't going to hang around with him. "You'll make people talk."

"They expect it, Doll. Or we can find a motel and make sweet music together."

The arrogance of the man! Did he find women that easy? Then why kill unless there was a threat made to tell his wife? She'd go for direct confrontation to get answers. "Craig, I heard you dated Jewel, the young woman who was murdered. What do you think happened to her?"

"Huh, what?" He slugged down the rest of his beer and muttered, "That's a lie. I didn't know her." He started to stroke her knee while rubbing his leg against hers.

Erin eased away. "I heard the victim worked at the betting booths. Someone mentioned you went out with Jewel."

He looked shrewdly at her but shrugged the conversation away, still intent on seduction. "Not me. No way. I don't waste time talking, Doll." He leaned into her, and his hand rubbed higher along her pant leg. His speech was nearly slurred. She hoped it was from the drink and not desire for her. "I'm ready to head to bed somewhere, and the pleasure won't be all mine, I promise."

Getting nowhere, she lifted his hand off her upper thigh when his fingers inched closer to her groin. "I heard you liked blondes, Craig. I'm a redhead: not your type."

"Any dame with your boobs is my type, Doll. Why not take a ride with Craig? I'll show you a real good time. You'll be begging for more."

Erin looked for a quick exit and spied Luke leaning against a rail, observing her. Looking to the other side of the bar, Bill stood at the canteen listening to horse owners he tolerated. "Oh, there's my brother." She jumped up, said goodbye to Craig, and escaped to join Bill. She was pleased when Craig swore, grabbed for her arm, missed, and almost toppled off the barstool.

Luke sauntered over to Bill and Erin, who had moved away from the group of horsemen. "Erin, why the come-on with suspect number one? Bill, did you sick your sister on Craig?"

Bill grimaced. "She has more sense than to cotton to the pretty boy. She probably wants to find out who he'll murder next." He glanced about to ensure no one was too close and spoke in a lower voice. "She wants to keep up with her divining rod reputation for discovering corpses. Maybe she thinks he's the next one to be found dead?"

Erin, exasperated with Bill, felt the flush rise in her face and refused to glance at Luke.

Luke whistled through his teeth, then spoke in a low, indignant voice. "Are you trying to do my job, Miss Rine?"

Erin spun around, glaring at him. "You've got Mark's grandmother upset with questions about him—your best and likely only friend—being a murderer. Celine and Gladys said we should find something to help clear him."

"Don't Aries people ever learn? You're jumping into an explosive situation with a man who has a lousy reputation—one your brother thinks is a pervert." Luke took a deep breath. "And one who the police are investigating as a possible murderer."

"You're so right there, for a change. He's more of a suspect than Mark." Erin's chin rose. "Besides, I only flirted a little with the guy.

"Flirted? A little? The guy's hands shook wanting to feel you up so badly that he looked like he suffered from palsy." He gazed ruefully at her. "I sympathize with the poor slob. You're far too dangerous."

Bill chuckled at them before turning to walk away and discuss horse racing with another stableman.

"Well, he's too dumb to be a murderer anyway," Erin muttered. "Rape is more his speed, but he thinks women will fall into his bed, begging for his attention." Erin pulled her hair back over her forehead. The nervous gesture strained her sweater tighter against her breasts.

Luke's eyes dropped as he surveyed the scenery. He gave a crooked grin. "You are lethal. Good thing we're in public 'cause what I'd like to do now is against the law."

She glared at him, turned, and stomped off to collect Marge. She found her friend parked in front of one of the slot machines biting the tip of her tongue.

"Hi, Erin. I haven't won crackers. Are you going to try again to see if you can win?"

"No excitement in pushing a button, Marge. I tried to do some investigating about the murdered woman but got no results."

"This is a timid sport compared to finding bodies. But trying to flush out a murderer will likely push someone else's buttons: someone dangerous."

"I'm not good enough at this detecting business to cause anyone to worry."

"This button pushing is more fun than sitting at home staring at my belly button. Of course, I need to be able to find my naval to push that button."

Erin laughed. "How much money are you down?"

"A day's wages, but that's my limit. The décor is nice, but there's no sexy men nearby."

"Well, on our way back, I'll point out our suspect. He's supposed to be sexy in women's eyes."

Marge stared at the tipsy man leaning on the lounge bar. "Oh, he's way too cute. I much prefer rugged men. But there's no way he'd drag me off to his cave nor look at me twice."

"He seems to like busty women, so you're a go. He's the type of guy who talks about nothing relevant while he leers at your chest."

"Remember that funny joke I told you about English men and ugly women?"

"That crude one about sex? Oh no, Marge."

The older woman laughed and whispered. "Yes, that one. 'What man looks at the mantle while he's stoking the fire?'"

Luke drove to the trapper's cottage. He greeted the barking Chum and rubbed behind the grovelling animal's ears before sitting down.

"Mr. Fraser, you've lived in this area all your life. Can you tell me anything pertinent to our investigation about the people around here?"

"Not about those in the new housing developments. Some of the older crowd moved into that retirement place across the river. Probably where I'll end up."

"You mentioned the summer lodge up the river. You work as a guide for the boarders during hunting and fishing season and keep an eye on the place for the owners in the off-season."

"The Reynolds only bought that empty place about three years ago. They return for the spring opening during the long May weekend to cater to the fishing crowd." He paused. "They're an older couple from Timmins way and wanted outdoor summer work to look forward to in retirement."

Luke appreciated that the trapper wanted to talk, likely because he was often alone.

"About two miles north of here is the old ghost town of Milnet. A few families have huts up there used for target shooting and hunting. Another seven miles up was the bigger town of Sellwood, which became a ghost town and was razed by a company. Nothing there now except an overgrown graveyard and a few rusted metal crosses. They both used to be mining and lumber towns on the CN railroad line."

"You said you did a lot of trapping over the winter?"

"Sure. I always do. I got pelts from otters, mink, martins, and weasels, though no lynx this year. The beavers are nuisance animals and, alongside rabbits, can be caught year-round. Only eat beaver and muskrat since they're vegetarians and don't taste fishy. And rabbits make for good stew."

"Do you clean the skins yourself?"

"Course I do. I skim off fat and gristle, stretch the pelts out on boards, and tack them down to dry. I use the small sheds out back. There's good income from pelts."

"What about bears for rugs or decor? I heard Americans like to think of themselves as big-game hunters and wanted to bag their own animals."

"I don't encourage hunting bears. The northern resorts drag stale garbage meats into the bushes to attract animals that like carrion. Not me. Bears don't scare me, but I don't want to attract them either. I have a healthy respect for the animals and prefer to keep them a good distance away."

"I think you met the daughter of the lodge's owner years ago. Her name is Sheila Gibson."

"Sure, Sheila Erickson back then. The old fellow that I helped, Bob Wallace, used to manage the lodge for them. He taught me all I know about the wilderness. His boss, Erickson, owned the place then. Their daughter, Sheila, married that lawyer fellow in town, Gibson."

"Have you seen her about the area lately?" Luke asked.

"No. She phones sometimes: called to check on me after this body was found. She came around a few years ago to check out

BETTY GUENETTE

the place, considering if she'd like a cottage, then decided the place was too wild—desolate was the word she used."

Mr. Fraser paused. "I spent some time with her friend last year. She likes to hunt. Growing up, the young Wallace girl hung around with the boss's daughter. She lived with her father in one of the cabins and the two bussed into Capreol for school in good weather. They took correspondence courses from T.O. when weather and road conditions soured."

The older man scratched his head and continued reminiscing, not spotting Luke's intent focus on this new information. "Good company for each other. When the weather improved, Sheila's dad brought in a couple of horses for them to play 'Cowboy and Indian' to keep occupied all summer. Course, the poor one always played the Indian, as she boasted a Cree grandmother. Typical girls, thick as thieves, could get nasty at times. Well, one girl was rich while the other was poor. But they roped and rode well, especially the poor one." The trapper smiled. "Gave their dogs a scare when they caught them with the lasso. The rich girl, Sheila, acted daintier and a bit uppity-like, you know."

Luke eyed the man, surprised by and interested in the name of the other girl. "Was the Wallace girl's first name Cathy?"

"Yup. She works as a secretary for Sheila's husband. She stopped in last year and wanted to act as a guide for the hunters. I told her that idea wouldn't fly. These guys can get pretty rowdy, especially when drinking. They know all sorts of swear words and spew raunchy jokes."

"That old town past the lodge you said is used by hunters. How do I get there?"

"I told you that Sellwood was razed, but Milnet has a few shacks standing among the mill ruins that belong to the older families. You follow Hwy 545 to Milnet Road. A couple of guys there might have seen someone. They wander through the forest and hunt. Old Marcel tracks small game but prefers target shooting. I think he collects and treasures guns. But nobody would've been tramping about that night in the pouring rain."

Luke left and drove past the empty lodge and up Hwy 545 to the deserted town of Milnet. It was a good thing his truck had four-wheel drive with all the potholes and eroded lanes. He slowed his truck to crawl over an old Bailey bridge, then heard rifle shots in the distance. "Hope they're target shooting or the MNR will come down on them."

He drove into a clearing alongside rusted train tracks, parked the truck, and hiked up an overgrown trail past grassy mounds and crumbling stone chimneys. Two burly, older men fired at cans in the distance.

The heavier one waved his rifle in the air and yelled, then pointed the gun at Luke's feet. "You have no business here. *Partez*! This is our patch. No poaching allowed."

Luke strode forward and flipped open his jacket, allowing the men to see his badge and gun holster. "Want me to arrest you for dangerous handling of firearms? Is your safety on? And how about your licenses for them?"

"Got them. This isn't hunting season. We're only target shooting." The hefty man opened his hunting vest and pulled out a card.

The smaller man took out his card as well and sneered. "We watch out for wild animals and need the guns for protection."

BETTY GUENETTE

"Have either of you spotted anyone around here or by the lodge? You must have heard about the murdered woman's body found buried along the river?"

They stared at him. The heavier one answered. "*Rien,* except on that rainy night, before the lodge, closer to town. I heard a car, a grey or beige van on my way out, but that's all. It must have got turned around. I come out more often than Leo here."

"And your name?' Luke asked.

"Marcel Gagnon. This is Leo Guerin. That's my shack over there."

Luke glanced over to see a dilapidated hut sprouting out of thick brushes and weeds backed against a rock wall.

Marcel spoke again, "I heard about the buried body, didn't see nothin' else. I heard nothin' and know nothin'."

The other man scoffed. "I was nowhere 'round here in that bloody downpour."

25

Erin woke up to a rainy Sunday morning and planned a hellish workout in the basement. Bill outfitted their gym with weights and machines to tone his large frame. Her taekwondo class was on Tuesday night, and she hadn't kept up with her exercises.

A couple of hours later, she trod up the stairs with her yellow shorts and tank top plastered to her body. She needed a shower, but a light tapping sounded at the door. Holding a towel in front of her sweaty outfit, she hurried to the door and heard the dogs yelping on the porch before hearing an answering bark she didn't recognize. She opened the door to see her visitor. "Oh, Adam, come in. You're soaking wet."

The tall policeman huddled on the porch with all three dogs sniffing and greeting each other.

"I'll leave Major out here on the porch with yours. He's too wet." With a sheepish look, he followed her into the kitchen and stood, shifting from one leg to the other on the doormat.

Erin grabbed a light throw and draped it over her damp outfit. "What are you investigating now?" She took a bottle of water and handed one to Adam, who declined.

"I drove by this way and figured the dogs would like company, and I wanted to talk. I didn't realize how hard the rain was coming down. I don't want to drip on the floor, so I won't stay."

"Do you have a specific problem you need help with?"

Both of them were startled when Juno started a barking chorus, joined by Rhea in happy unison, all of which preceded a light rap on the door. When she opened the door, Luke squeezed in to keep the dogs out. He must have recognized Adam's truck and spotted the dog.

Luke frowned at the two and spoke in frigid tones. "I assumed another crime was committed here, and I'd hate to miss out on the action. Or am I missing out on something else?"

Erin felt herself bristle. "Did you think to join an orgy, inspector, or are you being insufferable, per usual?"

Ignoring her comment, he turned to the young fellow. "Adam, are you following another line of inquiry?"

"Oh, no, sir. The dogs like each other. I stop by on my days off now." He shifted his tall frame alternately on his legs. "I'll be going. Bye, Erin."

Luke watched him leave, then turned back to face her.

She felt his reaction to the boy's visit was rude and irrational, and he had to know it. But maybe he was jealous? No way!

"Why was Adam here, Erin?"

"Like he said: he cruised by, stopped, and chatted."

"This is his route anyway. He's always passing by. Has he stopped before?"

Erin flung her arm out, and the throw slid off her shoulders. Her temper flashed. "That is none of your business. He's not on duty."

"I don't like my officers being under stress during an investigation. I'm sure he's got a major crush on you."

"Don't be silly. I'm thirty years old, much older than him."

"You're not dressed. Flaunting your body at his impressionable age can wreak havoc. You're the stuff of wet dreams."

"I've just finished exercising, so I'm all sweaty. But shorts and tank top are a far cry from nudity or sexual enticement."

"So, you walk around, your clothes plastered to your body, and entertain male visitors."

Her fury rose at his condescending tone, but she stiffened and smiled, leaning her perspiring body in against him. "Why, Luke, I think you envy Adam. Does my fire sign disturb you? Does my hot, damp body set you alight?"

"Damn it!" Luke's pupils dilated. He pulled her tight against him and pressed his lips harshly against hers. Feeling her body edging into his in response, he held the back of her head and explored her mouth with his tongue while his hands rubbed up and down her back.

"Are you satisfied, Erin?" He pushed her away, his breathing harsh. "You shouldn't tease. You know we're sexually attracted, and you're dynamite."

Erin gulped in air and willed her body heat to lower. "Sorry, all that exercise must have gotten me hot and bothered. I'll behave, but right now, I need a shower."

"And I know you don't want me to get in with you. I'll follow Adam and go stand outside in the cold rain."

Later that day, Erin sat across from Celine, already having told her how she got nothing out of Craig. "Luke shows up at odd times. He doesn't have much information about Craig that he'd share. He'd likely learn more from Mark, but they're not on speaking terms these days."

"I phoned Gladys, and we discussed the case," Celine said. "Mark told Luke to consult his partner, Craig. He refused to say anything to support the investigation."

"I bet Luke can't understand why Mark is hostile when he's questioning him about the case. He considers it doing his job. At least he's being pleasant enough to me, this time."

"If I was in your shoes, I would make the most of this—what you call—pleasant."

"Right," Erin answered. "You know he only wants to sleep with me."

Celine rolled her eyes. "Darn that man. Shame on him! More than the sleep, *je pense.* You will not admit that you want the same... *mais* more of the commitment, *non?*"

"No, and I have no intention of discussing my lack of a love life with you."

26

Luke didn't wait for Beth to file her report on Friday's visit to the law office. After he buzzed her, she entered with a questioning look.

"Beth, did you get to question the staff at the lawyer's office Friday afternoon?"

"I haven't written up my account yet. I would've called you if I'd found anything interesting or important to the case."

"I figured that, but now we have a variable in our equation. Cathy Wallace, the secretary to Craig Gibson, grew up near the trapper's cabin along with Sheila Gibson. Did she volunteer that information?"

"No, not a word. She didn't seem worried about my questions either."

"Celine, Erin's friend, seems to think we don't ask the right questions." He shrugged at her wide-eyed look. "Check your conversations for discrepancies or calculated omissions against this new info."

"Wonder why she didn't mention this. Likely a guilty conscience about something." Beth grinned. "Celine is that psychic friend of Erin's. Is the woman foretelling anything vital for us this time?"

Luke drummed his fingers on the desk. "Don't get cheeky. Anyway, Cathy Wallace will likely say we didn't ask and why should she invite questions that suggest her involvement."

"She must have known we'd find out somewhere down the road."

"Maybe she hoped she'd get lucky and we'd miss it. Give me a verbal report before you write up your notes."

"Well, I showed the picture to the firm's staff again. The receptionist and gopher girl insist they never saw her, and they appear excluded from the office's clique. They just come to work to earn their paycheques. Same with the two secretaries, Lois and Cathy, but they run the place efficiently. They're the right hands of their bosses, and they speak frequently. I didn't see either lawyer, as both were in court all afternoon. And the lobby security guard who saw the victim wasn't on duty."

"Any of your questions yield any new answers?" Luke asked.

"No. Lois and Cathy seemed annoyed I interrupted their work again to question them."

"Pick up different vibes from either of them?"

"No. Lois is the old-fashioned, reticent, and loyal worker you implied. Cathy has a daredevil attitude like she finds life a silly joke," Beth confirmed.

"Or she's laughing at us."

Ralph entered with some papers. "Trevor reported in. Someone at the food bank on Elm Street thinks she spotted Lester a while back. She said they don't pay close attention to the people coming in. Some are shy, others down on their luck and embarrassed, and a few are downright scary. They try not to make eye contact with most of them."

"Did the woman give any special reason why she remembered him?" Luke asked.

"Only that the man seemed 'furtive.' They worry with addicts and other bizarre types coming in. She said you'd never guess when they'd explode or take affront at imagined slights."

"That's a central area downtown. I wonder if he lives in one of the local boarding houses or he could be homeless."

"She had nothing else to add and couldn't swear to his identity."

27

Erin pushed all thoughts of murder out of her mind and concentrated on her workload. Her patients complained about the persistent rains and their muddy yards, but being a mining town, they were lucky the city had solid bedrock. At her last stop, she needed to flush a drain in an abdominal cavity. A young man lost control and rolled his ATV down a hill after getting stuck in mud. A rectangle of his skin needed to be removed from his upper thigh and grafted to cover the open abdominal wound. A drain to a pouch kept the swelling down and allowed the graft to grow into and over the area. She observed the skin flap for colour and warmth and picked a spot with a sterile needle to check for blood flow. Everything checked out. When she placed supplies back into her nurse's bag, the patient's skinny, hairy friend staggered into the apartment with a case of beer.

"Well, well, a visit from a sexy angel of mercy," he mocked while overtly checking out her womanly features.

"Behave yourself, Ron," her patient said. "I need nursing care for a while. Don't go rocking the health care system."

Erin ignored the unpleasant arrival. When she turned around from packing her bag, the visitor stepped directly behind her, his breath of booze and drugs wafting into her face.

"I've got a pimple on my lip, Nursie. How about kissing it to make Ronnie feel better."

Erin, in no mood for oversexed idiots, felt her temper flash. She didn't plan to count numbers here to relax or diffuse the situation.

"Back up, little boy, or you'll get a fatter lip and need a surgeon for your genitals, and I won't be in charge of your aftercare."

"Ah, don't talk so sexy, Nursie." He edged sideways, managing to crowd her and block the exit.

The patient started to rise from his chair. "Ron, don't start trouble. I told you to cool it!"

"Don't want to. She's hot stuff. Doesn't realize how good Ronnie can make her feel." He leered at her. "Some women like to play hard to get."

Erin weighed her situation. Since she wasn't able to default to her flight instinct, she'd have to switch to fight instead. She picked up her bag and offered him one last chance to behave and stepped forward to leave. She moved sideways, and he shifted to intercept her. When he latched his grubby, tattooed hand onto her arm, she pulled away and used the hard edge of her hand to land a side blow against his arm. He yelped but reached out with his other arm to grab her. She kicked his feet out from under him.

When the obnoxious man fell, he banged his head on the chair and lay unmoving on the floor. Erin reached down to check his wrist for a pulse, hoping he wasn't dead from an internal head injury. His hand snaked out, grabbed her wrist, and pulled. She tottered, then pulled back fiercely and hit his arm with her free one. No question about it: he was down. She readjusted and kicked him between the legs. "I did warn you." Not bothering to stay and watch him writhing on the floor, she turned to her appalled patient and told him she would file a report. He would need to guarantee being alone if they continued his medical care.

Safely back in her car, she called her director to report the incident. On the matter of finding Jewel's body, Mrs. Hildeforce had called Erin in to severely reprimand her for jeopardizing the reputation of their nursing office. On the remainder of her nursing route, it seemed her patients regarded her suspiciously. Some acted cranky, while others offered misgiving looks. A couple snuck muffled, leading questions that she avoided. She guessed everyone had heard about her unusual findings again. She arrived home early for taekwondo night and found Bill leaving for his afternoon shift.

"You know, Bill, I should change jobs. Not work as a nurse anymore."

"Go into the private detective business," he answered, striding toward his truck. "The way you fall over bodies, you'd be rich in no time."

She placed her hands on her hips and glared at him. "Keep up with the jokes, Billy-boy, and when I find your body, I'll feed it to the dogs."

He laughed. "Well, that would keep them well-fed for a long time."

28

Luke set out early to visit *The Final Touch*. The bell tinkled when he entered. A woman meeting the description of Craig's wife stood behind the counter talking to a customer. He scanned the shelves and tasteful décor, impressed with the exquisite merchandise. However, he preferred a rustic style and outfitted his Panache camp accordingly. His apartment was simply a place for him to crash between working hours.

When the customer left, he looked over to see cold, dark eyes watching him.

"Can I help you?" she asked.

Luke moved closer to the counter. "I hope so, but I'm not a buyer. Mrs. Gibson?" The woman nodded. "I'm Inspector Landry. I told your husband we needed to question you about the recent murder case."

"I know nothing about some little tramp at the racetrack." She handed him a card. "People sometimes carry my card, but it doesn't mean I murder them."

"I see your husband told you the circumstances of our investigations. I'm interested in your familiarity with the area where they found the victim."

"I haven't gone back to the old place in years."

"Has your vehicle? Someone spotted a lightly coloured van out there when the rain started."

Her eyes widened. "What are you suggesting? How dare you! I will not discuss this nonsense further. You may leave now!"

BETTY GUENETTE

"This is a criminal investigation, Mrs. Gibson. We can request that you come to the station if you aren't willing to co-operate today." Luke watched the woman strain to channel her built-up fury. Her hand shook with enforced control.

She spat out words at him, "I have friends in high places, inspector, but I am willing to co-operate. What was your question again?"

"I want to know if your van was in the Capreol area that night."

"What night? I don't follow this low-class sensationalism."

"Last Wednesday evening. Someone spotted a van similar to yours."

"There are many vans like mine. I only use it to travel to shows and collect items for my store, not night driving in the deep woods, and I have the only keys."

"Your husband usually drives a sporty Cadillac, and you drive a Taurus. You also wear an emerald ring. Does the Taurus car relate to your astrological sign?"

Sheila looked thoughtful. "You're not the only person asking me astrological questions lately. Am I missing some significance about this month's sign and the murder?"

"The murdered woman wore an emerald ring, too, a sign of her Taurus status. But now we're stretching for clues. When did you last visit your old place?"

"Not sure. At least a couple of years ago. I checked out the chalet to see if I wanted a nice hideaway spot. Too woodsy and wild now, and the ownership has changed hands many times. I stopped by to see old Mr. Fraser when I went out there."

"He mentioned that. He said you grew up in the chalet near the caretaker's home with Craig's secretary, Cathy Wallace. Is that correct?"

"That's one way of putting it. Her father rented a cottage on our land, and he worked for mine. The isolation threw us together a lot. My father leased a couple of ponies for us every summer. The guard dogs kept bears and other wildlife away."

"Did you attend school from there?"

"Only in good weather. Once the snow started, I stayed with my aunt in town, and Cathy took mail-order courses to keep up with her studies."

"You must have built quite the friendship over the years."

"We're friends, not bosom pals." Her chin went up. "We travel in totally different circles. Sometimes, I allow her to accompany our elite group."

Martial arts night. After the usual sit-ups and exercises, the evening followed with self-defence lessons. Master Cheung explained both women and men needed to feel stronger and self-assured. They should learn to develop strategies and protective measures to minimize dangerous encounters, and learn what actions to take when all these measures fail. He said a large person seemed intimidating, but someone small could outmanoeuvre and unbalance a larger opponent. He reiterated that, though surprise and offensive responses tended to disarm an attacker, avoidance should always be the first response mechanism.

Master Cheung called one of the regular woman participants, Lani Harper, up to demonstrate. "Pretend you are a timid woman heading home at dusk, all alone. Now, a man follows and grabs you from the back. Many women cry for the man not to hurt them, which often feeds an attacker's soul." Master Cheung shook his head. "Do not beg. Years ago, women carried an old-fashioned hatpin for defence. Now, I would advise a jackknife and pierce his gut for the softest point of entry. But it's not legal to carry if you're planning to use it as a weapon. Now, if he has you by the throat, he will expect you to grab his hands and try to release them. Most people attempt that reflexive action. Not an appropriate manoeuvre. Use the element of surprise. Drive your body into him, knock him over if you can, and scream. If he wants your purse, throw it far away, but if there's a gang after you, then that's dangerous.

Lani, who was tall, slim, and blonde, tried the different manoeuvres. "Nothing is ever this simple. I know I'll be in big trouble if the guy has a knife or gun."

"That is a problem. A knife is easier to camouflage. You can kick his arm to dislodge the knife once you break free. If he has a gun, why does he not shoot you right away?"

Lani worked through a few more defence tactics to demonstrate to the group.

Master Cheung turned. "Women are the most vulnerable; however, men must learn to evade attacks as well. Now, Erin, I want you to walk out. I cannot imagine you acting frightened. You are bold and would get angry and retaliate. But now, I am following you. You sense the person trailing behind and become worried. You pick up speed and try to reach a safe haven. But, if no shelter is around, when he is almost on you, flip around and kick him in the groin or knee. If he attempts to strangle you when standing in front, do not waste time and energy trying to dislodge his hands. Ram into him, mark him by scratching at his face, punch his nose, poke his eyes, or bite. He will let go to protect himself. You might say that'll make him angrier, but he planned to murder you anyway. You have nothing to lose. Mark him for DNA evidence. You may save a future victim."

Lani spoke up, "I can't imagine thinking about saving someone else at that point."

Erin demonstrated the different approaches and stances with Master Cheung in different scenarios, and then the group rose to practice in pairs.

Master Cheung continued instructing while moving around the practising group. "If they have a knife, you have a chance. If they have a gun, watch for an opportunity to run away in a zigzag path. You'll make yourself a harder target. Carry a whistle or bear spray if you travel a lot, especially in isolated areas. Be careful, as sometimes the predator can have a toxic spray to subdue you or will grab yours and retaliate." Master Cheung assessed and corrected their positions as he traversed the room. "Try to travel with someone, as there's safety in numbers. If you're knocked out or tied up, you have no chance to survive on your own without outside help. Try not to become a statistic. Above all, flight first, and then fight. Do not give in. It is a fact that an abduction is best foiled at the beginning of the attack."

30

Erin stopped to see Gladys Richards during her rounds the next day. "Any news from Mark, or have you seen the other two women from the apartment?"

"Nothing much, except that lowlife—probably the cousin—came by, but they must have told him to get lost. He stood outside their apartment for a few minutes and talked, making lots of angry gestures."

"You should have called Luke. They're searching for him."

"No, thank you." Gladys was stiff. "He was furtive, only staying a few minutes before he left. I'm cross with Luke right now, and I'm not going to help him."

"Finding this cousin might help Mark's case... or not. Hard to say."

"All he has on Mark is his firm's business card, circumstantial evidence at best. I talked to Celine, and we formed a plan to get evidence." She glanced out the window. "Oh, there are the two now, getting off the bus. Quick, Erin, go talk to them."

"Talk to them about what? Finding bodies?"

"You'll think of something. Hurry!"

Erin charged down the stairs. "This is stupid. I am stupid." She rushed out as the women passed the door. "Excuse me. Um, do you know where Hazel Street is? I'm the new visiting nurse for the area, and I tend to get lost."

Melanie gasped. "Are you the nurse that found Jewel's body in the ground?"

"Yes, sort of. Actually, the dog got upset and found her. I only followed him. He tried helping by digging around her body."

The other one frowned. "I'm Kelly, and this is Melanie. We roomed with Jewel. She was my best friend forever. Melanie's only rented with us a couple of months." She hesitated. "Was Jewel buried in that mud?"

Erin felt they deserved some information about their friend. "Except for her hands. They said the position of her body and the rain exposed her hands."

"I think we should find somewhere else to live." Melanie, the darker-haired one, shivered. "This place gives me the creeps now."

"You could look for a third person to rent. I heard her only relative was a cousin. I guess you wouldn't want a guy, though."

"And certainly not him. He's awful. Now he thinks he has evidence."

"Quiet, Melanie. Lester always brags like he's coming into money."

"How did Lester hear about her death?" Erin asked innocently. "The newscast gave the impression the police couldn't find him."

Melanie opened her mouth to speak, but Kelly nudged her and spoke first, "The story was in the newspapers and on the radio. The two weren't close. Sorry, we have to go." Kelly grabbed Melanie's hand and towed the other one behind her.

Melanie glanced back. "We don't know where Hazel Street is."

Erin hurried up the stairs and filled in Mrs. Richards. "I'll have to tell Luke. Darn! Now, he'll think I'm trying to get involved and solve his murder case."

"We wouldn't have to interfere," Gladys answered, "if he believed Mark was innocent."

At the end of the workday, Marge called Erin on her cell phone and asked if she'd care to go out for supper when she got back to town.

At the restaurant, Marge slumped in her chair. "I'm going to quit this stupid job. Our dragon of a boss is throwing her weight around. She wants everything done, stat."

"The work will get easier with the student replacements in the summer. But you're such an in-charge person that you try and manage everything yourself. Relax for a change. The place can get along without your constant surveillance."

"Right. By the time I get the temps' asses in gear, they'll be heading back to school." The secretary grunted. "The boss has her niece covering my three week holiday in August. Asked me if I wanted more time off—minus pay, of course."

"If she's giving you a hard time, she might hope you quit. Then her niece can take over your job."

"Bugger her." Marge pursed her lips. "Though I can try for a job in that new hospital."

"Great idea. When my friend Kayla returns from England, I'll go too."

"I need a guaranteed job before I can leave. I'm saving for the kids to go to college." Marge picked up the menu. "What to eat, menu or buffet?"

Erin glanced at the large buffet spread. "We can always go back for seconds at the buffet. I'll take my favourite healthier picks first. Then I hope I'll have no room for dessert."

"I like everything except the green salads and will try it all twice."

Erin grinned, stood, and approached the buffet. "But you'd feel better eating the chicken and vegetables first."

"I would not." Marge followed and grinned as she spooned

creamy macaroni salad, hot potato fries, and greasy breaded onion rings onto her plate. "I'd feel cheated. No way I'll go out for comfort food and nibble on rabbit leaves."

31

Lester snuck over to Jewel's apartment. Knowing the side kitchen window didn't shut properly, he stooped outside to listen when the two entered their ground-floor apartment. He peered up, able to keep hidden at that angle. He saw them in profile. Standing by the door, Melanie turned and fidgeted, rubbing her hands together. What a nervous ninny. She'd developed more bad habits besides biting her nails. She stared at Kelly, her eyes as big as saucers, and took a deep breath. "Kelly, why are you protecting Lester?"

"What are you talking about?"

"When he came to the door, he kept whispering about following someone. You haven't told the police about him and what he said."

"That bitch," Lester mumbled. "She'd turn me over to the cops in a minute."

"No, and I don't intend to, Melanie. Why let the police find him? He's dreaming of another get-rich scheme. He doesn't have information worth bugger all."

Lester believed they'd be surprised by all the things he managed to uncover.

"But you shushed me with that nurse and dragged me away. Why didn't you want her to know what he said?"

"I didn't tell the police he was here. Why tell the nurse and get myself in trouble?"

Melanie collapsed onto the chair. "This is awful."

BETTY GUENETTE

"You worry too much. It's bad enough that Jewel was killed without us getting paranoid about our safety." Kelly hung up her jacket and checked her purse. "I'm broke these days, but at least Lester couldn't rip me off. What do we have to cook?"

"Not much. I have a little money. Why not order a pizza?"

"Sounds like a plan. Get the meaty one." Kelly took a beer from the fridge.

He figured they wouldn't want to share that pizza or beer with him. That was fine. He needed to stay sober to plan his future.

Melanie cleared her throat. "I heard Lester tell you about someone. Something about Jewel meeting a lover at an empty lodge?"

"You heard wrong." Kelly took a long swallow of her cold drink. "Lester talked about a dodge, a way to evade the cops. He always keeps a low profile."

Melanie chewed her nails. "Please, be careful, Kelly. I'm scared. You should go to the police if you have information. What if you're in danger, too?"

"I don't know anything about Jewel's murder. You need to calm down and stop imagining things. Don't you think I want her murderer caught?"

Lester slunk away, grumbling to himself. The two hadn't an inkling about how smart he was. It wasn't the first time he listened from that kitchen window. Some of those old biddies across the way spied on the front door from their windows. They couldn't see the kitchen's exterior wall. He could bide his time before getting payback on the creep who killed his cousin. He had concrete evidence with the compromising photo. Those two women inside would quit calling him "Lester the Loser." Oh, he'd heard them, alright; they called him dumb and laughed at him.

Well, he'd teach the stupid broads some lessons in the brains department. And there was no way he was foolish like Jewel, going to visit a God-forsaken lodge in the wilderness and ending up in a muddy grave. No, siree, not this smart guy. Not Lester Lisson.

Erin checked on Mrs. Billings again. "Spotted any more wandering bears from your window?"

"No, but they've cut lots of brush away and banned all feeders except during wintertime. And they bought heavy-duty garbage containers to dissuade animals from scrounging." She grimaced when Erin adjusted her leg. "Bears are strong and will get into the bins if they're hungry enough, but they have motion detectors active at night. If all else fails, they mentioned getting a guard dog."

Erin finished her assessment and redressed the woman's wound.

Mrs. Billings was in a much better frame of mind today. "That nice Mr. Cresswell came over and thanked me for pointing out his predicament. He brought me chocolates that we shared. He said when the weather clears up, he'll push me around in a wheelchair on the pathways. As if I'd let him. I'm far too independent for that." She smiled with a faint blush. "By then, I hope I'm using a cane. It'll be pleasant to talk with someone when I'm out walking."

Erin smiled when she left. "Today, I feel like Cupid spreading romance in the air."

Next, she visited a sad woman in her early 40's, one recovering from knife wounds inflicted by a drunken boyfriend.

"He didn't really mean to hurt me, nurse."

"He stabbed you five times before he stopped, Lilly. All your wounds are on your lower abdomen and legs, but thankfully not your chest. Three are shallow and taped closed, but the two on your leg were quite deep and needed stitches."

"He did those last. He got real mad 'cause I ran into the kitchen and dialled 911."

Erin chewed her lower lip to stay quiet and not be judgemental when the woman's tears welled up. She stroked her patient's arm. "The police department is setting up counselling for you and charging him for the attack." The woman cried silently, the tears dripping onto her blouse. "Lilly, I'll take the stitches out next week when the drainage stops. The three small wounds don't need a bandage."

"But now he's in jail. What will I do here all alone?"

Erin found she couldn't respond to her plea and gave Lilly another pat on her back. She told the woman to take care and left. Shaking her head, she wished she understood anxious, lonely people better. She felt enough empathy for the ill and the downtrodden but tried not to be judgemental with the timid, dependent ones.

Next, she visited Eliza. Now, this woman was a force to be reckoned with.

The woman smiled on seeing her. "I think I'll miss your visits. The packing fell out and I see no opening or room to insert gauze."

Erin smiled back. "Let's check." After examining the sealed wound, she pressed the area around the nipple, noting no seepage. "You're right. I'll have to sign off and wish you good luck on your return to work."

"I hope my clientele stayed loyal and haven't run and found other interests."

"But they'll miss your nipple rings." Erin looked up. "You aren't putting them back?"

"No. Too risky." She frowned and tilted her head to look at Erin. "One of my admirers stopped by and mentioned you were the nurse involved with that lawyer, Craig Gibson; they said he's the number one suspect in that murder case."

Erin recoiled, thinking of the gossip spreading about her being linked with that man. "Never. That man's repulsive. Is he one of your clients, or should I not ask?"

"No. He's crass and can't afford me anyway. I've met him and his wife at a posh to-do with one of my single, rich clients. That pair think they're classy, Humph, I'm above them."

"That awful man's partnered with a lawyer friend of mine who's happily married." Erin paused. "I'll bet he stared at your chest when you talked to him."

"Most men do, but most are a little more refined about it." She buttoned her blouse. "With these implants, I get away from having to wear that torturous bra. No sag allowed. Besides, his wife didn't give him a lot of leeway with me; she watched him constantly and gave me the cold shoulder. I stuck my tongue bolt out at her when no one else was looking."

"Wow, you do live on the edge. My police friend has her on the list of suspects."

Eliza grimaced. "I don't think she'd get her soft white hands dirty. I could imagine her hiring someone to purge annoyances, though."

"You're right. I think she'd pay to eliminate a nuisance, maybe permanently?"

The woman smirked. "If you ever need another job, get in touch with me. You've got the boobs for the job."

"But not the stomach nor the desire. Anyway, thanks for the offer." Erin returned the vivacious woman's smile. "Well, I enjoyed meeting you, and I hope you have no recurring infections from those ghastly piercings."

Finishing her rounds early, Erin drove down the dirt road opposite Mr. Fraser's property. The road soon narrowed into a single lane, making her turn back, angry at herself. "What am I going to find, pray tell? As Luke insinuated, I'm a novice detective. I'll give Mr. Fraser a surprise visit to see if he knows anything else."

The man swallowed the rest of his coffee when she arrived. "I'm not scheduled today, nurse. Would you like some coffee?"

"No thanks, I'm good." She bent down and rubbed Chum's ears. The dog stretched and lay down on his rug. "I wanted to know if you've heard anything else about the murder. The police keep everything hush-hush."

"The only difference is that more cars are going by these days. People are curious." He shrugged. "I don't know what they expect to see. There's mostly wilderness further down that bush road."

"Have the police asked you a lot of questions?"

"No. It's not as if I'm going anywhere. I certainly didn't recognize the young woman's picture. I'm not much help." He scratched his head. "There were a couple of bears up the road, young-uns. The mother must be around."

Erin gulped. "Good to know. I'll make sure to drive slowly. Do you hunt them?"

"No, the meat isn't any good to eat, and I don't need rugs."

"We looked after a patient who developed trichinosis from poorly cooked bear meat. Being a bushman, he should have known better."

"I heard that disease always ends in a slow and painful death."

"Yes, he finally died. By then, the death was a relief for the family members."

"Don't need reminders, Nurse. I've lived in the bush a long time."

"Did you know Sheila Gibson when she was younger? I heard she lived at the big lodge."

"She was Sheila Erickson when she lived there. They played and hunted there in the summer, and they rode horses. The inspector asked me about the two women and how they grew up here."

"What two women? I didn't hear anything about there being two women involved."

"Cathy Wallace, the secretary to Sheila's husband, Craig. She was best friends—sort of—with Sheila. They grew up together on the large estate. Cathy's father rented a small cottage and managed the acreage around the Erickson's lodge."

Erin drove from the cabin, thoughts churning in turmoil. This Cathy couldn't have a motive for murdering Jewel. She blended into the edges of the investigation and appeared as a spectator more than a player. Sheila had the most to lose if Craig was either guilty or innocent, as being a suspect was damaging her social status regardless. She must've wanted him anyway, though she needed to be able to hold her head up in society, too. Gossip seemed most important to her and her fellow elite. Erin believed friends like that were fickle, unnecessary appendages.

The police wanted Lester picked up for questioning, but Erin believed they didn't suspect him as Jewel's murderer, as he had the most to lose with her death. Gladys had told Celine Jewel's car was leased, the apartment was rented, and the small trust for Jewel's education was exhausted. The elder brigade's grapevine worked well.

She drove down side streets, checking out the houses and surveying stores. There were some pleasant ones with a medley of old and new. She couldn't see the Sudbury smokestack, but its silhouette would stand out as she drove home. Small lakes peppered the area, probably the run-off from the nearby cliffs. Seeing the roads growing narrower and steeper, she turned around at a cul-de-sac and drove back into town. She would pick up some groceries on her way home.

Inside the large mall, she spotted Sheila entering a designer shop. "I'll never afford those prices." She liked to buy high-quality items but caught sales, too. She wasn't fussy—well, only about colours clashing with her titian-coloured hair. She looked like a disaster in most reds and oranges. She pushed back her hair, then decided she might as well aspire to join the rich in that expensive shop. What a lark! At least she'd be safe enough from the woman's antagonistic stares with other customers milling around.

Erin glanced at a few displayed items and moved hangers to the side. The rug on the floor muffled her footsteps as she observed Sheila in the store's rear with a saleswoman. The clerk bore a haunted expression as Sheila's lips tightened in a displeased frown. When she turned around, Erin bent her head to look at a price and gasped. So much money for this scanty piece of lace. A month of her wages for one brassiere. Eliza sure saved a lot of money with her breast enhancements. Sheila, her strident tone carrying, announced she would try the negligee on. Seeing her enter one of the changing rooms, Erin grabbed a couple of items in her size and asked the saleswoman in a hushed tone to let her try them on.

The clerk smiled with a usual artificial twist of her lips and directed Erin to the second stall. She tried to listen in on Sheila, but she only heard faint breathing. The clerk would soon return, so Erin pulled off her sweater and bra. She reached back to clasp on the lacy blue bra and, in dismay, noted that the almost nonexistent cup exposed most of her breasts, which bulged out and over the bra. She grabbed the other piece. Damn, this one had even less fabric.

When the clerk checked on Erin, who was dressed again, she offered to bring other items. Erin shook her head without speaking. Sheila next door spoke in condescending tones to the clerk. She demanded that a different size—a smaller one—be brought to her.

She heard a low, familiar voice and peeked out to see Craig standing by the door, asking for his wife. The man must've been meeting his wife for shopping or supper. Oh, goodness, she couldn't hide in here forever. Sheila wouldn't like to see her greeting Craig. And the clerk would start wondering about her stalling in the cubicle, and there was no way Erin was carting the brassieres out. She slid out and resolved not to run. She smiled at Craig, who looked dumbfounded before glancing toward the other changing rooms. Erin picked out a sheer blue blouse and returned to her dressing room. When she heard Sheila depart the cubicle, she peeked around the curtain. They left the shop without purchasing anything, and she felt certain Craig made no comment on her presence.

Erin figured she was already in trouble and trailed the couple. When Sheila stepped into another expensive store, Craig kept walking toward a small restaurant. Well, she didn't plan on following him. She dawdled at nearby kiosks before entering the store in time to see Sheila waltz into another changing room carrying a couple of sweaters. "No plan. Oh, well, I have a right to shop here, too." She selected a random top and matching vest and entered the other changing room. Bonus! She heard Sheila's talking to someone on her cell phone.

"I'm going to supper with Craig and burning time with a little shopping first. Of course, I'm picking the most exclusive shops. Where else?" Sheila paused to listen. "No, I'm not going to the theatre this week. The play didn't get good reviews." Silence again, and then she spoke angrily. "I'll tell that hussy to lay off my husband, good and clear. Who told you she played up to him at the racetrack? He wasn't interested in her? Good. I knew she lied when she told me she hadn't met him. I'll call you back tomorrow."

The spiteful words echoed against the wall. Erin guessed she must be the hussy in question. There was no sense in having a messy confrontation in public. It was time to be smart and take prudent action. She managed to slink away undetected.

34

Luke drove back to Capreol to question Jewel's roommates again. He'd get more lucrative answers if he separated them. No playing off each other, then.

He asked Kelly to sit with him in their living room. "I know we've gone over your story many times, but I want you to try hard to think of anything else that may help the case, even seemingly irrelevant matters."

"There's nothing else," Kelly answered in a sullen voice. "Jewel was foolish and too trusting in men."

"You don't think a woman is involved?"

"She wasn't a lesbian."

"That's not what I meant. What if the lover's wife got wind of her straying husband's indiscretions and threatened Jewel?"

"Jewel wouldn't like a confrontation, but she wouldn't care about the woman. She'd be sure the fellow loved her and expect him to leave his wife and marry her. No sense."

"Would your friend have gone to meet the wife if the woman called her?"

"I don't think so. She was meek. If the guy was a lawyer, well, rich enough to not bother with a lame-brain like her. She wouldn't pose a threat."

"What if she threatened the lawyer to tell his wife if he was trying to break up with her?"

BETTY GUENETTE

"I can't believe killing would be a choice when divorce is so easy." Kelly paused. "And the wife probably knows he plays around."

"Do you think Jewel would expect money to keep quiet about their affair?"

"I don't know for sure. It's possible if she knew nothing would be gained from mouthing off." Kelly shook her head. "Unless she accepted he didn't care for her long term, then she might want payback."

"Anything at all you want to ask?"

"Like me, Jewel had no relatives other than Lester. Can I have her clothes and a few items? They'd never fit Melanie, and she doesn't want anything: thinks the idea is morbid."

"I can't see why not. We've checked through it all. The clothes wouldn't suit Lester."

"Unless he wanted to sell them, but they're not expensive."

Next, Luke asked Melanie to sit down with him. Kelly took her time exiting the room.

"I want you to go over everything you can think of. No matter how trivial."

"I'm new. Jewel wouldn't confide in me. And that Lester guy always whispered to her. I didn't try to eavesdrop. He was scary... and smelly and... drank a lot."

"Did Jewel ever talk about married men or have strong views on breaking up a couple?"

"No. She kind of floated along, enjoying life." Melanie fiddled with a large brooch that held back her straight black hair. "She was greedy for life and affection. I don't think material things meant much to her."

"But she did wear that flashy ring."

136

"Only because the gift meant someone cared."

"You don't think she'd try to blackmail her lover?"

"If he was cruel or ditching her, maybe she might fight back. I think she'd only attack the man if she began to hate him."

When Luke left, he considered visiting Mark's grandmother, but figured she wouldn't have new information. She delivered barbs with quite the acidic tongue when she became annoyed and preached. He decided he'd play it safe and comfortable, not that he was a coward, oh no. Besides, what if he ran into Mark? His friend seemed aggravated by him as well.

35

Lester slouched in the bar, cradling his second beer. He kept his cap on, the visor at eye level, and now sported a scraggly beard. Kelly told him the police borrowed that old photo of him and put out an APB to pick him up if found alive. He wanted them to continue thinking he ran away or died. He always kept a low profile anyway; he had no friends anywhere and needed no one else.

That Melanie chick was such a wet blanket. Well, she wouldn't bother him except to snitch to the police that he was around. He made a point to phone Kelly on her cell, not their landline. The last couple of times, he snuck over and met her across the lane behind the Manor. That would have to change. Too many people and too close for comfort. He spotted an old guy from the home gawking at him last time. And the old biddies probably spent their day staring out the window, hoping for thrills.

Geez, in his school days, he ran around with a couple of buddies and flashed old ladies, scaring them shitless. It was loads of fun until they were caught and warned off. Later, his father found out and beat the hell out of him again. He finally buggered off. His old man—a mean, abusive drunk—always fell into a senseless stupor, his head collapsed on the kitchen table. Once, Lester came that close to killing the sopping drunk. He stood behind the chair grasping a knife, staring at his slobbering mess of a father. "Not worth the trouble," he muttered at the time. The old man soused himself daily and would destroy himself soon enough. Lester knew he needed to bide his time till he ran off and could take care of himself.

Jewel's father, his mom's brother, also excessively drank anything smelling of alcohol. He'd probably poisoned himself by now. Both their wives ran off when he and Jewel were youngsters, deserting them without a backward glance. He didn't blame either one. The yelling and beatings drove them away. He only wished they had taken Jewel and him with them. The two kids never spent much time with each other. He was a few years older and lived at the other end of town. Their fathers liked to meet and raise a drink to each other, cursing their wives and then belting their children if they hung around inside the trailers. One Christmas, during a cold and heavy snowfall, he remembered how the two youngsters snuck down to an empty house, heat turned low for the pipes, and smoked pot. He introduced the stolen stuff to Jewel.

A shame, but only the present mattered. Now, he needed to look after himself.

Kelly had listened to the couple's phone conversations more often than she first let on. He dragged the information out by scaring her, saying she'd be murdered next.

He planned to threaten Craig Gibson now that he knew the name. Kelly said the man didn't want his wife to find out about his affairs, and the dame held most of their money. But Lester wouldn't overlook the fact this Craig guy likely killed Jewel and was dangerous. But Lester was smarter than anyone. He rose and went outside for a cigarette. That guy wouldn't catch him napping.

36

Erin yawned and trudged through her workday, finishing up at last. What else could she look into about this murder? She knew she should try to forget the case but did the investigators miss anything?

Gladys and Celine seemed to think Lester was the key. However, no one had a lead on his whereabouts. They could discover more from the two women who grew up at the lodge. They would know the burial site and the surrounding region, but so would other people who lived nearby. At least Mr. Fraser couldn't manage the burial himself. He must be innocent. The roommates and Lester seemed out of the question as well: no motives there. Sheila appeared to be the prime suspect. Like her brother, Erin didn't believe Craig possessed the drive or recklessness to murder anyone. But if his wife found out about the affair? Divorce or failure to maintain her marriage would be detrimental to Sheila's reputation. Erin knew she should meet the secretary, Cathy, and dig for answers.

When Erin arrived in town, she stopped at Mark's office. The secretary, Lois, recognized her name and beeped her in. "He's tidying up."

Mark emerged and shook her hand before gesturing for her to enter. "Are there further complications with this murder case, or do you need an attorney's advice?"

"My neighbour and your grandmother are conniving to make me help clear you of involvement with the murder. I found out that Craig's wife and his secretary grew up together. I would like an excuse to meet Cathy, but I don't want to run into Craig."

"Why not? He's harmless. You're not afraid of him, are you?"

"Not at all. Celine and your grandmother convinced me to play up to him, only once." She held up a finger. "I almost vomited. Now he thinks I've got the hots for him."

Mark smothered a laugh. "You are good for my high stress levels these days."

"Well, in exchange, tell me how I can meet Cathy and what excuse I can give for wanting to."

"Craig's in court right now and doesn't usually return when they recess late. Cathy will be checking out soon. Let me ask Lois." He buzzed the intercom, and Lois came in.

"What can I do for you, Mr. Richards?"

"How formal. Erin is not our client. Can you think of an excuse to get Cathy over and meet Erin? My grandmother has questions. You know how persistent she can be."

Lois smiled, then stood quietly pursing her lips, obviously thinking.

Erin tried a few ideas. "What if I say the trapper, Mr. Fraser, asked about her?"

"We need more than that." Mark tapped his finger on the desk. "How about if you say the man chatted at length about her hunting prowess, and you wanted to meet her? She does bring her skills up in conversations."

Lois smiled. "Yes, that sounds good for her ego. I'll get her."

Erin and Mark stood as if leaving to make the visit look informal enough when Lois ushered Cathy in.

"Hello, Cathy? I'm Erin Rine, Mr. Fraser's nurse. He bragged about your hunting skills, and I wanted to meet you, though guns and hunting aren't my forte. Are you still fond of the outdoors?"

141

"I don't ride or do rodeo tricks anymore. I hunt occasionally for fun and still shoot like a pro. Did you want some facts, or are you looking for experience?"

"No way, I'm leery about guns. Mr. Fraser talked a lot about you two girls growing up in the bush and how capable you were. I was intrigued."

"Oh, yes, you met Sheila at her shop. I'm the thorn to her rose mentality. Craig mentioned that he heard you practised karate."

"Taekwondo, actually, and I try to work out. I believe women should be strong."

"So, you're the nurse who found that buried woman's body?"

"Well, the dog, Chum, did. Mr. Fraser couldn't get down the hill since he lost his lower leg in the shooting accident. I ended up following his anxious dog to the site."

"What an awful experience for you. But you're a nurse. I'm sure you see enough death in your line of work."

"Not violent death, not like that." Erin shrugged. "You must know the area, then."

"Sure, I've known it for years now. I'd like to act as a guide. Fraser thinks women's ears are too delicate to listen to crass drunken hunters and fishermen. Most of them spend more time drinking, swearing, and spewing dirty jokes than hunting or fishing."

"Do you know that other trapper up near Milnet?" Erin asked. "Apparently, he shoots his gun over the heads of people who trespass."

"I haven't anything to do with him. I heard about his eccentric behaviour, though. You'd think he guarded a gold mine in those shacks."

"He must be a character if he can shoot at people and not get charged," Erin said.

"Yes, I suppose so. Well, now it's Friday, thank goodness. Nice to meet you, but I'm off to find a fun party for the weekend."

"Is your boyfriend back in town, Cathy?" Mark asked.

Erin noticed Lois raise an eyebrow.

"Not till next week, but I'll find myself a good time. I'll go out to the casino on Saturday with Sheila." She glanced at Erin as she swept out the door. "Craig told me you often go out there to watch your brother's horses when they race at the track. We'll see you there."

Erin swept her bangs away farther over her forehead. She didn't like the ominous feeling she got from the woman about her visiting the track with Sheila. Did the words sound too much like a challenge, or were they implying a threat?

Erin stood on the threshold of the porch door, ready to go outside, when Adam arrived, and jumped out of his truck with his dog. She watched him approach Janelle.

Janelle played with Bill's dogs on the lawn, taking full advantage of the sunny weather. Juno and Rhea didn't listen to her stay command but loped over to sniff and jump around Major.

Janelle nodded to Adam, who said hello and held her hand, palm up, to the big German shepherd. He sniffed, then licked his tongue across the palm.

"Major likes you," Adam said. "He usually takes a while to warm up to people."

"Most animals sense friends. This breed of dog needs special handling to behave properly and act safely. Are you teaching him good control measures?"

"Of course. I do canine patrol training. I want him as my own, not out in the field."

"But you're in the field. Do you have a good education? Other languages?"

"Only English," Adam answered. "I have a degree in Geography and took law courses."

"And where does that get you in the police force? Do you not have other ambitions?"

"I like being a policeman. You don't start at the top in a job."

Erin kept silent inside the screen door, amazed at the young woman's direct approach—like she was going for the jugular.

Janelle kept on, "You don't speak French, and this is a bilingual country. You'd be able to apply for many jobs then and be promoted in your work. I have studied four languages. Italian and Spanish are easier if you already know French."

Adam scowled. "Well, sorry. I'm an ordinary guy, not super ambitious."

Janelle seemed to search for more fuel to attack. "Auntie says you're a Taurus. That means you're unwieldy, but you also carry a disposition of patience, kindness, and reliability. You need to push yourself more and do different things."

Adam pointed to Major. "You make me sound like my dog. Hey, I'm training Major to follow a scent to track people. Lend me your cap, and I'll show you."

Janelle paused a moment, then shrugged and handed over her cap.

"Smell, Major," Adam commanded. The dog sniffed the cap, then her pant legs. "Walk around the house, then into a few bushes. I'll wait five minutes, then send him to find you."

Janelle beamed at the idea and took off.

Adam smiled back, then frowned and muttered. "For such a bristly little thing, she's pretty when she smiles. Track, Major." The dog sniffed the cap again before he loped off, his nose unerringly glued to the ground. He caught up to her as she rounded a shed a few houses down and across from Adam. Major sat on his haunches, barked, and tapped her with his paw. The other two dogs watched the procedure in blissful ignorance.

Erin retreated into the house and brought out three cans of ginger ale. Adam seemed relieved to greet her and rushed to speak.

"Hey, Erin. I'm training Major to follow scents. He tracked Janelle around the side of the house. That's not too far, but he's learning."

"That's awesome. Bill's dogs aren't dumb—well, Rhea is a bit, but she practises at the role. We hadn't done much training till Janelle started working with them. We just like dogs and enjoy the exercise. Juno comes from hunting stock, but she has a timid nature."

Janelle crossed back over the road and emerged from the neighbours' cedar hedge, Major prancing behind her. "Good dog, Major. He found me all right."

Adam smirked. "Of course, I knew he would. I got myself one smart dog."

The three sat on the glider on the front lawn. Erin enjoyed watching the byplay between Janelle and Adam, the three dogs resting at their feet. The policeman held his hesitant ground under Janelle's forthright and bossy manner and answered her questions with his own. Erin smiled on seeing Celine's curtain twitch.

38

In the early afternoon, Erin accompanied Bill to the stables. John, the trainer, had already lightly exercised Chelsea Sky. A nervous and skittish gelding to begin with, he was on a temporary layoff from a track accident a few weeks ago. John now harnessed the trotter, River Lad. This gelding stood quiet and always behaved well. After a few jogs around the track, John guided the glossy bay to the entrance. "Don't put him in claiming races, Bill. Some scoundrel will grab and ruin him. Want to try him out, Erin?" the older trainer asked.

"I hoped for another offer. I brought my riding gloves in case."

She took the trainer's helmet, wiggled into the buggy, and spread her legs apart to hook her feet into the holders. John led them out and warned her to steer clear of the other drivers practising on the track.

"Turn him around, go both ways, and keep him from focusing on only the one turnabout." John turned to Bill before she led off. "I'm glad my son, Jason, is clear of this new murder. That sure was scary last month."

"Being Erin's brother, I'm surprised they haven't arrested me yet. They say murderers are close to home, and I live in the same house alongside a witch who has a body-attracting wand. Should make that plural; bodies."

She glowered at him and strapped on the helmet, too pleased to be driving the horse to contradict anything he said.

John leaned over and whispered to Bill, "She's a lovely woman and a good nurse from what I've heard her clients say about her."

She heard the comment, grinned, and set off. Her fingers played with the reins to trot around, pulling lightly to change and move in both directions. She slowed and turned, then sped up and turned again, riding around and around the track. River Lad's gait and rhythm always proved flawless as she sped to the finish line, reining in to pull him up to the gate. Stopping, she jerked in surprise to see Luke standing there talking to Bill at the fence. He waved to her when John took the reins, Bill following to unhook the cart and waiting to walk the horse around. When Erin disengaged her feet, she exited the bike with more speed than grace.

Luke gazed at her, his eyes half shut and whispered. "I didn't realize the position and spread of your legs in that contraption till I watched you coming around the turn."

Feeling herself flush, she hit her hand on the helmet when she reached up to pull at her hair. "That's rather a sexist remark."

"Depends on your view, and I must say mine was great. Celine's visions don't compare with my fantasies right now."

Erin pulled off her helmet and shook her hair before running a hand through it. "Why are you out here again?"

His eyes glazed. "What? Why am I here?" He blinked and straightened his shoulders. "I'm investigating a murder, yes." He spoke louder. "I came to talk to Bill about Craig."

John glanced back. "Are you hounding more innocent people, inspector?"

"Would you prefer we let murderers go free? How else can we solve crimes if we don't question people in the victim's circle?"

"You gave my son, Jason, a hard time last month, and he was innocent."

"Yes, and I'm sorry about that. Surprising what we don't know of a person's capabilities, what's important to them, and what they'll do to keep silent."

"So, how else can we help you, Luke?" Bill asked, coming closer.

"I want more insight into Craig's character and behaviour. We think he's the man involved with the victim. We're digging and hoping someone saw them together."

Bill shook his head. "I can't see him getting involved in murder, either with effort or inclination. John agrees. Craig's a surface player solely out for his own instant gratification."

"What about other dealers out here?" Luke asked. "Is he in on any joint horse ownership?"

"No. He gets chummy with some of the owners, mainly the well-off ones, usually with nothing more than a drink to solicit information for making sizable bets," Bill added. "He pulls off deals with a few less honest drivers. Likely wins as much as he loses. He ogles the women, mainly, and sizes up what wives are available for fun and games under the bed sheets."

That evening, Bill left alone for the track. Erin skipped going to the races. She didn't want the trouble of disentangling herself from Craig's wandering hands again, or a confrontation with Sheila. She disliked brawls, and women often acted out the worst. The way Cathy made her comment about visiting the track, she must have had suspicions based on something Craig said. The man was dumb enough to talk freely to others. You'd think he'd be subtle around his wife. Well, she deserved him. Erin didn't have the gumption today to deal with both of the women and Craig. He couldn't be a nuisance if she wasn't there. She knew she would have to confront him to squash any acquaintance once this murder investigation blew over. She couldn't shun him forever and miss all the Saturday night races, and she was the guilty one who baited his interest, thanks to Gladys and Celine's conniving interference.

Sunday, Erin and Bill drove to John's farm, jokingly called Johnny's Ponderosa. Though rain fell during the night, the sun now glimmered through the clouds. She convinced Jason and Jenny to accompany her riding, mainly as protection from wild animals. Safety in numbers, she believed. Jenny, a newly graduated schoolteacher, started working with the horses for the summer off and dated John's son. Jason saddled the large roan Bill usually rode, planning to take it himself today, and the women took the Pintos along the upper trails. The two dogs barked as they raced and cavorted ahead, scaring off any wildlife. They spotted no game or bears, but Erin kept them close to the main pastures, avoiding the thicker forest.

Bill refused to ride today. He wanted to watch John put their new colt, Elusive Dream, through his paces. The men planned to ready the horse for a classic race for two-year-olds. When the riders returned to the barn, Erin helped Bill lunge the two Appaloosas while the others removed the tack and cleaned up the ridden animals. Still young and excitable, but green broken to ride, the appaloosas required attention, making Bill persevere in their training. He held the reins while she mounted Geisha Girl, the brown mare, showing a classic, white-spotted rump. The mare sidestepped twice, but responded to Bill's strokes along her neck while he led her around the corral.

"We'll try neck reining today. Their mouths won't get pulled too hard. Let's stay in the corral for safety."

Erin laughed. "Safety for me or the horse?"

"Both. If you fall off, I don't want to chase a runaway horse."

"Thanks a lot. I may get bucked off, but I won't fall. They head for the barn, anyway."

Once Geisha Girl settled down, she was an enjoyable ride. Erin put her through her paces, attempting neck reining, and reducing the pressure on the bit.

Bill nodded at the mare's performance. "Soon, she'll tackle the trails. I'll get John to work her again during the week."

Next, Erin mounted Rebel while Bill held the reins and halter firmly. The gelding was grey with black spots that nature speckled onto him with no pattern. He was frisky and non-compliant, deserving of his name.

The gelding wouldn't settle. He shied and fishtailed, but didn't buck. Erin wasn't an expert enough rider to hang on without Bill's weight on the rope looped through the halter. Eventually, the horse sidestepped and reared, causing Bill to lose his grip. Not being a rodeo rider, she clung on. Sure enough, Rebel raced toward the open barn door. Erin's tugs on the bit didn't work. Rebel must have gotten the wedge between his teeth. She fisted her hand through the flying mane and grasped the saddle's pommel, while clamping her legs tighter around his sides. Should she jump off or ride into the barn? Neither was a good choice. She folded herself forward over his neck to clear the barn entrance. When he came to a jarring stop before the hay bales, she somersaulted over his head and tumbled onto the bales. It was a soft landing except when her helmet thudded against the solid wall. She squatted there, glaring at the horse while picking strands of straw off her clothes. The gelding ignored her and munched in the hay bin.

Bill lent a hand to help her stand, his lips twitching. "Well, at least the horse is alright."

"I'm getting back on him for one turn around the corral with the barn door closed this time. He needs to learn he's not the boss."

"Too bad I'm tall and heavy. He'd better behave, or he'll have to haul me around. The extra weight will slow him down."

After a quick canter around the corral, Erin jumped down, rubbing her arms. "He sure pulls, and usually the wrong way. If Luke comes riding again, I'll put him on Rebel."

"Are you two fighting? Kiss and make up."

"That's the problem, Bill. He wants more than kissing."

"Oooh, I don't need that much information."

"Why don't you date? I'm sure you're not gay, but you don't seem to like girls."

"Thanks for nothing. I don't like guys either, but women need too much maintenance. All those silly love games and socializing." Bill jerked around when he saw John leading a young horse out of the barn. "Hey, he's finally bringing him out. Let's watch the new colt work out."

Erin leaned on the fence, gazing at the dark, chestnut colt pacing around the smaller makeshift oval track. "You guys sure are good judges of horses. His rhythm seems effortless."

Bill waved at John, who drove the horse down the track again. "Look at that colt go. Totally flawless. He loves to run—an Elusive Dream all right. By next year, he'll be registered in a pacing race, wearing our blue and yellow colours."

She smiled when they returned home to see Adam leaving. Maybe Janelle helped him exercise and train Major. The couple seemed to get along as well as oil and vinegar. Adam didn't stay longer to chat with Erin, instead waving and leaving. Darn Luke and his suspicions. Adam was young. He didn't have an interest in Erin, herself.

Janelle walked over and grinned. "I don't think the dog learned much more, but he likes playing games and he's smart."

"Well, we love dogs anyway, good or bad." Erin rubbed the ears of both dogs winding around her legs after jumping out of the truck. They kept sniffing at the horse smells on her slacks, maybe remembering their afternoon fun.

"I hoped to pick up different training habits from Major for Bill's dogs."

"I hope something rubs off on them in time. Is Adam planning to visit often?" Erin asked.

"How would I know? Anyway, I'm working with the on-call vet for a couple of weeks. We check rural areas when called and respond to the SPCA's investigations."

"Wow, that's interesting but also hard. I've heard about some depressing cases."

"Hopefully, we can make lives better."

"Do you like Adam, Janelle?"

"He needs to mature and find his own way. He has promise and stability. Like your dogs, I think he's sweet, but that's all."

"I think he finds you mysterious and scary."

"He's nice, but don't go romanticizing about us. Auntie Celine is bad enough with all her suggestions and innuendoes. I'm constantly hearing about the Taurus people having such steadfast worth."

Erin grinned. She could well imagine Celine's ambiguous hints.

Luke rode the elevator up to the lawyers' offices. He got a fierce look from Lois when he asked how she was doing. She answered with blistering remarks.

"You don't need to care about my feelings, but Mark has been your friend for years."

"Everyone's under the microscope in murder cases, Lois. No one finds life pleasant when they're being investigated as a possible suspect."

"Then you sent that woman detective here to ask more questions. Are you going to fingerprint all of us?"

"Probably. One of my officers thinks you have a motive, Lois. You reminded him of a snarling pit bull. Would you kill to protect Mark from blackmail and exposure?"

Lois sat there frozen, her mouth agape when Luke turned and entered Cathy's office.

"Hello, Inspector Landry. A client just left. I'll buzz Craig to say you're here."

"Not yet. I have a few questions for you. I'm wondering why you neglected to mention you knew Mr. Fraser and grew up in the Milnet area."

"I know nothing that can help your investigation. Why ask for trouble? Why get involved?" Cathy drummed fingers on the desk. "The idea of me having evidence is farfetched. Are you looking for information, or am I joining the suspect list? Seems like it doesn't discriminate."

"Like I told Mark, I do keep an open mind and suspect anyone involved in a case, however remotely."

"Involved is a relative term. You're stretching to the outskirts of 'involvement' now."

"You visited the trapper a year ago and wanted to work as a guide for the hunters."

"That's right. I enjoyed my years out there hunting partridge and sometimes duck."

"No bigger game?"

Cathy frowned. "That's an odd remark. News reports said the victim was strangled, not shot. If you mean deer or moose, I have hunted them, but not anymore. What would I do with all that meat?"

"Another less veiled question then: do you order gifts for Craig's girlfriends like flowers or jewellery?"

"I can't be 'affronted' by that comment." Cathy made quotation marks with her fingers. "Everyone knows he flirts. Sheila thinks that's all. But no, I don't procure gifts for him."

Luke glanced at the diamond-like jewel on Cathy's right hand. He was checking everyone's fingers these days.

"I heard that you and Craig dated years ago."

"I never tried to hide that, inspector. I dated him before he met and married Sheila."

"The concept of infidelity doesn't bother you? That he cheats on his wife?"

"He's a handsome, virile man. That's a bonus for lots of women."

"You included?" Luke asked.

"I'm not immune to his appeal, but it's totally irrelevant to my involvement in murder."

Craig opened his office door and tried to control a bodily twitch when he seemed startled to see Luke. "You're here again?"

"Going to ask Cathy to buzz me in?"

Craig stood frozen for a minute and then retreated into his office with Luke following.

When they sat across the desk from each other, Craig raised his eyebrows. "Your show, inspector."

"We've confirmed you bought the victim that green trinket ring from your usual jeweller. The description matches. Did you know the real emerald gem's supposed to bring good fortune."

Craig kept silent, frozen in his seat.

"Jewel, the woman you didn't know, remember? I don't need to read out your rights, Mr. Gibson. You know them and can always call another attorney before answering more questions."

Craig cringed, and his brow furrowed. "I guess I can't deny that evidence. I didn't want to get involved with this murder. It's an unsavoury business for me."

"More for the dead woman, I'd think."

"Right... look, I had a fling with her, and we made out in the car a few times. She came onto me aggressively. How could I say no?"

"And now she's dead, strangled by a strong person, likely a man."

Craig wiped his brow. "I have no reason to kill her. You'll say she'd tell my wife. But to murder her? She wasn't that important, you know."

"No, I didn't know." Luke stood up. "Don't travel too far, Mr. Gibson. We're planning to up the pressure on you."

"Is that a threat, inspector?"

"No, Mr. Gibson. It's a warning."

With a new week starting, Erin sighed, looking at the gloomy, sodden skies. She drove to her district and did routine check-ups, while running IV antibiotics and changing dressings, glad to stay in the central area. With such short distances between patients, she fell back into her old habit of not fastening her seatbelt. The roads were slick, and she drove slowly around or through puddles. She sure didn't need more mud spattered on her car. Washing her vehicle had become a habit, though not quite as frequent as brushing her teeth. She visited Gladys for tea after her quick lunch on the road.

Gladys said she spoke with Celine over the phone, trying to uncover clues to solve the murder. "We're considering all scenarios. Those two roommates know something."

Erin looked out the window. "Well, I think Kelly does. There she goes now."

"Then Melanie will be alone." Gladys glanced out. "Go over and see her. She's scared and would talk more openly to you with Kelly away."

"But I can't..."

"Yes, you can. Tell her you want to check how she's holding up."

Erin shrugged her shoulders and crossed the road to knock at the apartment. "Why do I listen to everybody?"

Melanie peeped through the curtain before she opened the door.

"Hi, Melanie,' Erin said. "I'm working in the area today and wanted to check on you."

"Come in, nurse, right? I checked to make sure you weren't that creepy Lester."

"I'm Erin. Is he pestering you? The police must make visiting here difficult for him. They have a bulletin out to pick him up for questioning."

"Well, he hasn't shown for a while. Come in. How did you know where we lived?"

"You were going in the other day, and I checked the mailbox for your names." Erin gulped, needing to think quickly. "I've eaten lunch and must finish my rounds, but you seemed upset the other day. I wanted to check on how you're coping."

"Well, anyone would get uptight with their roommate murdered. Kelly keeps a lot in and seems relaxed, but she's not. I get scared and nervous myself."

"Is there a way I can help, maybe by listening?" She perched on a stool near the door while Melanie paced.

"Not really. Lester and Kelly were whispering about Jewel meeting a guy at a lodge. That was the last time he came here. Something about a secret rendezvous—no, a lovers' retreat—I think, somewhere away from prying eyes."

"Do you think that lawyer boyfriend took Jewel there?"

Melanie shrugged. "I don't know. She did meet someone secretly. That's why we bet the man was married. I don't know much."

"If Kelly knows anything at all, she should tell the police to make sure she's safe. Keeping secrets can be dangerous."

"Oh, I know. I begged her to—oh, don't tell her I told you that," Melanie wailed. "Kelly said I misunderstood the conversation and told me all kinds of false stuff to reassure me."

Melanie made a conscious effort to stop chewing her nails by twisting her hands together.

"But I need to let the police know what she said. They can be discreet in their questioning and cause you no trouble."

"I'm scared." Melanie wrapped her arms against her chest. "I'm looking for another place to live. Is anywhere safe?"

"Don't you have friends or relatives to stay with for a while?"

"No. My mother never liked living here and went back to China; she said I was old enough to live alone. My father was English but deserted us when I was young."

"Could you tell your mother about your problems here?"

"No way. She deserves a quiet life now. And I'm more Western than Asian. When I was starting school, my mother used to take me to the Chinese New Year parties, but she worked long hours in a coffee shop, so we stopped going. We didn't have a lot of friends. She was educated well in China, and she came over with my father, who worked there. He abandoned her when I was about eight years old. He didn't like her speaking Chinese to me, so I never learned much of the language. She always insisted that I work hard, get an education, and be English."

"I understand that newborn girls aren't welcome in China."

"Well, with only being allowed one child, parents always coveted a boy, mainly for economic reasons. My mother said families smothered or drowned infant girls, but many of the overflowing orphanages and temples found them wrapped on their doorstep."

"I heard a few lucky ones got adopted overseas. I know of a few families that went over to get a child, and the baby was always a girl."

"That's true. My mother often talked about the trials of the women in her country. I shouldn't complain."

"You have gone through a lot, Melanie."

"Well, I feel vulnerable and unable to protect myself."

"How about learning self-defence techniques? It would make you feel safer and more confident. I study taekwondo, a Korean martial art form."

"I want to be able to protect myself. I'll think about doing something."

Erin patted her hand. "Listen, Melanie. If you're ever in trouble, really scared, or need to talk, give me a call. I'll leave you my cell number." She tugged a paper from her purse, scrawled down the number, and handed it to her.

Erin left and hurried back to check with Gladys. "Melanie only knows that she heard Lester and Kelly whisper about a lodge as a meeting place for Jewel and her lover. She thinks Kelly knows more but doesn't want to tell the police. I told her that hiding facts and keeping secrets is dangerous. I'm sorry. I know I scared her."

"Don't fret about that. Being scared will make her watchful and help keep her alive."

Erin left, worried for the young woman and aware she would have to pass this news on to Luke.

She looked up a number and used her cell phone when she got in the car. She called the police station, and after many requests and transfers, Beth answered. Erin had spoken to the woman officer the month prior when she found a body.

"Hello, Beth. Erin Rine, here. Is Luke in? I'm calling with info on the murder case."

"He's not here right now. Can I take a message?"

"That'll work. Do you know Jewel's two roommates, Kelly and Melanie?"

"Sure do. I met them early in the investigation."

"Well, I spoke with Melanie while on my rounds today. She told me she heard her roommate whisper something to Lester about Jewel and the lawyer meeting for a romantic interlude in a vacant lodge. They were secretive about it, and Melanie doesn't want to get in trouble with Kelly for repeating the information."

"I'll give Luke the info. Did she say why Kelly withheld the information?"

"No, she did ask her. Kelly said that she'd misunderstood the conversation."

"Then, she'll deny the whole thing. She doesn't understand the dangerous game she's playing. Did she tell you anything else?" At Erin's negative response, Beth continued. "We should meet. I've heard a lot about you and more about your intriguing clairvoyant neighbour."

The darkening day promised more rain, and Erin hurried, heading home early before another storm descended on their soggy city.

Luke and Bill exited the front door as she pulled into their side parking space and emerged beside their parked trucks.

"Has something else happened?" she asked. "Do you have new information?"

"Not a damn thing, sorry to say," Luke answered. "I'm digging more info out of Bill."

Erin remembered her conversation with Melanie. It was safer to mention it in front of her brother. Luke often got testy and unreasonable with what he considered interference. "Did you get my message from Beth about my talk with Melanie?"

"Yes, she mentioned your call. Where did you see her?"

"I met and talked to them both on the street a few days ago. Melanie seemed upset. So, I stopped at her apartment today to see how she was managing."

Both men stared at her.

"You wanted to go and check on her? Did Celine or Gladys ask you, or was that your Good Samaritan role kicking in again?"

"Well, I visited Gladys, and she happened to see Kelly leave and..." Erin pulled at her bang. "Well, I did discover something. The kid's scared, and I don't pose a threat."

Luke held himself rigid. "You and those elderly women are interfering again. This is not a game for them to play from their rocking chairs." He regarded her defiant expression. "Tell me again what she said, the exact words... please."

Erin fumbled through her answer, probably not getting it correct. "She heard Lester tell Kelly that a hidden lodge was the lovers' meeting place. She said Kelly denies saying that."

Luke pursed his mouth. "Thank you for letting me know."

"One other thing. I forgot that Mr. Cresswell, the older resident Mark and I warned about the bear, said a woman—Kelly, I think, from the description—waited for someone on the trail. He said a shifty-looking guy wandered around near the lodge, too. He didn't know if he was the person she planned to meet."

"When did that happen?"

She shrugged. "I'm not sure. Recently, I think. He said he'd keep an eye out for the shady guy and tell Mrs. Richards."

"Why not get the whole nursing home facility involved in the investigation along with Gladys and Celine?" Luke retorted.

"Elderly people are often bored. They notice unusual activity."
"Murder is not a simple game of 'Clue' or 'Who Done It,'" Luke responded.

Bill stood, watching the warring couple. Despite being a big man, he seemed to know how to fade into the background, preferring to stay quiet.

Luke looked exasperated. "You're sure that's all? You haven't forgotten or waited to tell me something pertinent?"

Erin bristled. "No, that is all, inspector. Good day." She stormed up the stairs.

Kelly met Lester at the start of the trail and lit them each a cigarette. She turned to peer into the bushes, keeping a nervous lookout for bears and more nosey old-timers. "Why do we have to meet over here?"

"Cops would keep an eye on your apartment. This is secluded." He sneered. "Well, are you going to cut me in on the loot pickup? I'm your only protection. If Jewel asked me to tag along, she'd be alive."

Kelly seemed to be thinking hard. "Since the lawyer likely murdered Jewel, I will need you around when I confront this Craig guy. So, keep him in your sights. I'm not too sure how much to ask for. I don't want to sound pushy."

"Ask for a large amount upfront and add that you're willing to receive installments later. Don't let him think he's off the hook. He owes us for Jewel."

"I love your use of the word 'us.'"

"She was my cousin. And you need me, or you'll end up like her: dead."

"But I'll expect trouble. She didn't, the innocent. Besides, I'm no pushover."

"I'll get his picture meeting you." Lester drew heavily on his cigarette. "That would be a good hold to have on him."

"I forgot about your camera. You should take a picture in case we need more funds later." She flicked ash from her cigarette. "That kind of camera must have cost a lot."

"Free as a bird. You think I won the lottery or found the thing?"

"Like everything else you seem to find. Someday, you'll get caught."

Lester didn't tell her he already took a secret, damning photo of Craig and Jewel. He used the telescopic lens and recognized the man leaving the building when he scouted the area but hadn't known his name. He needed a spot of money changing hands. Would the wife pay more to have grounds for a divorce? He shouldn't hurry. "The scheme might work if I go ahead of you and shadow the guy. I'll find a spot near the rendezvous. Do you think he'll meet you in his office?"

"Only after hours, probably. I'll call him there. We must keep the secret from the wife if we want future profits. A public place would be safer, like a coffee shop."

"So, you'll call him soon? Strike while the affair is hot?" Lester spit in the bush. "I'm getting poorer by the minute."

"Tomorrow, when I'm off, I'll call. I can arrange to meet him after his day is over and the staff go home."

"He'll need time to get to a bank for cash. No cheques."

"Well, we aren't waiting too long." Kelly shivered and ground her cigarette in the wet earth. "I don't like dillydallying, and I keep looking over my shoulder."

"Not to worry. You look back, and all you should see there is me."

44

Another long day turned up no clues. Jewel's death seemed to have been shelved by the media, if not forgotten. The only glimmer of info Erin unearthed surfaced at the local diner near Gladys' place where she stopped for lunch. Erin asked the chatty, older waitress if she met the murder victim or her roommates.

"Only to say hello. Sometimes two or three of them came in for a meal. Those two dark blondes seemed a trifle hard-looking; a rough life, I'd say. The thin brunette was different. She was a shy, tiny kid, and she seemed... not afraid of them, only careful-like, you know.

"Did you ever see a man with them?"

"Once. I wouldn't recognize him again. The police questioned us and other shop staff in the area. He was a seedy sort: kept a cap on while eating and hid his features. The women didn't seem to like him either, and he ate double portions. I was surprised the murdered one paid. I heard later she was his cousin, not a girlfriend. Do you think he's a suspect?"

Erin shook her head. "I heard she was kind to him and often gave him money. Why would he be dumb enough to kill her?"

"Who knows these days? Seemed like the type who's positive everyone's against him. Unsavoury character, and not too bright looking."

At the end of her workday, Erin drove down the road past Mr. Fraser's. What to do? What to look for? She slammed her foot on the brake when a form moved along the side of the road. Her first impulse was to believe it was a bear, but she smiled when she spotted the deer jumping out of the ditch to scurry off into deeper bush. Sometimes, they travelled in pairs. She kept her speed low, then turned the car into a narrow sideroad. She had to stop searching for clues in the woods. Did she think the answers would jump out at her alongside an animal? At least it wasn't raining now. The sun barely shone through the encroaching clouds, promising more rain. The road was too soft and wet, and the ditches were too close. She shook her head at her foolishness. When she spotted an opening ahead, she drove in and up to a wider space in the driveway that enabled her to turn the car around.

Before she drove on, a van pulled in behind her car. A middle-aged couple sat inside the vehicle and stared at her, then looked back toward their house.

Erin exhaled, not aware she held her breath. They looked suspicious of her in their driveway. The man exited and checked her license plate, likely memorizing the numbers in case she was a thief. Erin got out and called to him, telling him she planned on turning around in their wider driveway.

The man spoke. "We're back from our holidays. Who are you? What are you doing here in our yard in the first place?"

"I'm Erin Rine, a nurse who works around here." She held out her phone. "You can check my credibility with Mr. Fraser, back down the last road. I did his leg dressings, and I got turned around."

The woman stayed in the car, listening with the window down. The man approached her. "I'm James Mortimer, the dirty son of a gun who shot him by accident."

Erin relaxed, then bristled at the revelation and the matter-of-fact way the man spoke about the injury. "Well, your actions caused terrible results. A higher angle, and you'd have killed him, not just maimed him forever."

"I know, and he'll never believe or forgive me. He thinks I drank too much and got careless with the gun. I was shocked, not hallucinating." He shrugged and gave a rueful grin. "I didn't think he'd want me to send him a postcard from my vacation villa."

"He didn't give me solid details about what happened."

"No, he wouldn't or didn't believe me. I fretted about that accident while away, and I should have told the truth then. But who would believe my story anyway?"

"I'll listen and keep an open mind. In my profession, I've heard everything."

"Well, I'm not squeamish. I know what these old eyes saw. After all the mess and getting help out there, I couldn't prove I wasn't nuts. So, we said I fell."

"But were you drinking at the time?"

"Well, that's the problem, you see. I drank a couple of beers at least an hour apart."

"Can you tell me what you saw? A woman was murdered by the river, and the police need help with their investigation. I followed Chum to her burial site."

The man pursed his lips. "That's awful, but I can't see a connection with our accident. You'll laugh at my story. That day, I heard some movements in the bush near the lodge. I stopped, released the safety, and waited to see. I felt the loud rustling must be a moose or a bear." He paused. "My foot was down on a rocky area for traction."

"You're going to tell me there was a monster—a Sasquatch—barrelling through the bush."

"I wish." He took a deep breath. "No, a naked man and woman were laughing and cavorting, playing touchy-feely with each other in the bush."

She stared hard at the man before her, eyebrows raised in astonishment. "And?"

"See. You think I'm nuts, too. Well, I was so startled that my foot slipped off the rock into the mud, and the gun went off. Fraser didn't believe me, told me to shut up, and said I drank too much. He was suffering from the pain then, but later, he still said I was nuts. We were good buddies. Now he doesn't want to see me at all."

"How did you manage to get help?"

"Sometimes the cell phone works up high by the lodge. Lucky for me, I managed to call and give our location. Fraser made me tie a rag above the bleed, then release the tourniquet off and on and hold pressure against the wound. But the damn wound got infected, and he needed the leg amputated."

"You know I'll have to pass that information to the police. They've investigated the area, and the inspector will want to question you. What did you hunt that day?"

"Damn noisy crows. Too many protection rules now for much else. I wouldn't mind a bearskin, though, if one charged. We often see them fishing by the river."

Luke was annoyed more at himself than Erin when she called to explain what she heard. Her travelling all day on her route gave her an advantage. However, the police, and he in particular, should have found the information. He'd need to question both parties to gain an accurate account of the incident. He called in Beth and Ralph. "Listen, both of you. I got another call from Erin Rine. Alongside the elder community, they are going to solve this case before we do or get themselves killed by interfering. They don't realize this is not a game of 'Scrabble' to find the right words that suit the crime. And if the civilians are finding out more than us, we'll need to put them on the payroll."

"You mean Erin and her older psychic friend, Boss? Well, I can see people tending to talk to a nurse. They usually have a kind, receptive demeanour, and she sounded pleasant enough on the phone. Our officialdom can put a person's guard up."

"And we don't have ESP to figure this stuff out." Ralph delivered that comment tongue in cheek. "My being a Sagittarius may mean something. Other worlds, you know."

"Don't scoff at some people's higher antenna power, Ralph." Luke then gave them updates on the case.

Beth frowned on hearing his recital of the facts Erin unearthed. "I followed up that story of the shooting accident. The incident was filed, and I didn't research the facts again."

"You shouldn't have to. I'm not assigning blame here. It likely doesn't affect the investigation. I'll check up on those two hunters.

I'm just mad at myself for knowing I'm way behind this woman in our investigation."

Beth smirked. "And her being attractive *and* smart doesn't help, right?"

Luke sighed. "You've never seen her except for the photos we got of her last month. She can be most irritating."

"And captivating and gorgeous and a sexy Aries," Beth grinned, "like me."

"All of that, too." He nodded. "Anyway, you'd understand her better, being a woman and an Aries, to boot. So, where are we going from here? Call and have Trevor and Adam stop in."

Trevor ambled in, nonchalant as ever. The man could be a good officer if he put his mind to it. Adam shuffled his feet behind him and stayed quiet.

Trevor spoke up. "What's on the agenda besides touring our bright city today, Boss?"

"How did the pub crawling go? No news on Lester Lisson, yet?"

"Well, a few employees recalled him. Some said the guy didn't talk much, and he wasn't a regular."

"Where else have you looked?" Luke asked.

"We canvassed the neighbourhood where the women lived and visited its bars." Trevor continued. "The waitress at one recognized him. Said he always had a scheming look on his face but didn't chat much with the staff. He drank plenty but not enough to become inebriated."

Adam spoke up. "One waitress said the man often looked over his shoulder nervously."

"Then the manager heard the staff talking to us and became annoyed and told the workers not to discuss their customers with the police." Trevor swore. "Likely only get damn lowlife customers in that dive."

Adam nodded. "He said discretion on his patrons' habits and character was more important than helping the police."

"We may have to lean on him. I want both of you to keep searching. I don't think he's homeless, but check with our downtown and undercover officers. This man may have a room somewhere. Beth can't find his means of income, so he either begs or steals."

"We checked the soup kitchens again," Trevor said "He must disguise himself somehow; he could look different, or the regulars and staff aren't telling."

Ralph nodded. "They often close ranks against the police to protect their own crooked buddies. Who said there was no honour among thieves?"

Luke thanked them and told them to keep searching for the elusive Lester. He would check out the seniors himself.

Erin smiled when Samson entered the taekwondo class. This large black man, whose real name was Andy Wharton, held a fourth-degree black belt. However, she was interested in hearing about his flying career. "Samson, how's your aviation business doing?"

"Not too well for the fishermen wanting a fly-in with all this rain. Good thing I have a regular job flying the hospital's transport team. Brought a young child down from Kapuskasing last week with a nurse attendant. Why not work as a nurse in the air?"

"I'm considering it and will put myself on the call list. I mean it." She smiled. "I can do weekend jaunts, or I might quit this job before I'm asked to leave. My boss would give a glowing recommendation to get rid of me. She thinks I'm trouble."

"I've heard some rumours. Are you an unpaid appendage for the police force?" He laughed at her rueful look. "We hold flight training classes for new attendants."

"In England, I took emergency transport training and helped move patients between England and France a few times. I'll call this week."

"Class, attention, please." Mr. Cheung entered the room. "We will do the push-ups first to limber up the body and free the mind."

Lani, the tall, slim blonde woman, sidled up to Erin after the extensive warm-up, breathing heavily and stammering, "I'm out of shape."

"I'm not bad today. Are you too busy at work to exercise between classes?"

"Doing ladies' manicures and pedicures leaves me with a lot of time sitting down." She smirked. "Did you find that new body in the mud?"

Erin raised her eyebrows, thinking fast. "I heard on the news that a dog dug her out."

"Along with a caregiver, I heard. Nurses are caregivers, right?"

"There are a lot of aides caring for homebound people here." Erin knew Lani was predisposed to gossip and embellishing stories. "I'm not the only one around, Lani."

"But you probably got in the habit and can sniff out bodies now like those cadaver dogs. And you know how to sleuth."

Mr. Cheung clapped his hands once. "Quiet, please. Everyone must practise their forms for the competitions next month."

Lani gave her a speculative look before taking a stance on one of the mats. The woman was able to contort her lithe body in all manner of ways.

Erin moved away to a corner to avoid further questions. She managed the two forms with only minor difficulty and repeated the exercises a few more times while Mr. Cheung paced around the group, checking their manoeuvres.

Lani edged her position closer to her. "I'm going to check with my nurse friend about this murder. She finds out everything. You should tell what you know."

Erin sighed and gave in. "I don't really know anything. You're right, I was the caregiver who spotted the murdered woman's hands in the muck. My elderly patient and his dog begged me to check the woods, and he called the police." She shrugged. "That's the extent of my knowledge." She faced the other way and practiced a few more forms before hurrying home once the session finished.

Luke drove out to check on Mr. Mortimer's account of the shooting. The man seemed resigned to repeating his story. His wife brought them both a coffee, cream, and sugar on a tray before she patted his shoulder and left them together. Luke stirred his black coffee and looked at the man.

"The nurse told you about us not being upfront about the hunting accident?"

"Yes, and now I want the true story," Luke stated. "Don't leave anything out."

"Well, I can't see this having anything to do with that other murder. I heard she was strangled recently."

"The bare facts, please, of your earlier episode."

"Okay, *bare* is the right word. The time wasn't hunting season. The winter felt long, and I wanted to get out. It was gorgeous weather: a hot, sunny day with the snow mostly gone. I convinced Fraser to go with me and shoot crows or rabbits."

Luke sipped his coffee, not directing the man.

"We didn't spot anything, and I got restless, wanting action. We sat on a rotten tree limb, and I drank my second beer. Fraser prefers whiskey, though he doesn't drink when he's hunting."

Luke nodded while the man seemed to get his thoughts in order.

"I pondered the event enough while we were away and should have the story down pat by now. We started back up the hill near the lodge, and I joked about getting a beaver. Fraser said he preferred trapping them for the pelt. They're harmful with constructing dams and are considered nuisance animals and open season prey."

"Go on," Luke said when the man stopped to think and exhale.

"All of a sudden, down below, I heard rustling in the bushes near the lodge. I took a stance and readied my rifle, released the safety, and watched for a bear. The tree movements were too high up to be a beaver, you see."

Luke nodded again. It felt like pulling teeth to get the man to the point.

"Well, this is the hard part. I spied through my scope to aim, and there, in my sights, was a man and woman butt naked in their boots, frolicking in the trees, grabbing each others' privates, and playing tag-like sex games."

"You're sure they were the figures of a man and woman. Could you recognize either one if I brought you pictures?"

"Not a chance. Uh, I was kind of shocked. You tend to look at the woman's body, especially a nude body, right? She had a good strong, build and was well-endowed. I didn't want to tell the nurse, but her hair looked dark you-know—uh—where."

"You didn't look closely at the other one?"

"Only that the second one was an aroused man, definitely."

"Then what happened?"

"I jumped in surprise, slid backwards down the slope, and the damn rifle fell and shot Fraser below the knee. What with calling for help and tying up his bleeding leg, I never looked again." The man gave a mortified shrug. "Fraser kept swearing at me, called me a bloody fool, and said I was drunk and hallucinating. But I know what I saw. What I saw was unsettling and too weird. I couldn't have made that nonsense up. And I don't believe in elves and fairies."

Lester left his rooming house clutching the camera under his armpit. The landlord never checked on his tenants. Lester figured the guy would expect he took porno pictures or planned to catch illicit partners' escapades for divorce cases. As long as he got paid the rent money, the man was content and didn't interfere with the tenants. Lester planned on following Kelly, too, rather than just watching Craig. He didn't trust her. He didn't trust anyone to not cut him out of a money deal. He wanted ready cash. He deserved payment since the fancy lawyer squelched his only source of income—well, handouts. Family should help each other out. Jewel always gave him cash when he was low on stolen funds.

Kelly called him to say she would meet the lawyer fellow outside his office during his lunch hour. She couldn't get past the secretary to speak with him on the phone and didn't want an out-and-out confrontation. She said she left a cryptic message on the tape, sure her voice was muffled, and didn't leave herself open to blackmail charges. On the phone, she lied, saying she had information that tied him to the murder victim. She hoped for a substantial reward or bonus from him, of course. She also said she'd wear a red cap and sweater to help the lawyer spot her.

Lester parked his car at a two-hour meter. He spotted Kelly waiting at the door. He approached her, looked furtively around, and whispered to her that he worked on their deal. She would need actual proof to get their money. He handed her a copy of the damning picture. She frowned, agreed it was good leverage, and then demanded to know why he hadn't given it to her before. He said he felt it was time to donate to the cause. He expected a fifty-fifty cut, and if she tried to double-cross him, he'd find her.

Kelly said she'd be able to recognize the lawyer. She had found the man's picture in the newspaper archives when his wife opened a charity function. Lester held onto the original picture of the lovers and planned to do his own fiddle later.

Lester waited till the guard rounded the corner before taking the elevator. When he entered the receptionist's office, he asked for a lawyer's card, saying he might need to retain someone later. There were two other doors, and he spotted a woman's figure moving behind one of the glass partitions. It wasn't easy to track someone in here. He'd have to hang around outside.

He avoided the bank, knowing they installed cameras and entered the computer store. He felt conspicuous and out of depth and strolled into the small hardware store. Only a few people were shopping there. The clerk watched him, likely suspecting him of pilfering the merchandise. He left to follow the stairs down to the basement. The door was locked and on alarm. He ran back up, sliding outside to check on Kelly. She wasn't there. He glanced around and didn't spot her anywhere. His panic settled when he spied Craig exiting the front doors and entering the corner store. The man came back outside and stood, puffing on a cigarette while he looked around. Lester figured the lawyer was searching for Kelly's red hat. Where did that dumb broad get to? He watched the man grind the butt into the sidewalk, look around, and then re-enter the office building.

Lester was too conspicuous to idle in this upper-class neighbourhood. He opted to stay out front and seclude himself in the doorway of an empty building advertised for rent. He lit a cigarette and watched the front for the man to leave. Then he'd follow... unless there was an underground parking lot. Hey, what if the rich guy's chauffeur picked him up? Lester felt uneasy, realizing he should have researched the guy's routine. Nah, that was Kelly's job. She'd better know what she was doing. Where was she? No way would she go off alone with the guy. Kelly wasn't naïve like Jewel.

Lester nodded his head. He'd wait and see. Dumb broad likely got scared about the whole thing and took off. He knew better than to count on a dame to do something right. Lester had all the smarts among people he knew. He'd find this Craig guy later, with or without her help. And, if that damn Kelly dared to scoot off with all the dough and ignore him... well, he'd find her too.

The next afternoon, Erin revisited Mrs. Billings. When she opened the door to leave, the older woman settled herself by the open window. "Finally, we have sunshine, nurse. And there's that lady's nephew going down the trail again. I wonder what he's looking for. No one has spotted any more bears around."

Erin glanced out the window to see Mark disappear around the corner. "Why would he go down there? I'd better bring him my bear spray." She hurried downstairs, threw her bag in the car, grabbed the bear spray, and sped down the sloping trail. When she raced around the corner, she almost collided with Mark. He stood immobile, fixated on the bushes. He turned with a stunned expression, seeming to stare right through her.

She shook his arm. "Mark, what's wrong?"

He pointed a hesitant, shaky hand to the underbrush. She shifted closer, then shoved a hand against her mouth to stifle a squeal. A body lay sprawled under the trees, partially covered in mounds of leaves. The dark blonde hair, red sweater, and one booted leg protruded through the bushes. Erin stepped closer, held her breath, and placed her fingers on the cold wrist to check for a pulse, but the swollen, discoloured face with embedded rope dangling from the neck proved a testament to their death. Erin stepped back, not wanting to damage the crime scene. "Do you know who she is?"

"Probably Kelly, one of the roommates." He gulped. "Oh, damn. She called me this morning to meet and return a clue that tied me to the murder of her friend. I figured she wanted money, but I didn't know what she found."

"The murderer didn't have time to dispose of the body. I bet they tried to frame you for this one. Luckily, my patient spotted you. After you found the body, I found you."

He looked terror-stricken knowing his timing and presence bade ill news.

"She's dead, Mark, murdered. You know I have to phone Luke."

"Someone called me, Erin. Someone's out to get me."

"But why you? Did you anger someone?"

"The only one I can think of is Craig. I tell him off when he intercepts my clients." Mark rubbed his hand through his hair. "The police—Luke—will question me. It feels like I'm being set up."

"I think you're right. The body looks like Jewel's friend," Erin whispered, trying to get a profile glimpse of the swollen face.

"I think she called—or was it her?" Mark babbled. "She said her name was Kelly. She told me she had something of mine that the police would want." He shook his head. "They covered her in leaves and piles of dirt—didn't even bother to bury her."

"They wanted you to find the body with something that could incriminate you. Do you have any idea what?"

"No. She only said that I'd recognize it."

A siren heralded the police before she finished dialling 911. The officer arriving said they'd received a call about screaming and murder. When Luke arrived later, the men cordoned off the scene and began checking the perimeter. Minutes later, Luke approached Mark and Erin sitting on a concrete bench. Luke held out a taped bag, a ring showing through the plastic. "This was clasped in the woman's hand. Look familiar, Mark?"

"My old, synthetic emerald ring. Haven't worn it since I got married." He showed his gold wedding band. "I thought I left it in my desk at work." Mark swallowed. "Lord, my initials are inside the band. The mythical centaur for Taurus is etched into the stone. I'm in deep trouble."

Luke asked her how long Mark was there before she followed him. She narrowed her eyes. "Less than two minutes, inspector. Check with Mrs. Billings. There wasn't enough time for anyone to talk, murder, and partially bury someone." Sarcasm was lost on the man. "Also, neither of us heard screaming that would lead to calling the police. Someone planned this, and they wanted Mark found with the body and suspected of murder."

"The burial was either interrupted or clumsily covered up." Luke looked them over. "Either the murderer planned for Mark to arrive, or Mark heard you and rushed the job."

Erin pursed her lips before replying. "I'm surprised you aren't suggesting we're a murdering duo, inspector."

Mark wiped his sweating brow. He blurted out the information about the bizarre phone call he had received. "You know I can't improvise that quickly, Luke. Cripes, a divorce is easier than murder. And you can check what time I left the office to drive over here."

"I'm thinking you wouldn't have called the police to be caught red-handed at the scene," Luke added. "If someone is trying to set you up, then we need to find a reason for this elaborate plot. Could you tell for sure that the voice on the phone was a woman?"

"No, I can't swear to that. The words were muffled."

"They wanted a red herring, and Mark's an easy target." Erin shoved her cold hands into the pockets of her fleece jacket. "Someone, like Craig, is trying to relieve pressure from being the number one suspect by calling the police with false information to have Mark caught at the scene."

Luke watched his officers check the scene before looking back at them. "Thank you again for telling me how to follow up this investigation, Miss Rine." The police photographer arrived, waved at Luke and took shots. "Mark, you may turn out to be the fall guy. It might not be that someone's out to get you personally."

Mark sighed and relaxed. "Thanks for the vote of confidence, you two, but I know Craig's not smart enough to plan this sort of hoax."

Luke stared at the murder scene. "No, but if not him, someone else was ready and willing to set the stage."

50

"Erin, I shouldn't ask, but Beth is tied up with another tangent of the investigation. Would you come across with me to see Melanie?" Luke swallowed his pride. "I think she would be more comfortable with another woman around, and she knows you and—"

"Of course I will. Oh, poor Melanie. She'll be shattered."

The two walked across the street, knocked on the door, and asked Melanie, who peeked out the window, to let them in.

The woman's pupils dilated when Erin took her arm and led her to the couch. "We have bad news for you, Melanie."

Luke sat across from Melanie. "We found another murder victim. We think the body is Kelly's."

Melanie screeched, then covered her face with her hands. Her body shook as she rocked. After a few seconds, she peered at them through her fingers, glanced around furtively, and then latched a hand tight onto Erin's arm. "I'm leaving at the end of the month. I already gave Kelly my notice."

Luke leaned forward. "I need to know everything—no matter how trivial—if we're going to find the culprit. There must be a connection."

"Not with me," she wailed. "It was Lester and Kelly's plan. All I heard were whispers about a lodge and a lover's tiff or something."

"We're trying to locate Lester. Do you recall your roommates talking about where he lived or who he hung around with?"

BETTY GUENETTE

"No, and I don't think he made friends." Melanie shook her head. "He always seemed to plot and look for easy money, never expecting to work."

"What about Kelly? Did she have close friends or a significant other?"

"No, I don't think so." Melanie grabbed a tissue and wiped her tearing eyes. "She just worked and watched television. She didn't go on dates. She hung around Jewel, mostly." She sobbed. "Oh, no! I can't go and identify her body. I won't."

"You don't need to. We have her fingerprints on file."

"And mine, too." Melanie sobbed and hiccupped. "I'm probably next."

"Not as long as you've told us everything you know." Luke glanced at Erin.

Melanie withdrew her hand and stared at her. "Why are you here with him? Do you help the police, too? You said you worked as a nurse."

"I am the district nurse, Melanie, but I know the inspector and Mark, the other lawyer under suspicion. I was visiting a patient across the road, and Luke asked me to come over with him as a comfort for you. He's searching for answers."

"I keep telling you I don't know any answers." She fixed a blank look ahead, then took a deep breath. "I'll ask Sara downstairs to stay with me tonight."

Erin hugged her. "I'll stop by soon. I'm not just a nurse, Melanie. I'm a friend."

Luke stood up. "Sometimes, Melanie, we don't always ask the right questions."

Melanie chewed on her fingernail. "How was Kelly killed?"

188

"We're not finished with the crime scene yet, so I can't make statements. The murderer hid her body under leaves on a pathway. Did Kelly tell you where she was going today?"

She left earlier when I was in the shower. This wasn't one of her regular workdays." She closed her eyes. "I assumed she took the bus to go shopping."

51

Lester sat in the seedy bar nursing his beer, trying to ignore the twitch in his eyelid. Next, he'd start biting his nails like that dumb twit, Melanie. What the hell happened with Kelly, anyway? It must be her. He heard on the radio that they found a woman's body along the path where they met. No way she went there alone or with a possible murderer, not even in the daytime.

He didn't trail that Craig fellow. It wasn't his fault. What had they missed? Lester bet her lifeless body was transported to the path, or she was tricked and killed there. Kelly didn't go into the building after him. Who did she meet? Or did she get cold feet and leave, then get caught unawares? Another problem was his stolen vehicle's motor coughed up and died. It was a big hitch in stealing old cars, but they proved harder to trace and easier to hotwire than newer models. He was temporarily without wheels to trail the man, but not for long. He left after spotting Craig leaving the building alone and went searching for Kelly. Could the man have killed her in the office and hidden her body before managing to carry it down the lift to the underground parking? Sounded farfetched to him. He should have trailed the lawyer to see if he parked a car somewhere else.

What if the guy sent a note saying he switched the meeting place at the last moment? He sure didn't see them get together. What if he met her at a bar near the trail by the senior housing? The closest would be the Drake Inn. He'd boozed out there loads of times while waiting for Jewel to get home when he wanted to hit her up for a loan. No IOU, of course.

He needed to think quickly and get his brains back together. If Craig wasn't the killer, then another man was involved. Another lawyer? Once he lured her into the car, the guy likely knocked Kelly out and drove her unconscious to the site, strangled her there, and covered her body. Would she have gotten in the car? Not likely. The guy must have tricked and surprised her somehow. He waved to the bartender. He needed another drink badly.

52

Gladys and Celine were worried about Mark having more incriminating evidence surfacing against him. They were devising tactics to prove his innocence when Erin came in.

Erin spoke up. "Celine, why does Mark have a centaur depicted for the Taurus sign on his emerald ring?"

"The sign for Taurus is the bull, *mais* their mythical sign is the centaur."

"You are knowledgeable about Astrology, Celine." Gladys shook her head. "I only match you in religious studies."

"We will not go there to show my lack of the biblical stuff." Celine twisted her body around to point a finger at Erin. "Gladys and I, we have a *bien* idea. It is idiot-proof."

"You mean foolproof."

"That is what I said. Fool or idiot, *quelle différence*?" Celine patted the seat beside her on the couch. "We have many of the *problèmes* to discuss and solve."

"No more brainstorms for me, ladies." She glared at Celine. "I get into enough trouble on my own. Why would you set me up?"

Gladys gazed at Erin with a reproachful look. "We have to help Mark now."

Erin pursed her lips. "Well, at least I'll listen."

"We want to disguise you and make you *pas bonne*." Celine waved her hands in the air. "You are too *chic* looking for what we have in the plans."

"Sure, and do you want to make me look like a hooker?"

The two elderly women stared at her, no reply forthcoming.

She gaped at the two older women and gulped a breath. "Now, wait a minute. This sounds sleazy and outside my expertise. Ladies, this could be dangerous."

"*Mais non*, we will protect you while you do the investigating." The woman wasn't joking. "Adam and Janelle, they will be your bodyguards."

"Have they agreed to this farce?"

"Not yet, *pas de problème*. I do not want you in the position *dangereuse* or me to get the bad vibes *maintenant* when I am to blame. Adam acts protective toward you and Janelle."

"Not a hooker nor a harlot type," Gladys cut in. "We want you to act like a woman of the streets and hit the bars to look for that cousin who must have some answers."

"Nothing to this foolish notion at all." Erin made faces at them. "I go around asking for some guy I've never seen or know anything about." She paused, her nose twitching. "Geez, I'll need to take lessons from Eliza."

"*Comment?*"

"Nothing. I didn't say a word."

The two women went back to discussing their plot. Erin made a wry face at them and twiddled her thumbs. "Don't I get a say?"

"You will put up the blocks in the road, *Chèrie*."

"Roadblocks. I think I should do that; in fact, I should veto this sordid idea now."

"The police cannot find this man, Lester Lisson. Celine and I think a slightly immoral woman wouldn't be suspected of subterfuge by the bar patrons."

"*Oui*. You can get clues or the pointers, I think the police say."

"But..."

"D'accord. You must possess a tight short skirt, a sexy blouse, and heels, correct? And I have that long black wig. *Pas de* worry about anyone recognizing you."

"Why do you have a long black wig?" Erin asked.

Celine bit her lower lip before answering. "At our elder's Halloween party last year, I played the fortune teller. I used an upside-down bowl. I never mentioned it as you tease me about using a crystal ball *tout le temps.*"

"You will need to wear lots of make-up," Gladys added.

Erin never agreed to the farce that landed her in this dramatic leading role, but that wasn't an issue for them. The two older women steamrolled her regardless.

Later that evening, Erin met Adam and Janelle at Celine's. They talked of protective manoeuvres for Erin's bar hopping. Adam didn't appear keen on the escapade when coerced by Celine, but Janelle's eyes probed into his disparagingly. He only agreed to follow and chaperone when Celine said poor, tiny Janelle would have to tag along after Erin by herself. The bar scene wouldn't be safe for her. Though both Erin and Janelle were strong women, Celine emphasized that he was a man, his role being a woman's protector. He agreed if Inspector Landry didn't learn about their exploits. His boss would shred his hide.

The next day, Luke frowned on seeing Adam jump or jerk a limb whenever he appeared in the younger man's vicinity. The lad wasn't assigned to work this shift on patrol. While Trevor trained a rookie on daily routines, Luke set Adam to file and absorb facts on numerous open cases in an adjacent office. He told him to check for avenues that no one else considered in solving these cases. Luke observed the young man and deduced Adam was suffering from a guilty conscience. But what was he up to? Another time, he caught Adam whispering into the phone before he blurted out goodbye and hung up quickly when he spotted Luke looking through the doorway. Near the end of the day, Adam fidgeted, waffled, and kept glancing at the clock. He didn't seem to have finished any work.

Adam glanced at Luke, who feigned shuffling papers and working while managing to keep a discreet eye on his young officer. Adam slipped away to the outer office, and Luke guessed he meant to phone someone again. With no qualms following and listening to the conversation, Luke hid from view beside the doorway he left ajar purposefully. Luke's lips tightened, and his eyes squinted angrily when he heard and understood the gist of the one-sided conversation. Thinking deeply, he settled for something besides confrontation.

After Adam left quickly and sheepishly for the day, Luke checked the downstairs lockers and found a few tools left by the surveillance team. Returning to his apartment, Luke picked a few essentials and donned some frayed jeans, a ragged black t-shirt, and an old denim jacket. Lastly, he added a dark beret over a cropped blonde wig with bangs before attaching a thin, pale moustache to his upper lip, items he had confiscated from the office. On the phone, he heard Adam saying that he would pick up Janelle and Erin at seven. Then, they would start their pub crawl at the Nickel Range Hotel and fan out to another couple of bars downtown to ask questions about the ongoing murder investigation. They planned to uncover information leading them to their quarry, Lester Lisson.

Celine and Gladys wanted Erin to parade about in her get-up all over town. She glared at them and lowered their expectations to three bars. She sauntered into the first dive on the strip, a smile pasted on her face. She kept her black wig hanging forward, the bangs useful for camouflage in fear that someone would recognize her. Dressed all in black with a tight low-cut shell and miniskirt from earlier, thinner days, she let out a nervous giggle. No one in her old nursing class would believe this. Erin glanced at the white cross on her nursing ring. Part of her felt she should take it off. No, she labelled this excursion under her duty to the truth. Besides, she bet lots of women dreamt of being wild and saucy for a night. She could relax and enjoy the fun. But it was hard to do with the butterflies playing volleyball in her gut.

Adam and Janelle followed inside a few minutes later. They didn't sit at the bar but slid onto chairs at a table facing the room. The primarily male patrons swivelled to glance at Adam's marked height. Celine had instructed the couple to dress down, and both wore tatty jeans and sweatshirts. Adam sported a ball cap over his dark hair.

Erin attracted a lot of attention, the wrong kind. She asked a few questions but got no answers. The bartender slid a hand with her drink alongside her breast, and a couple of customers lewdly propositioned her. Erin wished she had a picture of the guy to show around. Then she wouldn't have to waste time describing the man and avoiding wandering hands. Some fun, alright. Taking short breaths to minimize her intake of the stale odours of sweat, booze, and drugs, she slid out the door without getting a single response to her veiled questions.

She had no luck at the next bar either, as she kept evading hands and drinks—some of which she suspected were doctored. She bet Eliza wouldn't show up at a place like this.

At the third stop, Adam and Janelle couldn't find a seat together in the crowded bar. The couple opted to stay outside and keep a lookout through the window. But Erin found a bartender who knew the cousin— or said he did, anyway. The man drawled, his eyes assessing her. "He's usually here whining and begging for money or caging a free drink, but lately, he bragged about coming into easy money. I told him easy come, easy go. Check out Hairy Earl over there. He often listens to the bloke."

Erin got a lemon water and sat on the barstool beside the ape-like man in question.

"I've got no money, babe, and I don't need to pay for my tricks."

She managed a sickly smile. "That's okay. I'll buy you a drink if you answer a question for me."

Hairy Earl looked her over and guzzled his beer. "You an undercover cop or something? Not that you'd say, of course."

That idea hadn't occurred to her. She shook her head. "I'm scouting out news for my boyfriend who's in trouble with the police. I need to find Lester Lisson. I'm sure he'd help clear my boyfriend with what he knows about a murder."

"I'm all for that, helping a friend. Another beer, Charlie. The babe's paying."

"She can't like your ugly puss, Earl. Careful, lady. He's a mean bastard."

"I'll tell her not to leave you a tip." The man turned to her. "That Lester fellow you want, he came in this bloody joint last night." Hairy Earl took time to look her over, undressing her with narrowed eyes. "Bragged about a mark he planned to hit on for payback money."

She gave a shaky laugh. "You mean like blackmail someone?"

"Well, nah. Let's say favours in return for a closed mouth about certain activities."

"Did he mention any names to you or say when he'd be back."

"Nah, but his car's outside. He often leaves his old jalopy here, never locked if you want to look inside... for clues of his whereabouts, you know."

She shrugged, wary and on edge while following him out the back door, her senses on full alert.

He slammed the heavy door closed, turned, and grabbed her, pressing his body up against hers on the brick wall. "Like I said, whore, I don't pay. I take what I want."

When his wet mouth touched hers, she bit down on his lip hard. With a howl, he jumped back and raised his arm to strike. Erin high-kicked his arm and smacked his head with an arm chop. It wasn't easy kicking without exposing her underwear in this miniskirt. The man dropped to the ground and stayed there. She checked for a pulse to see if she knocked him out, noticing her shaking hands after her adrenalin rush. She glanced around, sneered at the human garbage below her, and tossed a few quarters onto him before re-entering the bar.

Fixing her dishevelled wig and proceeding toward the darkened bar, she smiled at the old cleaning woman in the hall.

The woman peered up at her. "You're a phoney, Duckie. You in an initiation group or doing a government job?"

"Neither. I'm trying to get information on Lester Lisson to clear my boyfriend."

"Sure. All your lies and shit stink, you know. Only losers in here."

55

Luke glumly trailed behind the group. He hoped smoke wasn't coming out his ears. He approached Adam and Janelle and asked about another bar's location in a thick French accent. Janelle answered him negatively in French. Adam paced before the bar windows, trying to peer in without being observed.

"The lad will never become an undercover cop, even if he was shorter," Luke mumbled before speaking up. "*Entrez-vous,* Monsieur?"

"No. It's pretty full. We're waiting for someone."

"I can find her for you, Adam," Luke spoke in clear, restrained English.

Adam's eyes widened, and he sputtered, clearly alarmed. "Inspector Landry, what are you doing here and in that getup?"

"Our amateur sleuth has more than two protectors tonight. Go wait by your car. I'll deal with you both later."

Going into the men's bathroom, he stepped up and peered out the high window when Erin went outside with the man. Luke muttered, let out his breath and jumped off the toilet seat to take off after her. He spotted her coming back in, talking to the cleaning woman and entering the women's bathroom. He eased open the alley door and witnessed the man lurching off the ground, holding onto an arm. "Listen, turd. I'd best advise you to take off home, fast, before I smack that ugly bod upside-down, too. I'm an undercover cop, and we're keeping an eye on you. Don't make that mistake again."

BETTY GUENETTE

Inside, on the cramped bar dance floor, Erin danced the twist, looking miserable. She evaded her partner's pawing hands. Her questions met only evasive grunts and further manoeuvring of bodies. When the dance ended, Luke touched her arm and proceeded to match her steps. He spoke broken English to her with thick French innuendoes. "Which man you wish to *cherchez*?"

"I can speak French if you're more comfortable, *Monsieur*."

"Not the *parler* I wish for, but the ac-tion. What you are liking to drink?"

"Nothing now. I'm expecting my boyfriend to show up." When a slower number started, Luke pulled her into his arms and rubbed his hand up and down her back. "*Encore,*" he whispered in her ear. "*Combien vous chargez, femme?*"

Erin tried to pull away from the tight hold. "I think this is *fini, Monsieur*."

Luke grasped the risk of injury if he kept up this charade. He spoke in soft, clear tones. "High time you went home, Cleopatra."

She froze, then pulled back. "Luke? What are you doing here in that silly getup?" Her face flushed beet red when he glanced casually over her attire.

Luke pulled her back and raised her arms on his shoulders to dance. "We're disguised, so let's take advantage of being here incognito." He rubbed his hands along her sides, slowing by her breasts. "No one knows us, so let's not restrain ourselves."

Erin gasped, and he was certain waves of yearning assailed her senses as they did his. Instead of pulling back when he kissed her roughly, she responded, and both devoured each other.

Soon, she managed to pull away. "Luke, stop this nonsense," she sputtered, fanning herself.

"Why stop? It's the best entertainment I've had in ages. Great fun after your contretemps outside."

"You saw that? Well, I handled it. Stop it," she whispered as his hands roamed over her body. "There are people here, and Adam's right outside."

"Who'll care? I sent Adam back to his car till I can decide on an adequate punishment." He pulled her back into the slow dance when she tried to leave. "They'll all think the lucky frog caught the luscious bug and gets to take her home."

Erin kept up with his movements. "I'm not going home with you. How did you recognize me, anyway?"

"The vampire look, I think. The fair skin and black hair made me want to bite your neck. Hmm, I think the cleavage view and tight butt swaying in the short skirt also clued me in." He grinned. "But I think you do want to go home with me." Luke wanted her body so badly that he got angrier at himself more than at her. He clamped both hands against her bottom, pulling her tight against him, letting her feel his arousal. "Don't trust yourself after parading your sexuality all over town," he whispered and slid kisses down her neck, nuzzling down to the exposed cleavage.

He felt her shiver and knew she wanted to push him away, but her fickle body responded in the dark bar, and she seemed to savour the thrill. Their breathing was loud and harsh.

Luke spoke again, "I don't think you planned this escapade all by yourself. We are going to visit Madame Lauzon, then I'll take care of Adam."

She pushed back and flounced away. He followed. "If you did your job properly and left Mark—your friend—alone, then I wouldn't have to go behind your back to help."

"This kind of help I don't need. I watched that guy take you outside from my perch on a dirty toilet seat. I wasn't close enough to help if he drove a knife into your gut."

"Well, he didn't, and I figured he'd try something. I took a chance to try and find out relevant information."

Luke knew that Erin was aware she was in the wrong. He was also aware that she damn well wouldn't admit it.

She pushed on the door. "I didn't enjoy this vulgar act and these lowlifes' attention, much less being called a whore. Besides, this is all your fault."

Luke, following her outside, raised his eyebrows in disbelief and spoke in a stilted voice, "This farce of a masquerade is my fault?"

"Yes, we're trying to help you solve the murders."

"Then quit. I like your body warm, not cold in a muddy grave." He strode toward Adam. "My men have already canvassed this route searching for the guy."

"And I bet they had a picture," he heard her mutter to his back.

56

Adam showed up, knocking on Erin's door Saturday afternoon. He seemed hesitant and looked more timid than usual.

"Oh, Adam. I'm sorry. Did Luke give you a hard time last night?" Erin asked.

"He sure did. I deserved the bawling out. But I'm here to check on you and Janelle."

Erin smiled. Janelle was an independent observer and had minimal involvement. Adam was focused on Janelle's discomfort, but he didn't need to worry.

With another knock, Janelle burst in. "Did you get sacked, Adam?"

"No, my boss is lenient, but he sure told me off for agreeing to that charade and allowing Erin to place herself in danger."

"I acknowledged the risks, Adam. You and Janelle watched my back."

"The inspector told me about how that guy assaulted you and how you defended yourself. I wasn't much help outside."

"Well, neither was I. We couldn't go in since no seating was available," Janelle said. "Auntie Celine wasn't pleased with Luke. He ticked her off for interfering in a murder investigation and placing Erin in danger. He told Auntie that the guy meant to rape her."

Adam gave a sheepish smile. "How did your aunt respond to that?"

"She asked him if Erin was tied up or unconscious. When he said no, she told him she did not understand why he made such a fuss. She did not see the *problème*."

Adam shook his head. "Well, I've been sworn to behave. Anyway, I've got Major in the car. I hoped you wanted to train Bill's dogs with him."

"What a great idea," Janelle said. "Let's do that."

Erin smiled. "Will you practice his tracking again?"

"Yes. He's great at following scents. I'll need a subject. You, Janelle?"

"How about me?" Erin spoke up. "Then Janelle can follow and pretend my dogs are tracking too, with Major."

Adam beamed. "That's better. Give me your sweater for him to smell."

Janelle's mouth twisted in a wry smile as she peered at Erin. "Where are you planning to lead us then, so the two of us can follow—um—together?"

Erin grinned, knowing Janelle recognized her machinations. "I'll zigzag up the small mountain behind the house and hide myself in the trees. It's not too woodsy here. We don't have a bear problem in town yet."

The plan worked, and the dog unerringly sniffed and followed her trail till he gave an excited bark and dove into the bushes to repeatedly lick her face, slobbering all over it. Juno and Rhea played with a bone they'd found in the fenced-off portion of the yard, oblivious to Major showing off his tracking expertise. The blissful dogs hadn't a clue.

57

Luke and Adam visited Mr. Fraser again. Adam petted Chum in the small entry while the dog sniffed, catching Major's smell on his pants. "I'm sorry," Luke said, "but I need to go over some points again. This area seems to keep popping up in our inquiries."

"No problem, inspector. I'm always here these days."

"Your neighbour, Mortimer, is home now. He told a different story about your accident, mentioning a couple playing sex games in the woods."

"Not that story again." Mr. Fraser banged his cup on the table. "Don't believe the idiot. I've never seen nudists running around amongst the trees, not even in my dreams."

Luke shook his head at the man and sat down. "About this murder, the resort property may have been used as a playground for sexual escapades."

"The wildlife around here tends to discourage people romping around. This is no bloody garden of Eden."

Luke grinned at the cantankerous man. "Are you running a private nude resort when the owners aren't around?"

"Don't be ridiculous. My neighbour's only trying to excuse his carelessness with these outrageous lies. It won't work." He rubbed his beard. "Besides, the end of April may not be bug season, but the damn weather's cold enough to keep your clothes on."

"We did have those few hotter days," Luke said. "Tell me about the Ericksons again."

The trapper shook his head in disgust, tried to refocus. "Well, they owned the big lodge up there years ago. There was a younger boy, but he was a sickly lad and died early. Sheila lost her mom to pneumonia when she was around ten years old. I don't remember Cathy's mom. I heard her parents divorced, and her mother died in a car accident later. Cathy would have been too young to remember. Her dad, Wallace, was the caretaker."

"So, the girls got thrown together a lot?"

"Sure did. Reminded me of a queen and a devoted subject. Sheila, the rich one, usually left Cathy to clean up the horses and tack. After all, they allowed her to ride their horses. It didn't seem to bother Cathy, though. That girl was a natural with animals and the outdoors. I worked at the INCO smelter and would drive my old jalopy up there to pester and learn from the owner and old caretaker. Both Erickson and Wallace died quite a few years back."

"We think Craig used the lodge as a meeting place for entertaining women. Do you have a key? I have a search warrant but would hate to break in."

"Yes. I'll call the owners up north after you check it out. Not as if they can do anything." The old man pointed at the hanger by the door. "It's that big one there on the wood peg. There's also a spare one at the lodge, under the corner post of the railing."

Luke and Adam left. Jackson Weevil, another officer, had been waiting in the car and drove them to the lodge. They carried flashlights and checked outside for broken windows or signs of forced entry. Luke stopped to gaze at the view of water and pointed across at the view. "Look at the lake. The sun's trying to break through the clouds, and there are a couple of loons diving for fish."

Jackson glanced around the shoreline. "The ground's rockier here, shouldn't get too wet and muddy like other campsites."

The three men donned gloves. Luke unlocked and entered the cabin ahead of them. "No power on, but some light is coming in from the upstairs windows. Check the main floor and basement for signs of habitation, and I'll go check the suites upstairs. Mr. Fraser said there were about ten bedrooms in all."

Adam found a two-month-old fashion magazine wedged between the couch cushions and bagged the telling item. The kitchen looked tidy except for an old, stained cup in the sink. It'd likely been there awhile and was good for fingerprints. He shone his light in the cupboards. There wasn't any perishable food left, but a few bottles of unopened red wine dated a few years prior sat on a corner shelving unit. No help there except for fingerprints.

Jackson shone his light around the basement crawl space. Besides cobwebs and old tools, he reported nothing important.

Luke wandered through the bedrooms. There were no linens or covers on the beds, and plastic dust covers protected the mattresses and furniture. He checked the closets, but they were empty. A fine layer of dust on the floors remained, save the gaps left from their footsteps.

When Luke finished and joined Adam, they checked the owners' suite on the main floor. The fireplace contained ash residue, and logs were stacked alongside in a bin. The closet contained a packed bag of wool blankets.

"Sir, he may have carried pillows and comforters in his car."

"That makes sense if he's habitually seductive. Test for fingerprints here and in the kitchen."

Cathy and Sheila drove a similar, lightly coloured van, and they'd checked Sheila's out. Forensics said no blood was found, but they detected rug fibres and indents where boxes once sat. Maybe Cathy copied her friend's ways and lifestyle and maybe even borrowed her friend's husband. Both women possessed the ability and conviction and were tied into a complex relationship with Craig. If he wasn't the murderer, he must still be pivotal to the case. Sheila was the repressed and tightly controlled one and he was unsure about Cathy.

58

Luke returned to the track on race night to talk to Erin and Bill. "Bill, you're sure Craig has no close male friends I can question?"

"He chats up a couple of drivers and trainers, but I'm sure he doesn't see them socially. I know his wife insists he attends the theatre with her and their elite group. She's one of the patrons, but he complains, saying the theatre scene is stuffy."

"Have you seen his wife, Sheila, here making bets on horses?"

"Rarely, and not betting." Bill said. "She thinks the track's low class, though she certainly visits the casino. Last week, she came out with another tall woman and watched one race. She seemed to be looking for someone.

Erin cringed. "Darn. I hope they weren't going to make a scene if I'm the person they were hoping to spot."

Bill glanced warily at her. "She's icily cold and not into making a public spectacle, though she holds contempt for others. Craig tries keeping up top-notch behaviour but lays on the charm between races."

"Do you think she knows how he carries on with other women?" Luke asked.

Bill grunted. "She'd have to be blind and stupid, and I'm sure she's neither. If he's circumspect and not an embarrassment to her, she'd turn a blind eye to his indiscretions and keep up a bold front to the world."

"Oh, oh, look who's arrived. Keep close to me guys, please. I can feel her waves of loathing flowing my way," Erin said.

Bill faced the entry. "That Sheila's one wicked-looking woman."

"They're both aggressive women. Cathy is just less prickly." Luke watched Craig saunter over and hook an arm under each woman's elbow, steering them in another direction.

Erin peered sideways at the trio. "I'm not afraid of them, but I hate confrontations and listening to barbed innuendoes, especially in public."

"Looks like pretty boy Craig is herding them off to the casino."

"I hope you're avoiding him, Erin," Luke admonished in a steely voice. "He's high on our list of suspects for the murder."

She smirked. "I'll ask Celine to create a talisman to protect me from predatory men, including you, Luke."

"You'll need more than that for protection if you continue disrupting my investigation."

"How about I get Celine to stir up a witch's brew or cast a spell to make a killer confess."

Bill shook his head. "Geez, remember that witches were burned at the stake."

Erin laughed. "And me, a fire sign. Glad I wasn't born in those days."

"Your ancestors probably passed along a weird gene," Bill said. "Wait, no, that would mean I have it, too."

Luke shook his head at the siblings. "Well, I'm going to find Craig and rattle him."

Luke spotted his quarry drinking at the bar, eyes raking the women passing by. The instant Craig spotted Luke heading his way, his body went rigid.

"Hello, Mr. Gibson. Let's find a quiet corner for a few minutes."

"What more could you want to know, inspector?"

"I'd like to tell you that we picked up yours and Jewel's fingerprints at the lodge near Mr. Fraser's. The lodge that your wife's family used to own."

The man's face blanched. "I have confessed to my association with Jewel. I did have assignations out there with her. The key left in the deck post isn't a big secret. Cathy and my wife know where it's hidden. The old man wanted Cathy to check on the place when he left."

"You do realize failing to volunteer this relevant information has impeded our investigation and makes you seem very suspicious," Luke added. "I presume your wife doesn't know about your trespassing."

The man gulped. "No, of course she doesn't." Craig threw his head back. "There's no reason for my wife to find out, inspector, unless I need to address the issue in court." He turned to return to the bar.

"We make no guarantees, Mr. Gibson. If I need to pressure anyone further, I will use everything I've learned to solve this case."

Craig stalked off, his body tight and unyielding.

59

Erin spotted the two women returning. They veered toward her after seeing Luke talking to Craig while Bill turned to talk to one of the owners.

"Hello, Erin," Cathy spoke first.

Erin smiled back. "Hello, Cathy, and you, Sheila."

Bill turned back to face them.

"This is my brother, Bill. He owns a couple of racehorses. I often accompany him and watch the races."

Bill nodded to Sheila. "I've met Craig's wife, but not your sister."

Sheila fumed. "She's not my sister, merely an acquaintance."

"Sorry. There is quite a resemblance."

Erin grimaced at Bill's faux pas, thinking he was deliberately goading her. He didn't realize how dangerous and malicious the woman was—and now there were two of them.

"You do have the same hair colouring and physical presence," Erin said.

Cathy smiled. "We just played slots in the casino and want to watch a couple of races. Standing around is boring. Sheila and I used to ride at a young age: regular rodeo riders."

"I enjoy riding too," Erin replied. "Have you tried the different stables?"

"I think we outgrew those childish pursuits," Sheila said.

Bill grunted. "Hope I never grow that old."

Sheila's lips couldn't have thinned more as she scowled at Bill.

Luke sauntered over. "Hello, ladies. Is Bill bragging about his horse, River Lad, coming up in the eighth race?"

Cathy glanced at the inflexible Sheila and then looked back at them. "Craig told us you owned a couple of racing horses here."

"One is recovering from a track mishap, but he'll be racing again soon." Bill flashed a deadpan look at Sheila. "Do you want a tip for the races?"

Sheila drew herself to her full height. "Certainly not."

Erin stiffened. "Betting is the same, whether at the racetrack or the casino. But this is more fun than pushing a button."

Sheila looked down her nose at them. The feat proved difficult, as everyone was equal in height or taller.

"Let's go, Cathy. To each their own."

The two women turned and marched to where Craig sat hunched alone at the bar. The man pretended he hadn't seen them talking to Erin's group.

Erin whispered to Bill, "You sure put in your two cents worth."

Bill shrugged his broad shoulders. "That woman's attitude made snakes slither up and down my spine."

Luke waved. "I'm out of here. Erin, you should be safe enough with Bill."

Bill scowled. "Thanks for nothing, Luke. You should be worrying about my safety."

215

60

On Sunday, the one day that promised to be dry and sunny, Erin smiled, knowing she would be horseback riding at the farm. She felt she needed to repent for her masquerade at the bar, and after asking Janelle to accompany her, she checked with Bill and asked Adam and Luke if they wanted to go riding, too. Janelle, intrigued by all animals, wasn't sure what veterinary specialty she'd follow. Now, at the farm, she shook her head and stared at the horses' muscled physiques.

"We haven't done vet work on larger farm animals yet, only the pet ones. I was a horse fanatic like most kids, but we rode ponies."

Erin grinned, more pleased than usual about the men coming riding with them. "The pintos are gentle, and I can help you up on Spirit."

"But you can't help me hold on once I'm up there. The ground's a long way down."

Luke and Adam showed up shortly after with Major. The dog took in the new scents, seeming leery of the horses' hooves but romping with Bill's dogs. Adam wore an old cowboy hat and, though grinning, fidgeted and glanced back and forth at the horses. He had only ridden when quite young.

Bill saddled his large placid roan for Adam. "Come on, Cheyenne. You are getting a workout today, you lazy hay eater."

She whispered to Bill without looking over at Luke. "Can't we put Luke up on naughty Rebel this time?"

Bill glowered. "I don't think so. He'll ride Chico again. You'll have your hands full managing Geisha Girl. John said she's ready for the trails. Don't let her get spooked."

Bill spent time with Adam, giving him pointers and easing him into a comfort zone.

The four rode through the newly green pastures and entered a wide, wooded trail. The three dogs raced ahead, sniffing and barking at ecstatic volumes and only once flushing out a partridge. They didn't know what to do when the thing kept fluttering in the air before landing a short distance away from them.

Adam glanced back at Janelle, then forward quickly, his body posture stiff as he hung onto the saddle horn and reins. "Major is having a field day, running wild with his nose to the ground."

Erin trotted ahead and led the way alongside a small lake. The willow trees dotting the shoreline drooped over the water as if admiring their sombre reflection, waiting for a breeze to enhance their presence. "John said he'll clear some new trails through the woods. It'll give him plenty of logs for winter burning. Let's gallop here. Lean forward and hang on. The other horses will follow the lead."

Slowly pulling up later, Erin turned in her saddle to see Janelle coming to a halt when they rambled up behind her. Janelle looked radiant. "You look like you had fun, Janelle."

"Oh, yes," she answered. "And Adam seems more relaxed now. More than when he first took off."

Luke manoeuvred Chico beside Erin. "Will I make your horse skittish if I get too close?"

"She has to learn." Erin pointed to the dogs. "I'm not worried about bears for a change. Major is better protection than Bill's dogs. Ours run around in a delightful frenzy. Major's running around, but he keeps checking back and sniffing for different odours."

"Probably thinks he's gone to heaven." Luke pursed his lips. "We haven't said too much in the news, but we think Kelly was knocked unconscious and dragged over rough terrain before she was strangled. The coroner thinks someone hit her on the side of the head with a blunt object and knocked her unconscious."

"I'll bet you think the killer kept her alive till he set up Mark as the culprit."

"That's a reasonable assumption. The Manor's pathway was disturbed and covered by leaves. Mark's office knows when he goes out to visit his grandmother, and his car was parked in the Manor's lot. They likely lured him toward the backyard."

"Sir, look at the big stork—or crane—I think." Adam pointed to the far bushes. "It's standing quietly, almost totally camouflaged."

The two men rode over and halted, gazing across the shimmering lake. Major, mesmerized by the scents, kept running around in circles, sniffing every blade of grass.

Janelle looked over at the men. "If Adam became a good rider, maybe he could work with the RCMP. Riding a horse is like riding a bike as a child: it comes back to you later."

"At least he's able to stay in the saddle," Erin added "He looks more comfortable than when we started. He's a rookie in more ways than one. I bet he'll make a first-class man."

"He's got a lot of maturing and learning to do," Janelle said.

"You have, too, Janelle. The more I learned at university, the more I realized how little I knew, even in nursing."

"Are you playing matchmaker?" Janelle asked.

"I hope I'm not patronizing you. Don't be too hard on that nice boy."

"See. You said boy, not me." Janelle laughed.

"Sorry, some men, like Adam, need longer to grow into what they'll become."

Erin urged the horse forward. "And some I met never grew up."

There was little chatter on the way back through another trail. Janelle and Adam learned the feel of the horses' rhythm, how to handle the reins, and how to stay in their saddles. Erin stayed apart and kept a tight hold on her reins.

Nearing home, a hawk flew out of the bushes, startling the horses and riders. Spirit and Cheyenne didn't blink, but Chico sidestepped. Erin held onto Geisha Girl, who danced around, showing the whites of her eyes. Erin managed to keep tight control and stopped the whirling. The horse didn't know which way to take off to anyway. The dogs barked, chasing the hawk and racing into the trees for more fun and games. Before Erin settled the horse down, another hawk flew out of the bushes, and the horse freaked out, spun around, and wheeled toward the distant forest.

Erin pulled harder on the reins, but the horse accelerated frantically. She leaned forward onto the mare's shoulders and hung on. She knew she should stroke and soothe Geisha Girl but couldn't change her unstable position to pull harder on the reins.

The horse finally slowed in the thickening bush and came to a stop, the animal's hefty form quivering all over with its head hung down while it panted and slobbered. Erin patted the mare's neck and debated dismounting and leading her around, but she didn't trust the dark, forbidding trees surrounding her and felt inclined to tremble alongside the horse. She heard rustling in the far bushes and worried about another bird taking off and spooking the horse again. Her eyes widened at the sight of the bear of her nightmares standing on all four legs, watching them from a rocky point. When Major raced up to her, barking in greeting, the bear raised its head to sniff around, then turned and scrambled down the far side of the hill and disappeared into dense bush. She pulled out her jackknife—her only defence—and waited, praying the animal wouldn't work its way around to surprise them with a sneak attack from the rear.

Erin heard Luke calling her name and answered, only then realizing how petrified she was by hearing her shaking and croaking voice. She cleared her throat and called out again, turning her horse toward the rider coming over the hill.

On the ride back, the appaloosa glanced furtively around and shook her head more frequently, checking out the surroundings while Erin weaved her in and out on the side paths to settle her down. The other horses, used to wildlife, carried the riders safely home, unconcerned with the frolicking, tiring dogs.

Bill grabbed the reins and caught Erin as she slid to the ground, wobbling on her jittery legs. "Wow, I'm getting a late adrenalin rush." She shivered. "Bill, I spotted a bear out there."

Bill clamped his lips together, knowing her childhood fear. He listened to the others telling him about the hawk startling Geisha Girl into a gallop. "I'll put her in the corral to quiet down, and she can enjoy some peaceful surroundings before she gets settled in the barn."

Luke came over and offered his arm to Erin for support, and she hung on, grateful for his closeness and warmth.

61

Monday morning, Luke sat at his desk checking all the information they'd tabulated.

Ralph strolled in and handed him a few more sheets. "More faxes with zilch info."

"I've scanned everything multiple times. Does anything pop out at you?"

"A few robberies I followed to see if this Lester's involved but turned out to be mostly underage delinquents. They'll probably get a slap on the wrist and be back working the streets."

"Are Trevor and Adam on patrol today?" he asked Beth when she came in.

"Sure. Did you want them to check in?"

"Ask them to stop in before their lunch break."

The two arrived in a short time. Trevor, the older, jaded one, rocked on his toes.

"Any luck on finding Lester Lisson's haunts, Trevor?"

"Not a one, Boss. You're sure the guy exists, right?"

"You have his picture and all the details we've uncovered. Someone must know him."

Trevor scratched his head. "Those fingerprints we found at the victim's apartment aren't on file and don't match any of the women's. They must be his."

"Probably into petty pilfering and hasn't got caught," Luke answered.

BETTY GUENETTE

Adam spoke up. "I talked to our snitch by the overpass near the soup kitchen, but he seemed cagey today. Course, he wasn't sober."

Ralph frowned. "The jeweller Craig deals with was surprised but didn't question his customer when he bought the cheap emerald ring. The man must buy his wife the good stuff with her own money."

Luke spoke. "Lawyers make good salaries, though Mark said the man's lazy."

"You'd think he'd have enough smarts to go to another jewellery store." Trevor shook his head. "Lucky for us, some suspects are dumb."

"Ralph, get Jackson to take fingerprints of the lawyers' staff: the four women there and the wife, and photos, too." Luke shrugged. "They won't be happy."

When he left, Luke drummed his fingers on the desk. They found another set of fingerprints at the lodge that didn't match Mr. Fraser's, Craig's, or Jewel's. "We're not making headway with any of the suspects. I'm thinking there might be others involved."

"You mean someone we haven't met? I was hard on that nurse, Erin, last month." Trevor pursed his lips. "Unless she's switched from fires to burials. No cause, though."

Beth sauntered back in, hearing the last comment. "That nurse could have died. And remember her interference solved our last murder case."

A voice interjected. "That elderly psychic woman next door helped."

Three heads turned, and all eyes stared at Adam, who flushed beet red. "I'm repeating what Erin said." He stuttered. "I... I didn't say I believed it."

222

Luke narrowed his eyes when he stared at Adam. The young man was getting too personally involved. Of course, Luke managed to control his own desires. Right!

Beth handed an invitation to Luke. "Don't forget about attending the mayor's charity event."

"Damn, I hate those dress-up parties. I have to make chitchat with the elite crowd."

Beth replied in a suggestive voice, "Take a sexy date with you as a diversion." She grinned wickedly. "I suggest you take a hot Aries. Sorry, not me. I'm married."

After her busy day, Erin headed home and detoured to check on Celine. "Are the exercises too hard on your leg with the new therapy?"

"Not at all. I feel like the young *poulet*."

Erin grinned. "I brought you some chocolates a patient gave me. I'd rather you indulge than me."

Celine huffed. "I made the green lemon tea. Good for cleansing of the *système*."

"I need more than my system cleansed. With all this rain, I haven't done much exercising. We have a lot of rock in town, but the outlying areas are muddy, and my car gets bogged down on those back roads."

"The rain seems to have *fini, ce soir*." Celine, looking out her window, chanted in a bemused fashion.

"*Earth does move, so watch your feet,*
Take care, and don't be caught asleep."

"Thanks a lot," Erin said. "An earthquake is scary whether I'm awake or asleep."

Celine pondered a moment. "Too many Taurus earth signs floating around. A word of advice I've heard is to 'never second guess a Taurus.' They are always *plus* steps ahead and are persistent and inflexible."

Back at home, Erin broke out her windbreaker and pulled on her high boots. Juno grabbed her leash and trotted over while

Rhea jumped around in circles yapping. The lab already waited at the door. The spaniel kept chasing her tail.

Leaving the driveway with the excited dogs, she spotted a young-ish fellow from the apartment building across the road approaching her.

He called out. "Hello there. My girlfriend says you're a nurse."

Erin glanced at her young neighbour beside him, then back at the man. "Yes, I'm a nurse." And here we go again with another free consultation, she thought.

The guy, saying his name was Ross, lifted his jogger pant leg to show a swollen, red-yellow lump below the knee. "I hoped you could tell me what this boil thingy is on my leg?"

"Yep," Erin answered. "It looks like a boil all right."

He dropped the pant leg. "I have another one of these ugly lumps on my bum."

Erin stared upward in exasperation. "I don't want to see it."

The fellow shrugged a few times. "Well, they're sore and get really itchy, and I don't know what to do. They hurt if I try to scratch them."

Annoyed, Erin untangled the dogs' leashes and fixed a fierce gaze on him. "Maybe you have lice, ringworms, or an infectious disease that could spread all over your body?"

He gaped at her and stuttered. "You think it's really bad—that I might die?"

"And contaminate everyone, killing us all." She added, "You should see a doctor fast."

He stared, unblinking, before sighing. "You're kidding, right?"

"Yes, I'm kidding," she answered, shaking her head and restraining the excited dogs. "Go see a real doctor at a clinic. The lumps may start to drain pus soon and spread. You likely need penicillin shots for the infection."

BETTY GUENETTE

She left in a lurching gait, dragged onto the side of the main road by unrepentant, anxious dogs. She watched out for oncoming cars to avoid getting splashed from the springtime potholes filled by the recent rains.

Erin took a different route to avoid running into Adam to defuse Luke's belief that she led the lad on. How silly. He was enamoured of Janelle. The dogs loved the new smells and barked at the various dogs they met leashed on this route. Beside one yard, a large Rottweiler jumped the enclosed gate and charged toward them. She yelled and grabbed up tiny Rhea, trying to stand in front of Juno. The big dog was a male and only interested in checking the others' female scents. Bill's two were spayed, but lots of anal sniffing occurred before the owner was alerted to his dog's escape and shouted to call him back. The dog flipped around and loped away, returning through the now-open gate.

"Geez, girls, did you see that? His dog listens." Erin unscrambled the leashes.

The young man came out after tying up his dog. "Sorry about that. He's young and excited about everything. Our fence is tall, but I didn't expect him to jump the gate. I often let Caesar loose while I work in the yard."

Erin smiled, recognizing him. "Aren't you the foreman constructing that new apartment building?"

"Yes, Dave Hamish. Are you looking for a place to rent?"

"My neighbour, Celine Lauzon, and another elderly couple bought the building. I'm Erin Rine. I checked on it for myself and a couple of friends."

"Well, we hope to be done by the end of August. Our company is keeping the maintenance contract for the place. Handy with it right around the corner from my house."

226

"Handy for both parties. May see you around then." She waved and trotted the dogs back home before they got their leashes tangled up again. The fellow seemed pleasant.

Janelle, on her way home to her grandmother's in Hanmer, dropped her Aunt Celine off to visit Gladys. Erin and Mark arrived after work to discuss the murder with them. Then Erin would bring her elderly neighbour home.

Mark looked askance at Celine. "I've heard strange tales about your skills in clairvoyance. You look like such an innocent, sweet lady."

"*Mais, in-no-cente* is not a word to apply to *moi*."

"So, you were a wild one in your youth?" Mark asked.

"Still am, young man, and *rien* of the old timer jokes."

Mark placed his hand on his chest. "I promise to never think of you as old."

Celine became businesslike. "*Maintenant,* we need to check other things. Erin says this Sheila, Craig's wife, grew up at a lodge further down from Mr. Fraser's. That area seems the focal point for these murders. You two must look around and check for the disturbances."

"Like what, Mrs. Lauzon? I'm not a detective like Luke."

"Call me Celine, *s'il-te-plaît*."

Gladys frowned. "That lodge is a summer retreat for city dwellers. I understand that the log building kept a rural charm, yet they upgraded with numerous amenities."

"Vagrants wander through areas *tout-le-temps*. You can *chercher* for the cooling coals outside or windows forced open or broken.

Ask that injured trapper for what you can expect to see. Hunt for *les différences*."

"I don't know what we can find when the police have already searched the place."

Mark nodded, agreeing with Erin. "Traipsing through the bush seems excessive."

"*Mais nécessaire.* We need to see the place through your eyes. You must pay attention to everything around you."

Mark almost stuttered. "I don't have a gun or know how to use one."

"The killer, he will not be hiding in the bushes to *attendre* for you."

Erin crinkled her nose. "No, but bears might. They live in those woods."

"Take Bill's dogs with you. They make *toujours* the racket." Celine got up.

Gladys put down her cup. "Why are you leaving so early, Celine? You've only been here over an hour."

"But I drank two cups of tea and ate pastries. Are you sure the clock is *cor-rect?*"

"See what I mean." Gladys nodded her head. "Timing getting screwed up—early Alzheimer's. We need to exercise our brain cells more—like with this murder mystery.

Celine patted Mark's hand on her way out with Erin. "You are a *bon* Taurus and would be okay living alone. But, many Taurus people, like you, are conventional and committed to their family. You are steadfast and calm with a laidback, pleasant personality, not to push your buttons, *mais non*. On the niceness scale, the earth sign of the Taurus *personne* comes in at number five out of twelve." She stopped and stared fixedly at Mark.

"*Blessed soon with child, you need not fear,*

This one who comes, you will hold dear."

Erin didn't look back at him as she walked ahead of Celine out the door.

Erin met Marge at a diner on her way home from work the next day.

The secretary sighed. "I can see you more often now that my kids are older and involved in after-school activities. "Do you remember the sexy nurse, Lise?"

"I won't forget that angry woman. I dared to suggest her involvement in the murder last month to the police and implicated her creepy cousin. She's a Pisces and too emotional."

"Well, she got a transfer into town. See what comes from playing nice-nice to old Mrs. Hildeforce and dating the boss's nephew?"

"No simpering up for me, thanks. Is she man-hopping or settling down this time?"

"She says she likes variety and brought her new red t-shirt to the office to show us." Marge pointed to her chest. "The logo reads, 'So many men and so little time.' Geesh!"

Erin grinned. "She'll enjoy living up to that motto. The last shirt was worse, the one that read, 'Jump my Bones.'"

"Lise asked about you, not pleasant-like. She heard that you found the woman's body and likely ratted on you to the boss. She asked me if you were still chasing that attractive inspector."

Erin grunted. "I don't chase men. I like my single status."

"Sure. Say that to someone else. Tell me, though, what's new about your murders?"

"Not *my* murders, please. The police aren't getting ahead at all. Mark and his grandmother are getting worried and searching for clues."

Marge leered at her. "Are you involved with Luke again?"

"I was never involved with him the way you mean."

"Then you're losing it. When his eyes land on you—oh, yummy." Marge's eyes lit up. "My toes tingle, and some other parts too."

"My brief affair in England turned me off romance—no more temporary flings." Erin shook her head. "Him desiring my body is not the same as him wanting the whole package."

Marge sighed, resting her chin on her hands. "Boy, wish I had your packaging."

"Oh, Marge, you're very attractive. Don't put yourself down."

"I don't, but my eyes and the mirror wage a constant battle on what they perceive. I see what I am." She gulped her coffee and placed her hands at her waist. "If I was taller, I'd be slimmer. I need to squeeze my torso up."

Erin choked on her tea, wiping her eyes and forcing herself to refrain from laughing aloud in the public restaurant.

65

Luke blew out a held breath when Ralph handed him the document showing the fingerprint comparison matching the ones found at the lodge. They belonged to the secretary, Cathy Wallace. "Well, we see those two are still an item."

"And you can spot some of them superimposed on Craig's. Good thing you ordered the extra fingerprints. Not that the evidence indicates murder."

"She can't say that her caretaking duties are the only reason and can't deny their continuing relationship since his marriage." Luke hit the buzzer. "Beth, come in, please."

When she arrived, he handed her the damning sheet.

Beth raised her eyebrows. "I'm not surprised, though it's not a motive for murder. She seemed pleased about his virility and many conquests. I read that feeling as real."

"Mr. Mortimer said the naked woman was a brunette," Luke added.

Ralph grinned. "Guess we can't have an identity lineup if the old guy can only identify the body. A nude show would not sit well with head office."

Beth pondered. "You can confront her with the knowledge, but she's not likely to bend. I think Cathy knows how to control her emotions."

"She's not as vicious as Sheila," Luke said. "That woman would kill her husband and Cathy in anger, but little Jewel?"

"Do we need to find more background on Jewel?" Beth asked.

"We've travelled that road," Ralph said. "She didn't have a lot of other friends. She was a mousy thing and kept to herself, except for her cousin and roommates."

"Well, I'll go visit Cathy." Luke got up. "If she mentioned to Craig that we took her fingerprints, he'll suspect we found a match. I don't think we'll take her by surprise."

"We'd need a lot more proof than our knowledge of an affair with her boss to ruffle that one, Boss."

66

ark met Erin at the firm's office door near closing time. He turned to his secretary. "Lois, will you assist Erin with the information she needs? She's helping Grandma clear me in this murder case that Luke is possibly pegging me for. Bugger, I'm being framed. Craig's the only one that could possibly be involved unless his wife found out." He sighed. "I'm not pointing the finger here. Erin, I need you to investigate, since my grandmother and Celine want to play Miss Marple, using you by proxy. They're enjoying themselves. I'm not." He turned and went into his office, his head tucked down between slumped shoulders.

Erin sat across from the secretary's desk. "Lois, Mark has good reason to be worried and upset. Lots of clues are being planted that point toward his involvement. Have you seen anything out of the ordinary recently that could help with this investigation?"

"No. I know Mark is innocent, but the others are questionable." Lois looked mutinous. "I can't see a reason for murder, though. Sheila must know her husband's no saint."

"Would he fool around with someone visiting or working in the office, like a client or a secretary? Or did I get inaccurate vibes from you about Cathy?"

Lois pursed her lips. "Well, he and Cathy had a relationship prior to his marriage and they're close—too close, I think. He doesn't need to look further. She says she has this long-distance boyfriend, but I've never seen him. Craig and Cathy throw sparks off each other but circumvent their attraction when Sheila's around. I don't think their affair's over, and Cathy laughs about his enjoyment of 'nature's bounty.'"

"That's no reason to kill those women. There must be something else."

"What if his wife became fed up with his exploits? No, then she would have killed Craig." Lois seemed to hesitate, then veered off on another tangent. "Do you tell fortunes, or is it your friend who does? Could you ask her if I should invest money in that new stock for uranium mining? I'm a Capricorn."

Erin sighed and got up. "Sorry, that's not how her visions work. They're not dependable. I'm going to speak to the other office girls again."

"I'm sorry, but I have another personal question. Mark said you do karate."

Erin smiled at the pleasant woman. "I practise taekwondo. I believe women should be capable of protecting themselves."

"I'm small and getting older." Lois stood as well. "Would you show me something to help me protect myself?"

"Well, sure, only it's mainly evasive tactics. You try to avoid a dicey situation in the first place, scream, or run away." Erin walked behind the woman. "I can show you a few things. Now, if I came from behind and grabbed your neck to choke you, you would grab my hands as a natural response and try to break the hold. Don't bother. No chance that'll work." She placed her hands around the older woman's throat. "Usually, the attacker is a man, and they're stronger than you. If he's not wearing gloves, then rake his hands with your nails to hurt him. But what you should do is try something to throw him off guard. One response is to hurl your body backwards to try and unbalance him. Surprise is often quite effective." Erin grinned. "Or twist your body sideways and use your hands to grab something on him, something that hurts."

Erin turned her head to see Cathy watching them from the doorway.

The woman came forward. "Geez, Lois, are you planning to take us all on?"

Erin spoke up. "Cathy, I want to help Mark by uncovering new information. I'd like to ask you some questions, too."

"Sure. Let's grab a coffee and sit downstairs. I planned to get one and then head out."

Before they sat, Erin chose a decaf. "First off, I never had designs on Craig. I talked to him once to ask questions for Mark's sake.

"I believe that, but Sheila doesn't. You're too refined and self-reliant to get involved with his low calibre and lusty personality. I'm not."

"Someone said you introduced Sheila to Craig."

"My big mistake. She ignored our attachment and said it didn't matter. She fell for him and didn't care that he and I were in a sexual relationship. She's the original ice maiden and wouldn't satisfy his sexual needs. He runs around, and it's never mattered to her that I cared for him. What Sheila wants, Sheila takes." She sipped her creamy coffee. "I was her bridesmaid and warned her no woman would keep him satisfied. I didn't add it wouldn't bother me to share."

"She didn't believe your advice or didn't care?"

"She wanted him on her terms. 'Discretion always,' she said. Liked to look at his pretty face and call the shots. She knows her money will keep him on a leash, however long it is."

"So, Jewel became another conquest on the side."

"That silly Jewel, such a scrawny thing. She came on too strong for Craig to resist easy pickings. Craig has a strong appetite for real women." She narrowed her eyes, assessing Erin. "His wife has good reason to be wary of you."

Erin's nose scrunched up. "No danger of that. What about you?"

"Craig and I fool around a bit, nothing too suggestive. She's okay about superficial stuff and likes her husband being desired. We're okay as long as she keeps thinking our more intimate relationship is in the past and we behave. I date a fellow, Frank, when he's in town."

Erin glanced at the woman's hand holding her coffee cup. "You wear a diamond on your right hand. It's not an engagement ring?"

"No, it's my birthstone from another beau, long ago—and don't ask."

"You grew up with Sheila, didn't you?"

"We lived in the northern bush growing up. I enjoyed the rougher life more than she did. She personified the rich bitch and stayed in town during the winters with an elderly aunt. I can hunt, shoot, and ride better than many men. I've even tracked bears."

Erin made a face. "I'm terrified of bears and have a strong aversion to hunting and guns."

"Hunting is not most women's hobby, but I like it."

Erin persevered. "What if Jewel thought she was pregnant?"

"No way. Craig's sterile. He had mumps as a child. That fact suited Miss Prissy. Meanwhile, Craig can have all the extracurricular fun he wants under wraps with no worries of paternity suits."

"You sound bitter but resigned. Pilfering your lover must have hurt you at the time."

"I was nobody, a leech she once called me. Sheila was rich, the daughter of the Manor, which was actually a lodge, but same difference to her."

"We don't all embody that stereotype, Cathy, but to some people, money counts."

Erin followed the secretary out and checked at the office. She questioned Lise, the receptionist, and Annie, the gofer. Neither had any new information to offer.

Lois thanked Erin for showing her the self-defence techniques and continued to practise gyrating moves, unbalancing herself a few times before Erin turned to leave.

67

Erin visited Celine again. "Are you and Gladys plotting any more dumb schemes to get me into deeper trouble?"

The older woman, looking perplexed, shook her head, frowned, and pointed her finger.

"The Taurus stalks
To protect the mate,
And will not stop,
So check the date."

"Check what date? If he's a Taurus, what difference can a time frame or date make?"

Celine shrugged her shoulders and sipped her tea. "I do not know. A suspicious date for something does seem important. Gladys and I will try to figure it out."

"No more schemes. If you think of anything else, make sure to check with Luke, or he'll haul us all in for interfering with his case."

Celine sighed. "Luke will not let us get involved. We need to act under the hand."

"Underhanded. It's one word."

"Silly word anyway. We hide something under the hand; I hope we know what is there."

Erin forged ahead. "Mark said his wife, Sue, called from the east coast. He didn't want to worry her, so he didn't tell her anything about the murders."

"He would fear mistrust from her *avec* this woman. I wondered about all these Taurus people mixed up here."

"And? Do you have relevant ideas about them?"

"Most signs have *deux*—two sides—to the personality. Mark is the pleasant one. He is patient, reliable, and secure in his loving home with his family. *Mais,* that wife, Sheila, she seems burning with anger and carries on the pantomime of a stable marriage with the comfort of money. She is a bitter woman but keeps up appearances and holds tight onto what she has."

"Cathy is a tolerant person, or greedy for the fruits of staying Sheila's friend." Erin sighed. "Craig was her lover first, and she cares for him in an unhealthy way, I think."

"*Même pas*, that was in the past, I hope. Sheila is a jealous, possessive woman and has grounds for her insecurities with his continued amorous activities. She is inflexible and resentful: spiteful to others who she feels are her inferior."

"They seem okay with the status quo. You said the Taurus sign doesn't like change."

"*Vraiment,* and they are *très* cautious about life and money. They do not take an action without the grave *conception* and planning."

Erin stood up. "Someone's trying to get Mark embroiled in the case. The police have no reliable information to tie him to the murdered women. No one has ever seen him with either of the two victims."

"*Pas de* worry. We will prove him innocent, *bientôt.* We must find that cousin."

Erin didn't appreciate the emphasis on the "we" that Celine blithely mentioned.

68

At the end of the workday, Luke stopped at the lawyers' offices. Lois was facing away from the door, arranging files. He walked past to Cathy's office. "Hello, Miss Wallace."

"I'm sorry. Craig is at the courthouse and likely won't be back."

"That's fine. I'm checking up on you today."

Cathy stared without a change of expression. "Fire away, inspector."

"I think you know why I'm here. Craig must have told you about how we matched Jewel and his fingerprints at the lodge. I'm sure when we came back and took the fingerprints of your office staff—yours included—you knew we'd find evidence of your liaisons with Craig."

"Craig said that would happen. Our visit there was quite a while ago and I've checked out the place for Mr. Fraser. You can't pinpoint any time frame."

Luke perched on the edge of the desk. "What if one of yours overlapped Jewel's, implying a recent relationship and contact with the victim."

"I don't believe you. I never denied my attraction to Craig. He is a sensual man and has a healthy appetite for women. I don't care how many women he beds as long as I can wiggle my finger at him whenever I have an itch. He's sexy and easy."

"What if Sheila finds out about your continuing dalliances?"

"That would be most unsatisfactory. We both make a good living and aren't totally dependent on her charity. She's tight-fisted anyway. What she has, she keeps. Taurus people are a money-conscious group." Cathy remained seated behind her desk. "I can understand Craig and I being under the microscope if Sheila was murdered, but not for an easy, cheap mark like that young woman."

"But you're still leery of Sheila finding out about the two of you as an item?"

"We like what we have going on." Cathy raised her eyebrows and shrugged. "You're digging away and finding grunge but no malice, inspector. No motive or reason."

"Other news has surfaced." Luke stood. "Mr. Morrison accidentally shot Fraser in the leg because he was startled on seeing a nude couple running around outside the lodge. I'm presuming that was you and Craig."

"In our birthday suits? Naked? What a lark. Presume all you like, inspector. I don't think I care to answer any more questions."

"We can insist, you know?"

"Then I would have to get a lawyer, and I have a couple of them quite handy." She smiled and added. "I'll say one more thing. When Fraser got shot a few months ago, Craig never knew Jewel, so forget that fingerprint nonsense."

"Would the timing make any difference to our investigation? And how sure are you of his schedule?"

"I can do the arithmetic, and I'm his secretary. I handle all his correspondence and timetables. Besides, I've always read him like a book. His habits and appetites don't vary much."

Mark agreed to check out the summer lodge with Erin when she offered to take Mr. Fraser's dog, Chum, along for protection.

"He's big enough and knows the bush," Erin spoke on the phone. "I emailed my sister Maggie last night. She lives near London in southern Ontario. She's the oldest of my siblings and remembers going to the towns of Sellwood and Milnet when she was young. She skirted old wooden buildings and a small graveyard with metal crosses and worried about the ghosts. The town was abandoned, but a caretaker checked on the property to see that nobody stripped the place until a decision was made about the town's future. Later, everything belonging to Sellwood was razed. Milnet still boasts a few hunters' sheds.

"We'd best take my SUV," Mark said. The all-wheel drive works better if we get stuck in muck back there."

When they arrived, the trapper shook his head at their decision but gave them directions. Chum's tail wagged in excitement, anxious to go.

Mr. Fraser told her, "Nothing to see but Milnet farther along. Be careful if you see the owners of the shacks. They target shoot and threaten people away. I didn't tell the officers about their poaching, and that old bridge isn't safe to cross either."

"We need to find out about Craig and his wife in case Mark gets charged with the murder. I think there's something to find out there."

"The inspector said someone dared to use the lodge as a lover's refuge. They must have found the key I keep concealed in the corner post," he added, grinning.

Erin smiled at the older man and nodded.

Mark followed her out. "Why am I here?"

"I need you to protect me from bears."

"Me?' Mark raised his eyebrows. "Good luck with that. How am I going to help?"

"I think I can run away faster than you."

He gaped at her. "Why does that comment not surprise me?"

They arrived at the lodge without issue and sat in the car looking around. She gripped the door handle. "Do we inspect now?"

"What about our fear of bears or other wild animals?"

"I've got my bear spray."

"I have one of my grandmother's canes in back."

"Chum will warn us." She leaned over and blasted the horn. A cow moose jumped away through the bushes. "That should scatter the animals, and I have my whistle handy."

"Oh, goody. We can blow it and teach them to stay."

"Not if they're as clueless as Bill's dogs."

They let Chum lose. "Stay near us, Chum." He ran around, sniffing along the high grass and occasionally giving a soft woof.

"We can't find more bodies, Erin, or I'll be going to jail. Aren't you afraid of being out here alone with me, a prime murder suspect?"

"Too many people know we're here, and Celine said you're innocent. She and your grandmother want clues, so we're searching for evidence."

"You're more likely to protect me than the other way around. I only work out at the gym twice a week to keep moderately fit, usually with Luke."

They wandered around, calling to Chum whenever he strayed too far for their comfort. The two circled the rustic inn. Shutters covered the lower windows, and no break-ins showed. All the doors were locked.

"I think he told us about the key in the corner post on purpose," Erin said.

"I'm a lawyer. Do you think I don't know the penalty for breaking and entering?"

"If we use a handy key, we're allowed, right?"

Mark shook his head in annoyance and held his hands over his eyes for a second.

Going around the perimeter of the property, she was surprised at the dryness of the gravel walkways and lawn. She glanced down at the clear water. "A lot of higher ground here."

"Yes, lovely. Everything in the world is beautiful."

Erin wore her gloves and trailed a hand along the porch railing to locate the key under the corner post. "I brought my flashlight in case. The electricity will be off."

Mark shook his head and followed her in. "Not too dark here, anyway. The upstairs windows let light down the staircase."

"How about I check the upstairs, and you go down."

"No way, and not because I'm scared—well, not a lot. I don't want to be alone and a suspect if we stumble across another body."

"They've already lifted fingerprints, but we shouldn't touch anything. I don't think Luke would like to find we checked out the place."

Mark yanked his hand off the counter and rubbed the spot he touched with his coat sleeve. "I'm not happy to be here either. Besides, what did our elderly sleuths want us to look for? Right, clues to a murder."

Both slinked through the lodge but unearthed no clues and no bodies. They left, replacing the key in the corner post.

70

Mark and Erin wandered back to the car and started to drive across a bridge.

Mark stopped and got out. "I can't drive my car across that. It's not safe."

"We'll have to walk in. Mr. Fraser said it wasn't far, and we have Chum."

"I don't get this trip." Mark grabbed the cane. "Why are we here now?"

Celine and your grandmother think the old man who spends time out here may have seen someone or something abnormal."

Wearing their high boots, they trudged through mud and around a corner before a shot rang out. Erin ducked. Mark dove sideways into the bushes before edging back into a slouch.

"Erin, if you get killed and I'm discovered with another body, I won't get a trial."

"Mr. Fraser said the man shoots over people's heads to scare them away."

"Okay, I'm scared. Now what?"

"*Arrêtez!*" A short man, legs poised apart, glared at them while holding his rifle across his protruding belly.

"Hey, Mister, we only want to talk." Erin waved. "Mr. Fraser said you'd help us."

The stout man, clad in a checkered jacket, frowned at them and spat on the ground. "You have his dog. Fraser must have sent you. *Pourquoi?*"

"We need to find clues to that woman's murder so my friend's not considered a suspect. You're Mr. Gagnon, right?" Erin asked. The man nodded. "Have you seen anything or anybody around lately?"

"I always have trouble with people coming around chasing after ghost towns and wanting to explore." The man gestured. "What do they expect to find? Damn ghosts?"

Mark, cross now, took over questioning. "What about vehicles on the night of the storm when that body was buried?"

"I left that night. Can't hunt or shoot in the rain. I told the cop a lightly coloured van left near here when I drove out. Maybe the lodge owners came around to check on it."

"What about the next day? Mark asked. "Were you out here then?"

"Late afternoon only. I needed to make sure the shack didn't fall over. There was a mudslide by the crumbling mill last week. Lots of soft, hilly areas here."

"Did you notice tracks on your way in?" Erin spoke up.

"*Non,* and the rain would have washed marks away if I looked. *Mais*, vamoose."

The two thanked him and left, making their way back to the car.

"That was a total nothing," Erin said. "Celine was sure we'd find evidence."

"I don't know what discovery my grandmother expected, but we didn't find it."

Chum barked and veered off into a grove of trees down near the water.

Mark held up his cane in protection mode and peered ahead. "Oh, oh! He smelled something."

"I think that's way down from where the body was found." Erin walked and called the dog. "Chum, come back, she's not there anymore."

They pushed aside branches to see him race around and head over to a farther section, closer to the lodge, with his nose sniffing along the ground. He dug intently in the soft ground by the shoreline. He arched his back, woofed, grabbed something in his mouth, and ran back to drop the article at her feet.

"Looks like a wallet." Erin picked it up, scrubbed off the mud, and zipped it open. The cards and driver's license inside were issued to Jewel Martin.

Mark held up his hands, warning her away from him. "Now, you're in trouble, Erin. Luke will be upset if you smudged other fingerprints."

"Well, what else could I do? I didn't know the woman was missing a wallet." She wrapped it in tissues and placed it in her pocket. "And my fingerprints are on file."

"Well, I never touched the article," Mark answered. "I do think in terms of court evidence, Luke will likely say I wore gloves to return here and plant the damn thing."

"No, he'd think you buried it farther away when you murdered the woman, hoping if she was found, she wouldn't be identified for a while."

The two stared at each other silently before trudging back to the car.

71

On returning to Mr. Fraser's, Erin spotted a van in the yard. Chum let out a howl and barked at two women standing there talking to the elderly man. Erin emerged from the car and opened the back door for the dog. Chum barked and paced over to sniff and growl at their feet.

"I guess your dog isn't used to our city smell?" Sheila asked.

"Chum's not used to all the traffic we've seen around here lately." Mr. Fraser bent over and patted the anxious dog's head.

Both women showed surprise when Mark stepped out of the vehicle. Sheila reacted first. "Are you dating on the sly while your wife's out of town, Mark?"

"Nice to see you too, Sheila. Hello Cathy. I presume you both came out to check on how Mr. Fraser is doing since his accident?"

Cathy scowled at his implication of neglect. "We came to ask him about what's going on with this murder. They've been questioning all of us non-stop. I don't know why he was hunting out of season with his friend. And on top of that, they spotted some nudists? I blame the drink." She turned back to Erin. "Why are you two here?"

"Yes, are you interested in Mark now, as well as Craig?" Sheila sneered. "My husband told me you propositioned him at the track."

Erin flushed and managed to control a hasty and nasty reply. "That comment's not worth answering. And I don't think Mr. Fraser appreciates your critical words."

"Erin's my nurse." The trapper glanced from the women to Mark, who shook his head at their attitude. "She offered to check the chalet for me since I have trouble manoeuvring."

"You went into the chalet, my chalet?"

Cathy held up a hand. "We've no claim on the place anymore, Sheila."

"Well, you never had a claim, but the lodge was my home. I grew up there."

Mr. Fraser patted Chum, who rumbled in his throat, staring at the women. "The lodge was sold years ago, Sheila, and you haven't checked there in a long time."

Bored now with the women, Chum sniffed at one of Erin's pockets: the one that held the salvaged purse. Erin squeezed her arm tight against that side of her jacket.

Sheila took a deep breath and clasped a hand around Cathy's arm. "Let's go and leave these lessers to their boring lives. Like I said earlier, they know nothing."

Erin looked at the trapper when they left. "I'm sorry they were rude."

The man snorted in derision. "Not your fault. I know them well, and not a lot changes with either of them."

After Mark dropped Erin off at home, she drove her car to the police station and asked the receptionist to speak to Luke. Erin mentioned she had information on the murder case.

When the receptionist beeped in, she said there was no reply and told Erin he'd gone out.

"Would Beth—I don't know her last name—his officer, be here?"

"Who do I say is asking?"

"Tell her it's Erin Rine and say I have information about the murder case."

"I'll check." The woman spoke on the phone, then she told Erin to go past the grey door and enter the second room on the right.

Beth waited in the hall and pointed inside for her, then followed. "Well, Erin, I wanted to meet you. Luke mentioned last month we're both Aries signs. I like to remind him that we're hot stuff. But I don't think you're here for fun and games."

Erin assessed the pleasant-looking brunette. She was ten or twelve years older than her but in good shape. She thought it must help having an active job. Erin sighed. "No, I found a piece of evidence. Luke will likely get mad again at my so-called interference, so it's better that he's not here. I drove past Mr. Fraser's and picked up his dog to scout the lodge. Chum ran down and dug up the victim's wallet. I'm sorry. I touched, opened, and fingered the cards inside before I read the name of the person it belonged to." She pulled the wrapped, muddy wallet out of her pocket and avoided mentioning how Mark went with her. "I looked for an ID, but I didn't know Jewel's was missing. The dog must have got a whiff and recognized her odour."

"Could you find where it was buried again?"

"Probably not. If someone took the dog, I'm sure he'd locate the site. The area was past the gravel riverbed near the lodge, far from where Jewel was buried. We looked around after realizing the item belonged to Jewel. Nothing else seemed out of place nearby."

"You said 'we.' Who else went with you?"

"Besides Chum, I took a friend for protection in the woods."

"Always better safety in numbers." Beth picked up her pen. "I'll need the name." When Erin hesitated and held her breath, Beth looked up. "Is there a problem?"

Erin exhaled her pent-up breath. "I brought Gladys' grandson, Mark Richards, with me."

Beth held her stare for a long time.

72

Erin told Celine the next time she picked her up, they'd stop at a tearoom halfway between town and Capreol. "Lani, at taekwondo, said the place was run by a Chinese couple, and her young daughter helped after school. She said the lovely girl looked about ten years old."

The following day, Celine and Erin met Mark again at Gladys' place.

"Erin will drive me home, *mais* you said you feel spry, Gladys. Why not come to that new tea place Erin talked about?"

"Oh, how nice to go out for a change. Would you drive me, Mark?"

"Of course. I'm always trying to get you out and about. This murder seems to have brought colour and vigour to your life. But me? I've developed indigestion."

"Then you should try their peppermint tea," Celine said as they left.

The two cars arrived at the teashop. The four went in and sat at a table near the door and glanced around at the lovely Chinese designs.

As this was the year of the monkey, numerous artifacts pictured monkeys on the walls. Anchored fans and lanterns hung discreetly from the corners and the loft. Gladys and Celine studied the pictures on the wall next to them.

Erin checked the table. "The placemats have Chinese horoscopes, Celine. I know I'm the tiger. Beware my bite. What are you?"

"Gladys, do not tell them. They will figure out our *âge*."

"Oh, we can't have that."

Mark grinned. "I know your age, Grandma, but I won't tell."

Gladys patted his arm. "I can tell them that you and Luke are both pigs."

"Thanks," Mark answered. "And here I was being nice. I heard the older you get, the more you brag about surviving too long."

"*C'est correct,* but we are not old enough to do the bragging."

A young Asian girl in a pink kimono arrived and handed them card menus. She smiled shyly. "I apologize for eavesdropping. I am the sheep."

Erin smiled back. "A cuddly one, too, I bet."

Gladys looked back at the photos along the wall and turned to the young girl. "Is that a picture of you dancing?"

"Yes. I performed the feather fan dance in the green costume and the lantern dance in the pink one. The older girls do a ribbon dance, but that takes strong hand and wrist coordination."

"You have lots of growing time to practice," Gladys added. "What's your name?"

"I'm Shana. My mother will explain the list of teas. We can arrange a taste test if you're unsure what brew to order."

"Do you have a favourite tea, *ma petite*?" Celine asked.

"Oh, I like many. Being here after school, my mother lets me try all kinds." The girl did a slight bow and returned to the counter. Her mother, in a traditional black and gold silk dress, glided over to explain the selections. Whether due to the dinner rush or the novelty of the teahouse, the tables soon began to fill up.

Later, when they voiced pleasantly over their hot tea and delicate pastries, Erin's arm jerked, spilling a few drops from her dainty cup when she spotted Sheila and Cathy enter. She whispered this to Celine, who then relayed the news to Gladys. The older women studied the new arrivals with avid interest. Erin hoped they didn't plot more nefarious deeds because of her. The two women sat down and ordered before Cathy looked around and eyed their group. She gave them a thin-lipped smile and whispered to Sheila. Sheila's head whirled around, and her frosty eyes focused on each of their faces. She nodded at Mark and dismissed the rest.

Celine's ears almost quivered. She wouldn't let this opportunity get away. She traipsed to their table to thank Sheila for the lovely opal earrings she bought at her store. A client needed catering to, and Sheila bent enough to be polite.

Celine chattered about the woman's delightful shop and décor. She also inquired about their chosen beverage and commented on them, as Celine knew her teas.

Cathy and Sheila did their best to ignore Erin's party when Celine returned.

Gladys turned to her friend. "I wouldn't like to meet them on a dark night. Which one is the wife, and which one is the secretary?"

Celine twittered. "They do look similar. I find it interesting to see these players that are the main characters in the story. Like being right in the action, *n'est-ce-pas*. The one I spoke with is the wife. She did not introduce *moi*."

"We're not in a play here, ladies. This is real life and dangerous." Erin pointed her finger at the two conniving women beside her. "See the pleasantries you get me involved in."

"And here comes another major player through the door." Mark turned. "Hello, Craig."

The man glanced at the group, froze, and settled an uneasy look on Erin before spotting his wife and secretary. He only nodded to Mark and wove his way around the small tables.

The three seemed to talk little and didn't linger over their tea and sweets. They ignored Erin's group when they left.

"I will have to go out more," Gladys whispered. "I'm pleased to be near the action, if only observing the players from the sidelines."

"*Bien*. Now, we know who we talk about. *Mais,* I did not get the helpful vibes."

Gladys answered. "I found the two women quite similar in height and dark hair. I think the one is physically harder while the other is of a malicious mentality."

Mark and Erin both sighed. She spoke to him. "Well, Mark, I'm sure you felt the waves of animosity emanating toward us?"

"You're right on that. I can't believe they loathe me enough to set up this farce with my playing the starring role of murderer."

"*Mais,* if the plan is for their survival. I think all three of them are involved in the deception, and they need you to be the goat who gets blamed."

Erin gulped her last swallow of tea. "Celine, the term is scapegoat."

"*Mais,* if the goat escapes, how does he get blamed?"

Gladys smiled. "I like your reasoning, Celine. We need to uncover more clues to clear Mark, and I'm thinking my dear grandson needs to find another business partner."

Erin lounged around in her sweats after a short bout of exercise and weightlifting. The dogs snoozed. She guessed Bill must have taken them for an earlier run and gone back to his room. She pondered the murder cases but came up with no reason for someone to kill the two women. What motive was strong enough for murder? The cousin wouldn't inherit anything. Was hate a factor? But who did the women injure deeply enough to cause someone to make that final, deadly choice? Did the victims know something that led to them blackmailing the murderer?

She'd done enough thinking in endless circles and eased into the whirlpool tub to soak in the hot, sudsy water. She had no interest in the mystery book she tried reading. Instead, she breathed in the rich aromas of her glass of red wine and vanilla-scented water. She closed her eyes and dissected the clues surrounding the murder case. "What if Craig connived with one of the women in the plot? And if so, which one?"

When finished her bath, the phone rang. Surprised, she heard Luke's voice on the line.

"Erin, I need your help. I'm forced to go to this elite reception centred around the mayor's campaign for a new bill they plan to introduce."

She waited in silence.

"Look, I hate these boring things, but my superiors expect my attendance, and I'm asking if you'd go with me as my date? It's this Friday night."

Erin responded in an icy tone. "You're asking me to go to keep you from getting bored?"

"Well, if there's one thing I know: when we're together, we're never bored."

She hesitated for a moment, thinking she rather liked the idea of an evening out on a real date. "Is this formal?"

"Well, most women attending will be wearing some type of short cocktail dress, so it's a little fancy. I'll be wearing a suit, not a tux, though."

"Okay, it's only an evening out. No strings attached."

"I'll be on good behaviour if you come. Thanks, I mean it. I'll pick you up at eight. And no investigating there, please. Sheila likes to foist her presence with her husband. She feels the sham of mingling with the elite is necessary to her business."

"I promise I won't be the one making a scene."

The next day, Erin plowed through her busy job. Numerous calls in the morning almost made her miss lunch. The afternoon's schedule looked lighter.

She stopped to see the broken-ribbed logger who nearly had a tree fall on him. His son visited, having finished odd jobs around their place. He smiled a lot, and was quite talkative.

"I'll bet my dad didn't tell you how he plunged to the ground with the tree."

"No, he said when he sawed the trunk, the tree fell the wrong way."

He grinned at his father, who looked quite disgruntled. "It was a novice move for a seasoned lumberjack. He strapped himself to the tree halfway up and, for some reason, lost his bearings or his marbles, depending on how you look at it. He sawed through the trunk at a line lower than he was and fell with the treetop."

Erin gaped at one and then the other, and then she placed her hand over her mouth to try, without success, to stifle her outbursts of laughter, picturing the scene.

"Have axe will travel, but he dropped it, thank God. He rode the top half of the tree down like a bronco buster."

"I don't find the story all that funny," the older man huffed. "It was a slight misjudgement on my part."

In a much brighter mood, Erin left to visit her last patient, a young girl recovering from an ATV accident after an embankment gave way, tipping the girl and her father into a soggy ravine. The man suffered lacerations and bruises, but the young girl suffered a large gash on her lower leg that needed stitches and possibly cosmetic surgery later. She required dressings twice a week, but the once bright redness now showed a healthy pink.

"Have you finished the course of antibiotics, Amy?"

"Mom said tomorrow's the last day. I'm getting around better now."

"She only needs the Tylenol at night and when you bandage the wound," the mother stroked the girl's head. "Good thing they both wore their helmets. With this wet weather, the top of the ravine gave way and sent them down the embankment. Luckily, some sturdy trees stopped them from falling farther."

When Erin left, she pulled her wisps of hair back into the restraining band and drove home. Later, she picked up Marge to go shopping.

"Things aren't going well with this murder investigation. That Luke is anal."

"Now, spell it out, Erin. Tell me what you really mean."

"Well, he keeps harping at me, saying I'm interfering."

"Well, you are. He has his job, and you have yours. What if he told you how to be a nurse?"

"I'm not putting him down or trying to do his job." Erin turned in her seat. "His job comes with so many restrictions that impede investigations. I can help in unconventional ways."

"What, you want to become a private detective now?"

"I want justice for Mark. He's innocent and being set up."

"Don't you dare go bar hopping again." Marge wagged her finger at her friend. "Geez, you get yourself into more trouble, and a lot's your own fault—and Celine's."

"I don't ask for these problems. I just need to find some answers."

Marge held her hands up in surrender. "Curiosity killed the cat, I heard. Why not settle for a ravishing affair with Luke and forget the rest."

"Well, I'm going to a classy party with him on Friday. It's a date as an antidote to boredom, not a wild-ass affair."

"Bingo! And after the party and wine, you lower your inhibitions and become bare-assed."

Erin shook her head at her friend. "You think sex is the answer to everything."

"Sure helps. At least sex makes you forget your problems for a delightful while." Marge smacked her lips. "Am I getting you horny yet?"

Luke hiked up the trail, glad of his orienteering skills. He wasn't into organized sports or exercise programs but loved hiking and felt he was in shape for his job. He wore his holstered gun more to deter deviants or murderers than in fear of wild animals. He focused on the position of the sun and his compass, wishing he had his GPS. He kept that on the pontoon boat at his camp. Mr. Fraser advised him about the main roadways and railroad tracks and lent him his dog. Erin told him they drove up to the lodge and walked around. She didn't think she'd find the wallet's burial site again because it was far from the body's location. Luke was counting on Chum's keen sense of smell.

Mr. Fraser said a few overgrown trails led to lakes and rivers if he veered far away from landmarks. A young moose startled and jumped back into the denser bush. The dog loped the other way toward the river and sniffed vigorously through the bushes till he came to a disturbed area of ground. Luke carried a small trowel, not expecting to find anything else. Chum circled the area, sniffing, but ultimately didn't seem interested in any other spots.

He didn't realize he was following the trail Erin and Mark navigated the day before. Luke found easier footing by following the rusted train ties, stopping first at the lodge. He checked doors and windows. Everything was securely locked. Though the setting of the lake and woods appeared tranquil, with a light breeze causing the branches to dance, the desolate air of the dense woods behind weighed him down. Years of encroaching trees and bush narrowed the acreage, though the lodge appeared in good condition. Further on, he slogged along the tracks to reach the abandoned town.

Arriving at the Milnet huts, he blew out his breath in exasperation to find a damp blue scarf patterned with cavorting horses and dogs tangled on one of the branches. "I've seen this recently." Luke shook his head, vexed. Knowing her fear of bears, Erin would never check these woods alone. Mark wouldn't explore the forest either unless his grandmother and Celine impelled the two into their dangerous games. They must have felt brave enough with the dog, so they didn't stay near the lodge. Chum took off, smelling bushes and chasing dreams. Luke worried about Mark. He figured his friend was set up but couldn't let his inclinations disrupt the course of the investigation. It looked like he needed to talk to those two amateurs about interfering in his case again. Not that they paid him the slightest attention.

A few shacks sat silent and alone. Luke climbed a hill and glanced around to check for anything unusual. He didn't see the bear till the animal charged out of the far bushes. It ran toward him before doubling back and then paced backwards and forwards in a circling motion, eyeing Luke the whole time: a bear's classic danger signs. Maybe there were cubs nearby.

Luke pulled the gun out of his holster and aimed above the animal, yelling and waving his arms to make himself look taller. When he fired, the shot rang above the silent trees. Chum, sniffing in the woods, came charging back from his hunting foray and spotted the bear. He barked and snarled, feinting charges at the bear without getting within range of its claws. The bear veered off and raced down the slope in the opposite direction. Chum chased a short spell after the animal, barking, keeping a cautious distance behind. Neither man nor dog spotted any cubs. The bear may have been an aggressive male.

Luke wandered over to the huts with Chum guarding his side. The dog tilted his head sideways at him as if in apology for leaving him to face the peril alone. Luke glanced around at the rubble and encroaching forest. Why did the woodsman shoot to scare people away? There were no marijuana fields hidden out here. The old guy acted paranoid. Would he have wanted to keep everyone away to protect his meagre holdings or to maintain his isolation?

When he brought Chum back to the cottage, he was startled to see Mr. Mortimer sitting and drinking coffee amicably with the trapper.

At Luke's surprised expression, the trapper spoke first. "I called him to come over and bury the hatchet. With these murders and shenanigans, I may be missing something. I am caretaker for the lodge, but I haven't been getting around lately."

Mr. Mortimer beamed. "I told him I'd check on the lodge for him every other day. If someone's playing night games, we won't know unless we check regularly."

"We might see something significant now that we're alerted to trespassers and murderers." Mr. Fraser scratched at his beard. "The owners should be up in a couple of weeks to prepare the lodge for the season."

Mr. Mortimer grimaced. "I guess I should leave my gun in the truck."

"Well, if you're going out alone, better carry it with you. That was one angry bear out there." Luke shook his head and told them about his encounter. "Don't be heroic and try anything dangerous. We've too many amateur sleuths involved with the murder as is."

75

Back in town, Luke decided to rattle Craig again at his office and settled in the chair across from the man's desk. "We've checked phone records, and Kelly—Jewel's friend—called your office numerous times. What did she want or ask you?"

Beads of perspiration showed on the man's forehead. "Look, my secretary handles all incoming calls. I don't talk with everyone that rings up."

"I don't think she would mention your involvement with Jewel to your secretary, no matter your relationship with either of them."

The man bristled. "You're making bold insinuations, inspector."

"Whatever. We can prove it, you know? I'm sure Cathy informed you that we know of your continuing affair at the lodge."

"If I'm as indiscriminate as you suggest, then having to publicly acknowledge my affairs is no motive for me. Mark is as likely a suspect as me."

"We're aware of that. But now, we've added your wife and secretary to our list of suspects. Are you going to accuse Lois of being involved as well?"

"Lois? My wife and my secretary? That's impossible. I can't imagine a woman strangling someone, carting the victim around, and then messing around in dirt to bury the body."

"It's not that strange. Cathy and Sheila are both strong women, and they both have knowledge of these dumping grounds. I suspect you as the catalyst for these murders. But my question is whether you committed them or did others."

"Look, neither woman was involved with this. Isn't there a third renter and a lowlife cousin that you can investigate?" He sneered. "You can't see what's right in front of you, inspector. Quit focusing on us."

"You didn't mention Mark in your list this time."

"Well, I know he's your friend, why bother?"

"He's being treated and investigated in the same thorough manner as everyone else," Luke answered.

"Well, at least his wife is away on the east coast. You can't suspect her."

"We ran checks on his wife and Lois as well. I didn't want you to think we neglected anyone in our investigation. And we certainly didn't want you to feel too special."

76

Lester debated further actions. He needed to get a firm grip and plan a different strategy. He phoned the lawyer's office and tried to get through the blasted secretary, but she turned him down. Okay, he'd send the snotty lawyer a letter and mark it private. Should he send it to his home, office, or both? Lester nodded. That way, he'd show them. His cache of stolen money was drying up, and he needed to find or steal the rent for next month. Pickpocketing was not as lucrative anymore. Men kept attachments on their wallets, and women strapped purses over their forms. A windfall from blackmail would give him a ticket to endless comfort.

In the dollar store, he nicked a couple of cheap invitation cards, snickering at his own joke. He'd invite the snob to meet tonight at a bar in Capreol. He knew his way around there, and there was no way he'd get into anyone's car. Now, to write a message. Not too masked, but not obvious enough to get himself charged for blackmail if the note ever got into a copper's hands. He would sign it—hmm—"the murdered girls' friend." The lawyer would find it different dealing with a smart man like him this time around.

Lester wrote that he'd wear a black leather jacket—stolen, obviously—and a black cap and would be sporting a beard. He needed to mention some hidden details to get the lawyer into hot water with his wife or the law. How funny and fitting. A lawyer himself "in trouble with the law." What a great inspiration. He would add that murder didn't carry the death penalty if they weren't interested in a little restitution. He named the seedy Belfry Bar in Capreol as the meeting place that evening between seven and nine. He needed to give the guy a little space and not get too pushy.

Lester nicked another older-model car and drove to the lawyer's building. There were too many security and alarm systems to try and break in after hours. During the workday, he ambled into the main lobby behind a couple of repairmen and took the elevator to the third floor. Instead of entering the offices, he pushed the envelope through the mail slot and sauntered to the stairwell. Later, he drove to the suburbs, found the address he'd looked up, and dropped the second identical letter in the mailbox. That would shake the sucker up. Lester snickered. What a hoot if the wife opened it. He wished he could hear that argument.

Later that night, Lester sat at the bar nursing a single beer. He didn't want to take a chance on numbing his brain. He would restrict his drinking to one bottle.

A young fellow entered and approached him. "Someone gave me this note and pointed you out. 'All in black,' he said. Gave me enough change for a few drinks."

"What'd the guy look like? Where is he?"

"Oh, more information will cost you."

Lester yanked change from his pocket. "I don't have much."

"Well, this guy—I think it was a man—whispered for you to meet him in the morning. He was tall and wore a dark coat and brimmed hat. I didn't see much in the dark."

Lester scanned the note and swore. There must be a reason for the delay. The guy likely needed the extra time to get some money. He wanted to meet him by the bridge in Grover's Park

271

around seven in the morning. That was fine. The open area would be spacious and light enough. Better than meeting up with a murderer at night. He guzzled the last of his beer and ordered a couple more drinks with fries. He enjoyed the extravagance now, using the last bit of his money. He'd brought the copy of that lewd picture of Jewel and Craig to bargain with. The photo showed the extent of their chummy behaviour. Lester would be bright and alert in the morning. No one got the better of him. He would sleep in the back room that Al kept for drunks. Then he'd be close by for the morning meeting. He wasn't leaving now to get a nasty surprise in the dark. Not him.

He dozed till the morning light seeped through the dingy window and unfolded his scrawny frame in the small room with cots and tattered, smelly blankets. There was no room for drunks to wander around except outside, and he would have to pee in the alley. Lester checked the alley strewn with rotting garbage, wrinkling his nose at the stench. Sliding out, he aimed his stream of urine at the wall. He heard a scurrying noise in the garbage near the end. Rats. He lit a cigarette with shaking hands, took a puff and hurried down the fetid alleyway to get back to the stolen car, never sensing the figure behind him. He heard the swish a second before a noose landed around his neck. He choked as the rope tightened unmercifully. Gasping his last, he had no time to lament that he wasn't that smart after all. Lester died with both hands clutching the cord, trying to drag the tightening rope from his throat.

77

For her first visit of the day, Erin got out of her car at Mr. Fraser's cabin. "Hi, Chum. Where you such a bad dog today that he tied you up outside?" The dog wiggled his whole body in greeting and barked till she went over to pet him.

The trapper was curious as she entered. "We didn't get to talk after your trip because of my other visitors. Did you find out anything exploring the other day?"

"Not really, but I didn't like that bushman when we hiked to Milnet. He was threatening and annoyed by our visit. He only talked to us because of Chum."

"With all Chum's running around lately, I tied him up as a reminder to stay close to home. But yes, Marcel is leery of strangers, and lots of people want to view the ruins."

"Well, thanks for letting us borrow Chum. It was better with him there for protection."

"You and the inspector, both. He went out later and met a big bear. It might be a male, as he saw no cubs. It stalked him and seemed angry. The inspector shot the gun in the air as a warning and Chum routed the bear."

"I didn't know Luke came out again. Well, why would I?"

The trapper sat down for Erin to attend to his amputated leg.

Erin undressed the man's bandaged stump, telling him the wound was nearly healed. "When the swelling shrinks, they'll fit your prosthesis." Chum started barking louder. "Hey, quit wiggling around till I tape up the bandage."

"My dog's barking at something."

"That's what dogs do, Mr. Fraser. They bark." She stuck the last stretch of tape on the bandage.

"That's a bad bark. There's something wrong. Please check, nurse."

"I think I remember this conversation." She stood to look out the window. "He's straining on his chain toward that ravine and jumping around. Probably sees a bear."

"I'll grab my rifle and walker. Let's see what we can spot down there."

"We?" Erin squeaked. "I don't want to spot a bear."

"I got this feeling there was more trouble coming."

"Oh, you're psychic now?" Erin gaped at the man grabbing his coat. "Listen, Mr. Fraser, if it's more bodies, I'm out of here. Oh, Chum broke his chain and tore up the slope!"

With their coats and boots on, they both hurried out the door. A shot rang out, followed by a high-pitched yelp.

Mr. Fraser roared. "They shot my dog."

Erin raced ahead of the trapper, who pounded his walker legs into the mud, trying to balance the gun. When she reached the top of the rise, she heard a car engine rev up in the distance and take off with a screech of tires. She spotted the grey-ish animal lying near the grove entrance. She slipped and slid down the muddy slope, trying to keep upright. The dog raised his head, whimpered at her, and tried to get up when she reached him.

"It's okay, Chum. Stay down. Let's see." Blood oozed from a small hole in his upper hind leg. She grabbed a wad of gauze from her waist pouch and applied pressure to the wound to stop the trickling flow. He growled a few times while trying to stand. She patted his head, telling him to stay down again. She wasn't sure what commands he understood, but he became quiet.

At the top of the hill, she saw Mr. Fraser train his scope on her. A nervous thought arose that he'd shoot her. But why? Keep your cool, Erin. No stupid thoughts or dumb actions. She gave a thumbs-up and yelled loudly that the dog was okay. She pointed to her own leg, then at the dog, to tell him the problem. Then she made hand gestures to telephone for a sling to carry the dog back up the hill.

The dog kept trying to get up. With the bleeding stopped, she made a sling with her arms under his belly for support, thinking to work their way up the hill. But Chum wanted to go in the opposite direction, back to the old burial site.

"She's gone, silly dog. No one's buried there now. No, please lie down. I'll check later." Chum let out a blood-curdling howl, raising every hair on her arms, before he rolled onto his side, panting.

She peered around to note her isolation. Mr. Fraser had gone to telephone, and here she was, stooping down at the edge of the woods with a wounded dog. "Damn." Mad bears were roaming about, and she hoped whoever took potshots at the dog left in that car she heard. She had no bear spray with her either. Only a dinky knife and a whistle. The noise from that rifle shot would probably send an anxious bear skittering away.

A licking tongue against her hand made Erin reach out to stroke the dog's head and side. "Quiet, Chum. Stay down. It's okay. We'll find out who hurt you." The bone of his leg may have shattered, but with luck, he'd have a clean wound and little surrounding damage.

78

Erin started to breathe slower when the trapper reappeared at the top of the rise. He steadied his gun, hopefully to watch for attacking bears. Why would someone shoot the dog? A poacher was unlikely. What about the murderer returning to the scene of the crime, or someone committing a new one? She shivered. The dog stared at the thick pine grove and whined. The way he acted suggested another person was hurt down there. There was no thinking about that or going in there alone. Chum whined and growled in a repetitive, throaty whisper.

Erin heard later that Janelle was on her placement when the vet's hotline received the emergency call. The young vet trainer jumped in the van to tag along and help at the scene. Adam and Trevor arrived, saying Luke was on his way once he heard the address and about the shooting of a trapper's dog. The vet, an older man, stayed at the top of the hill while the younger professionals loaded the dog onto a stretcher. Janelle and Adam transported the quieter Chum, with numerous slips and slides, back up the hill. Erin trailed behind. The trapper let the tears fall, not embarrassed by the steady flow, and petted his poor dog. Chum licked his master's face before the vet sedated him for the trip back to the clinic.

Luke's truck pulled in, and he jumped out. "What happened?"

"I think someone is hurt in that gully," Erin answered. "The dog fussed, broke his chain, and charged down the slope. We heard one shot and a car's engine rev up. The dog took the bullet in the hind leg. I'll show you where he headed."

Luke frowned at her. "You don't have to go back with us."

"Yes, I do. I told the dog I would."

He snorted. "She told the dog she would, Adam."

"I understand that, sir. Lots of dogs think they're humans."

Luke raised his eyebrows at the two of them. "Figures. Both nuts!"

He told Adam to go with the dog and find out the extent of his injury. Adam smiled, likely pleased to help Janelle. She heard Adam tell the vet they wanted the extracted bullet.

Erin tripped and slid as she followed Luke and Trevor. Trevor tripped as well, and both slid down the hill toward the pine trees while Luke forged ahead.

Trevor glanced sideways at Erin and held out a hand to help her over a jagged section. "All that business you talked about horoscopes and sensing things. My wife told me that I'm a Scorpio. Do you have any predictions for me?"

"I am not psychic. It's my friend, Celine, who has exaggerated ESP. I think I could have guessed your sign, though. It's a dark one: it represents death."

Trevor frowned. "Thanks. Is that why I became a policeman?"

Erin tripped and righted herself. "Some become killers. But you could try and be pleasant for a change. You learn more that way. You were quite nasty to me last month."

"My wife keeps reminding me. She's a good sort and puts up with my mood swings."

"What's her sign?" Erin stopped to check for another murky foot placement.

"She's a Taurus like my partner, Adam. I get along with both."

"Celine says that's the polar sign for Scorpios: perfect compatibility. Most Taurus people are kind, reliable, and loyal. You're lucky."

They caught up to Luke, who stopped at the entrance to the glade, gazing across at the muddy slope. "Chum interrupted the burial this time."

Erin peered around the two men. Across from them, a man's body sprawled on his back in a shallow grave on the hillside: a skinny man in jeans, a black jacket, and worn sneakers. A thin rope, tied around his neck, trailed down over the outstretched arm. She only needed one glance at the discoloured and bloated face to know he was dead.

Luke trudged in high boots over the muddy bank and stared down at the body. "I think the murderer found Mr. Lisson before we did, or Lester went looking for easy money. The murderer chose the same hole in the ground, less work to excavate. He didn't have enough time to finish with the dog coming after him.

"You think that's his ID, Boss?"

"Well, there's the rope around his neck, the same burial site, and he matches the description."

"If the person carried a gun, why not shoot the victim?" Erin asked.

"They might be afraid we'd trace the gun. Besides, a rifle's hard to camouflage. The dog helped, though. We'll probably have a bullet—didn't look like there was an obvious exit wound."

"Lots of people haven't registered their guns," Trevor spoke aloud. "They'll be nervous about hanging onto damning evidence."

She left the two men, climbed back up the hill, and entered the cabin. The trapper sat slumped at the table with a bottle and glass of whiskey. "Want a shot, nurse?"

"No thanks, though I'm sure I'll be twitching all day. I'm driving, and I've only started my daily visits."

"I thank you once more. Vet phoned and said Chum will be okay. He may have a limp; it depends on whether the bone's fractured or not. He said it looks like it's only chipped." He took another drink. "They'll keep him for a couple of days."

Erin picked up her bag. "How old is Chum?"

"Only four, he's got years left. I rely on him for my hunting business." The old man wiped his mouth with the back of his hand. "In the future, we may both be hopping around in the bush." He looked at Erin, pushing his silent question on her.

"We did find another body, Mr. Fraser—a man this time. Chum interrupted the burial."

"I'm not surprised by the way Chum acted. I knew it was bad."

"Better start calling me Erin. If we keep up this business, we can name ourselves 'Finding Bodies, Inc.'"

The trapper shook his head when Luke entered. "Ever since my leg injury, I've had nothing but trouble. Weird. As if the devil himself sauntered through my open door."

Luke glanced at Erin with a rueful look. "Or herself."

She glared at him, daring him to suggest that she was a harbinger of disaster and death.

Luke leaned over and whispered. "I'm going to tell Bill what Mr. Fraser said."

At her last visit, Erin's phone beeped. She heard Melanie's shaky voice. The woman seemed agitated and asked Erin to drop by if she could manage to steal time away from her job.

Erin arrived and didn't have time to knock before the door flung open. She noticed Melanie hanging onto the door, then stepping back to take deep breaths before rubbing her trembling hands together compulsively.

Melanie reached out and almost grabbed Erin's arm to drag her in. "I wanted to phone my mother in China but realized I would only upset her and she's too far away to comfort me."

Erin told Melanie to grab her coat so they could go out for tea. The frightened woman needed a new, more comfortable venue when she told her about finding another body.

When they arrived at the teashop, Melanie sat across the table and viewed the Chinese décor. "I'm half Chinese."

The owner approached their table with the tea menu and eyed Erin. "I've seen you here before." She turned and stared at Melanie.

"Hello, *ni hao*." Melanie held up her hands. "I only know a bit of the language. My mother is Chinese."

The woman smiled and answered the same. "We are happy to welcome you to our little teashop in this year of the monkey."

"I've never been to China, but my mother returned there. She lives near Beijing with her sister. Have you lived in this country long?"

"Yes, for many years. We do travel back to visit. I am Mrs. Wong. My family lives in a village in the southern province of Jiangxi." She turned to Erin. "Excuse me, weren't you with those two dark-haired women last time? One of your elders was talking to them."

"Not with them, but we are acquainted. Why?"

"One of them dropped a picture and paper. I think it fell on the floor from the man's pockets. I will bring it." She left to greet more customers.

Erin sipped her tea and pointed to the placemat. "I'm born in the year of the tiger, Melanie. What animal sign are you?"

"I was born in the year of the dog. In Western astrology, I am born under the sign of Cancer."

"That's my brother's sign, too. It's a water sign, and I tell him he's all wet."

Melanie smiled timidly. "I don't think I'm a wet person."

Erin pointed to the wall. "Those pictures of a girl dancing are of Shana, the owner's daughter."

"My friend from high school did Chinese dancing. When she was older, she performed best with the ribbon dance. I practised with her at her house. You need strength in your wrists and precision to weave and trail the ribbon in patterns."

The owner returned to hand Erin a folded paper. "I didn't want to throw it out, but I didn't know anyone's name. It's not a pleasant picture, and my daughter found it."

"Thank you. I'll see they get the articles." Erin sipped at her cooling tea and opened the envelope. She stared at a photo of Craig with his arms wrapped around Jewel with both hands covering her breasts.

"I've never seen that picture," Melanie whispered. "How lewd."

"I wonder if one of the women carried it in her purse instead of Craig."

Melanie grimaced. "If it was in Craig's pocket, he'd be awful dumb to keep it."

Erin opened the accompanying letter and read. 'This picture is evidence to take to a gossip mag but'... Erin paused. "It says to 'persuade them not to do that with a little gift,' followed by a dollar sign." There was a dark line marked under the word little. "Craig's face is turned sideways, and his eyes are closed. I bet he didn't know about this photo. I wonder who took the picture."

"Well, I didn't know, and I don't think Kelly knew for sure who Jewel dated." Melanie nodded her head slowly. "Her cousin Lester owned a fancy camera."

Erin wouldn't rush to bring the picture to Luke. It proved damning for Craig, and it confirmed what they already knew. It was concrete evidence of his intimate association with Jewel. Sheila sure wouldn't like that picture publicized.

She got Melanie to try a soothing herbal tea. "This one's similar to chamomile."

"I know I need to relax. I'm trying to study for a mid-term exam, but my brain keeps skittering away. I get more panic attacks now, like today."

"Well, I've something else unpleasant to tell you. It's going to be on the news so I have to warn you it's scary." Erin laid her hand over one of Melanie's. "They think they've found Lester's body, which was in the process of being buried. He was placed on top of the ravine where Jewel's body was found."

Melanie's eyes opened wide with fright. "You mean, he's been dead for a while?"

Erin grasped Melanie's other hand. "No. Apparently, if the body is Lester, the man was strangled recently."

Melanie turned ashen. Erin worried the woman might faint and moved her hand to rub her back. "Take deep breaths, Melanie."

"The murderer must be unstable," Melanie gasped. "What other reason could there be for this farce?"

"Luke thinks Kelly and Lester tried to extract money from someone using proof of Jewel's relationship."

"You mean blackmail, like that picture?" Melanie sat quietly and seemed to relax. "Then I'm safe. I don't know anything that could threaten anyone."

"That's right. Well, you'll soon be in town and away from these bad memories."

"Not soon enough. Another week and the room will be ready at the university residence. This is an intersession period, so they are only keeping a small block of rooms open. The maintenance people have to clean and repaint because the student who left made such a mess. Some students act like wild animals when they're away from home."

Erin finished drinking her oolong tea. When business lulled in the teashop, she approached the proprietor to ask who dropped the photo. The woman didn't know and said they found it at their table since they clean an area after every customer. That day was hectic, with many customers coming to check out the new teashop.

Later, Erin drove Melanie back to her apartment. She watched till Melanie was safely inside her apartment and waved goodbye to her through the window. Then, Erin stopped at the police department and inserted the incriminating picture and note in an old nursing folder. She tore out a page from her notebook, wrote where the evidence was found, signed and sealed the package, and printed Luke's name on the envelope before giving it to an officer at the front desk.

80

The police checked over the newest victim's sparse belongings. They got lucky. The murderer hadn't removed the patient's identification, as he or they didn't have time.

Back at the office, Luke checked the reports. "We can thank that dog again, Ralph. He was shot, but the vet says he'll be good as new. I'll take Trevor and Jackson with me to check out this address since we got a key. It's a run-down area, not near the downtown hangouts."

The three men entered the seedy building undetected. Using the key, they found some belongings inside the room: a few changes of old clothes, some toiletry items, and a couple of small cameras. They were probably stolen along with the TV and microwave. There were a couple of cloudy pictures but nothing pertaining to the investigation. He likely hoarded his film, and they only recognized Jewel with Craig in one picture.

Once back at the office, Adam called in from checking a stolen car behind a bar in Capreol. They took fingerprints but found no signs of blood or violence. The only evidence linked to the culprit was an expensive camera with a picture identical to the one Erin found and brought to the station.

Ralph came in. "All you need is a rug to wrap up a body, put in your car, and throw it away. We didn't find any blood or hair. We checked out the secretary's van, too."

"Well, with three killings, we may find out who's buying or missing rugs." Trevor laughed. "You said no fibres, though. I'll join Adam."

"Bet he used plastic wrap." Luke spoke quietly. "Then he rolled the body in it and transferred the victim by car."

"If it was wrapped in plastic, they'd drag the body by the edges," Ralph added. "At the slope, you'd only need to grab the center folds and fling the body to roll out and discard the plastic. Otherwise, same scenario. He was strangled with a rope."

"The victims weren't large in size." Luke held the picture that Erin dropped off. "A woman could have surprised and overpowered them if they went after Craig using this picture as evidence. It's the same one. There are likely more copies."

Beth sat listening. "Either woman had motive if they wanted to keep the status quo and were okay sharing Craig quietly. This is a rather brutal solution just to hide his vices."

"When we left Lester's room, the custodian spotted us, but we got zilch info from him." Luke looked frustrated. "He said the man did photography with that first-rate camera. The tenants keep to themselves, and he doesn't bother anyone if they pay their rent."

"Lester's fingerprints in his place match the ones found at the women's apartment."

Trevor called back to the department after joining Adam "While Adam checked out the car, I questioned the barkeeper here. He recognized Lester from the picture and said he thinks the man used the room in the back he keeps for drunks unfit to drive. He must've stepped into the alleyway in the morning. I'll call forensics to check out where he might have been attacked."

"Good work, both of you." Luke said and hung up the phone.

"What would he do about money for food and rent?" Beth asked.

"He probably had a fake welfare card and travelled incognito among different food banks," Luke said. "He changed his appearance at the soup kitchen. No one there admits to seeing him. And I'm sure he was the culprit in plenty of small-house and auto burglaries."

81

Erin checked her closet for what to wear to this posh event with Luke. She settled on a brown silk dress with shimmering gold streaks. Spaghetti straps and a cowl neckline with a zigzag hem settling around the knees enhanced her figure. She went with her gold and diamond jewelry, a gift from her late parents for graduating from university.

Since the evenings were cool, she picked a warm beige wrap to cover her shoulders and carried a clutch to match her closed tan heels, a footwear choice made in case it rained again. Staring at her reflection in the mirror, she carefully applied her make-up. She fluffed and teased her red hair and applied bronze lipstick and nail polish.

When Luke picked Erin up, his eyes lit with a predatory gleam. Heat emanated between them. She wouldn't dare imbibe too much wine tonight.

Erin waved to Celine, who stood smirking in the window, watching them leave. "Luke, I gather you don't know many people there tonight. Are they from the town services or only bigwigs surrounding the mayor?"

"Lots of bigwigs certainly, and members of the city elite will be on hand. Some of the heads from the funeral homes and the top police and fire department staff. Numerous restaurant entrepreneurs and other bona fide businesses are represented, too. This isn't a sit-down meal, but hors d'oeuvres and drinks will be served."

"So, we mingle and talk to people we don't know. Oh, you mentioned speeches." Erin wrinkled her nose. "Now, that will be boring."

"Why not try to find a balcony and go outside and neck like teenagers?"

"You will not mess me up. I'm sure I can find someone to talk to."

Arriving at the reception, it looked like close to fifty people were in attendance. Everyone held a drink—hers was red wine— and some people gravitated to the few seats at the far end of the hall.

Erin picked a cracker from a tray, wondering what the delectable appetizer was atop it. She smiled at Luke on tasting it and nodded her head at him to try it. He did and took a second one. It must've been a salmon mix. She was inclined to test a few more.

A hand touched her arm, and Erin turned to see a gorgeous brunette dressed in a black sheath adorned with silver accents. Surprised but now smiling, Erin leaned in and whispered in the woman's ear. "Do I call you Eliza?"

"Yes, please, I'm working tonight."

Erin laughed and turned to Luke. "This is Eliza. I met her..." Erin stammered. "She lives out in Hanmer, where I do my rounds."

Luke stiffened and didn't smile back. "I'm Luke. And Eliza, you're with our retired fire marshal? Hello, Glen."

The large, florid man turned his glacial eyes to Luke, greeting them both, and rested a predatory hand on Eliza's hips. He focused his eyes for unnecessarily long on Erin's features, face and body, before speaking to her.

BETTY GUENETTE

"I'm sure I've seen you before, at the hospital, fairly long ago. Are you a nurse?"

"Yes, but I haven't worked in the hospital here for many years. I've been in England."

The man gave a lecherous grin. "I'm sure you took care of me a few years back when I underwent my adult circumcision. I'd like to have dated you and demonstrated my new sexual prowess."

Erin's body froze for a second on hearing the blatant remark. She didn't stop to think—maybe it was that second glass of wine—but she whispered back before turning away. "I don't enjoy circumcised men."

A choked noise from Luke made her glance at him. A member of the Elk's club ambled over and guffawed when he swatted the retired chief on the back, engaging him in conversation.

Eliza moved with her hand on Erin's elbow. "I know that look. I agree I deserve better, and I do. However, he's rich, and I don't tolerate abuse from men."

"The potential is there. I get a sense of his underlying brutality. Is he married?"

"Well, I'm not sure if he's divorced yet. He lives alone and has run off a couple of wives already. Our service manager does a thorough check and lays down lots of rules. It's like having our own selective pimp." Eliza giggled, glancing to Luke. "This is he, the cop you like?"

Erin grinned. "I'm here to keep Luke from getting bored. I do like him, most of the time."

"You haven't slept with him yet. I can tell from that animalistic look he throws at you and the way he peers sideways at your body when you're not looking."

"He does not." Erin gulped her wine. "Eliza, you are so bad. I'm involved with his murder cases, as they always seem to happen in my district."

"I think Luke guessed my line of work." She whispered. "He looked at me coldly and must disapprove of what I do."

"I got the vibe that he disapproves of your customer, not you. He probably thinks you're at risk dating that arrogant excuse of a man."

Eliza lowered her voice. "I considered calling you with information but didn't want to be too familiar." She looked questioningly at Erin, who smiled back. "Another man I date is high ranked on the police force, and they're thinking of arresting a lawyer involved with the murder case. Your Luke keeps telling the head office there isn't enough evidence."

"Not my Luke. Did he mention which lawyer? There are two under suspicion."

"No. There are also women being investigated. That's holding up an arrest." Eliza touched her arm. "And don't turn to look 'cause one of the lawyers just walked in with that haughty wife of his."

Erin didn't look and sipped her glass of wine. "I'll need to leave soon. I doubt she'd make a scene, but my wrap won't keep out the chill. The woman thinks I like her lecherous husband, who will likely try and stare down both our cleavages tonight—not that my breasts are anywhere near as magnificent as yours."

"But yours are natural. Ah, your friend Luke spotted them and is coming to protect you like a knight in shining armour. Are you in danger with these people around?"

"I've tried to help with the investigation since I believe the other lawyer is innocent. Members of our senior community are involved, too."

"And you're worried about me being in a dangerous position? Hey, if you ever get tired of nursing, remember that I can get you hired with our service. They take good care of us."

Erin burst out laughing and then covered her mouth. She didn't want people to think she drank too much and was becoming rowdy.

Luke came over and touched her arm. "I want to introduce you to our mayor. Nice meeting you, Eliza." He led Erin over to a portly gentleman. "He's a little old-fashioned in his views, so don't take offence. And please curb your responses this time."

"You mean he thinks all women should stay in the kitchen while the men do the real work? I've met lots of that type."

"And you probably annihilated them. That friend you met, Eliza, likely works for the date-on-call service. They provide everything a man ever dreamt of."

"Are you a snob, Luke? And how do you know? She looks classy!"

"She's alright. I know the ex-chief and don't like anything I've heard of the man."

"You're right. I wouldn't want to meet him alone in the dark when he's in a bad mood. Eliza says the men are warned about proper behaviour. She offered me a job working with her."

Luke twitched and glowered at Erin while they waited for the mayor to finish his conversation with an older couple.

Erin glanced around and whispered. "Eliza spotted Craig and Sheila."

"They're here. Sheila likes to be seen at these functions. I don't think we'll be able to avoid them. We'll learn nothing from them relatable to our investigation, so please don't ask loaded questions."

"You keep warning me of what to say and not to say."

"From your history of commentary," Luke hissed, "I have the right to cringe and worry."

Luke was right about how boring the event could be, and after speaking to the dull mayor, they turned and found Craig and Sheila standing next to them. Their encounter was civilized and low-key. Sheila kept her hand wrapped around Craig's arm while he greeted Erin and stared at what her gown displayed. He did the same thing when the couple walked over to meet the retired fire chief and his date. Eliza worked to contain a smirk and used enticing body language when Craig glanced at her frequently. Sheila pulled him away after their greeting, and Eliza turned and winked at Erin.

Erin managed to keep a straight and stoic face when Sheila glanced around to see who Eliza noticed. She'd probably thought Eliza was flirting with Luke or one of the other men. After a few speeches, Erin chatted with Luke and some other dignitaries, saying nothing memorable. She sighed when they left.

Luke started up the car. "Well, that was draining. Thanks for holding my hand and trying to keep me focused. Anywhere you'd like to go? How about my apartment for another drink?"

"Oh, no. Remember, we're friends tonight."

Luke glanced at her. "Do you really think so?" He reached over and tentatively pulled her into his arms, then thoroughly kissed her when she didn't try to evade him.

Erin felt the body heat between them both. She tried to push her body closer to him while his tongue explored her mouth.

He wasn't in control, and neither was she. His hand cupped her breast and slid over the filmy fabric of her dress while pulling her tight against him. She hardly breathed. She wanted him, all of him. His hand slid up her leg, but lights streamed out the entry door, and people were walking to their cars laughing and joking. The mood evaporated.

"I'd like to take you back to my apartment for the night. I want you in my bed, Erin."

"No, Luke. I can't do it." She exhaled to try and cool down. "It would turn into a cheap, tawdry affair. I have to face myself in the mirror in the morning."

"But you seem to want me too." He leaned over, whispering trivial nonsense in her ear.

Erin choked on a laugh and held a hand against her mouth. "Did you really say what I thought you said? Did you say you're uncircumcised?"

"Thought I'd get that little problem out of the way before we embark on a scorching affair if it's a prerequisite for you." He glanced over at her. "We're sexually attracted. I can't see why you don't want to date and enjoy sex on the side?"

"I'm not ready for casual sex." She took a steadying breath. "Please take me home."

Luke sighed and shifted gears to drive.

82

Erin called out to Adam the next day when he visited her neighbour after his shift. Erin asked him to go with her and Mark in the morning and to bring his dog and gun. Mr. Fraser wanted them to see if the old guy in Milnet heard or saw anything unusual when his dog was shot. Mr. Fraser said the man often drove around and hunted in surrounding areas.

"You can't go off on another wild goose chase," Adam warned. "I need to ask Luke."

"You're not on duty, and Janelle's worried about what happened with the dog. She's working, but she said you were off. The trapper can't go, and he said we could borrow his quad and trailer because the roads are much worse. Besides, going with two stable Taurus should be safe enough for me."

"Your brother warned us that *we'll* be unsafe going with you."

She stood with her hands on her hips, glaring at him. "Janelle said you'd help us."

Adam did show up the next morning. He was neither talkative nor happy. Erin jumped into the back seat of Adam's truck beside the German shepherd and gave him a few treats. They picked up Mark, who climbed in front. Adam drove up the old trail toward Milnet, stopping at Mr. Fraser's. All three hovered near the truck, expecting to see a bear, but they talked loudly to keep wildlife away. Major, with his nose to the ground, fervently sniffed along the terrain.

Mark glanced around. "If we find another body, we're with an armed policeman."

"But I'm not in uniform. I shouldn't be packing my gun."

The trapper handed the keys to her. "I didn't know there'd be three of you. Two can go on one quad, and my old machine can take a single passenger. With the hitch on his truck, you can pull the loaded trailer till you get stuck, and there's a ramp on the trailer to drive off."

"Let's take the road up to the lodge first," Erin said. "Shouldn't be anyone there."

"Then what are we looking for?" Adam asked.

"Clues or impressions from the past. We need to talk with the old French guy again."

An eerie stillness surrounded the lovely lodge. A porch ran along two sides and the back wall while a trail of railroad ties led the way to a small beach and dock. The rain stopped, but mist prevailed over the quiet setting.

Mark shook his head. "Not my idea of a fun vacation. Too lonely and wild. Luke's camp is nice and on a populated lake."

"I don't think anything's changed here. Celine wants me to look, and I'm standing here looking," Erin said. "The area around the lodge is clean, and the rest looks wild,"

Adam watched Major sniffing around down at the dock before the dog drank out of the lake. "Lots of people would think this is the perfect escape to the wild."

After checking around the building and the taller brush near the boathouse, Erin shrugged. "Seems like a wild goose chase."

They drove further down the trail and almost got bogged down near the bridge. Mark gazed around. "Grandma said we need to get to the ruins. There aren't any other vehicle tracks. Maybe the hunter came a few days ago, before the last rainfall."

Back in the truck, Adam drove back and slowed at a curve. He spotted a mother moose and her calf watching from a swamp. Worried the animals would attempt to cross, he came to a near standstill. The mother bellowed at them and then charged toward the truck, ramming against the rear fender of the trailer. Major barked, the cow moose pawed at the ground, and assumed a threatening posture. Adam honked the horn. A bleat from the frightened calf running off into the bushes deterred the mother more than the horn or the barking dog, and she trailed her baby into the forest. Adam got out to check for damage, took a wary look around, and jumped back in the truck. Erin didn't budge.

Adam spoke up. "Dumb animal attacking a vehicle. No damage. Good thing it wasn't a male with antlers."

"She was protecting her child," Erin answered. "Moose attack people too. I heard a bull moose killed a man in rutting season a couple of years ago."

Mark shook his head. "I'm out in the wilderness, endangering my life with bears and moose, all because I have to try and solve Luke's murder case since I'm one of the prime suspects. I know Luke has his work cut out for him, but I'm still miffed."

Erin smiled. "I got annoyed with him last month when he suspected me of murder. Once he got all the facts, he told me I was clear. The police have lots of restrictions. That's why Celine and Gladys wanted us to do some private investigating."

"I can't think of why you want to do our job," Adam muttered. "We're not that dumb." The wheels spun, and the truck tires churned up the ground, digging themselves deeper. Adam stopped, and they wheeled the quads down off the ramp. "I'll take the single one," Adam said.

"I played on one of these years ago. Erin and I should manage driving the damn thing."

"Don't count on me. I've ridden behind on a motorcycle a couple of times. I only know how to hang on."

Mark swore. "I can't believe I'm here. Damn that Luke."

Erin grinned. "Try to quit complaining. Pretend we're on an adventure."

Both men stared at her in disbelief.

"Hey, I'm here with two reliable Taurus guys. Why worry? We can travel along the train tracks," Erin gestured. "That'll set our teeth clacking, and not from fear. Remember, Mark, that Celine and Gladys want to help you."

Adam started up the quad and beckoned Major. "Those two old women are playing armchair detectives. They should leave the investigation to the police."

The trip took longer than expected after they crossed the bridge with the unfamiliar vehicles and sloppy terrain. Adam slowed down to watch Mark manoeuvre the bigger vehicle. When they reached Milnet, they stopped the noisy vehicles by a huge mound of loose earth across the track and shut the vehicles off to dismount. A yell shattered the quiet and their complacency.

"Who was that?" she whispered, wide-eyed.

Mark ducked down in case the guy took potshots at them.

Major barked and bounded forward over the hill.

Adam pushed through the thick bush at the side and rushed forward. The other two followed at a careful pace. The three paused in a semicircle, staring at the trapper's head and one arm protruding out of a thick mudslide.

Major sniffed at him and gave a soft woof.

"Get me out of here, *maintenant*," the man howled.

Mark glanced around for digging implements, but there was nothing around. "You must have a shovel somewhere?"

"The damn thing's in here under me. *Merde*! That's what I was doing, trying to get rid of the mud on the track, but the whole hill came down. I'm stuck. My gun's plugged with mud."

Erin crouched and checked the man's pulse and heavy breathing. "How long have you been trapped?"

"Had to hike in a long way from my truck," the man bellowed. "Stuck about three hours. Hard to say with no sun around in this misty weather."

Mark tapped his unresponsive phone. "Cells don't work out this far. Someone has to get help."

"You have a gun and dog, Adam," Erin said. "We should divide them for protection."

"Okay, I'll go for help, and Major can stay here with you. Erin should stay, in case the man has trouble breathing." He cautioned the dog. "Stay, Major."

Mark and Erin heard the motor start, and Adam left on the quad for Fraser's place.

Later, they learned that when he reached Fraser's and told him to call for help, Adam grabbed shovels, the first aid kit, and rope before returning. However, he got stuck and almost wiped out before dislodging the quad's wheels.

Erin and Mark used their gloved hands to dig the softer muck away from the man's chest but found the ground too packed further down.

"That's okay. I can breathe better now." The man gulped. "The way my neck stretched backward, I was afraid more rain would stream into my nose and drown me."

She glanced at his red-veined bulbous nose and wide nostrils. It very well could've happened. "This is such an isolated area. How would you get help and you're elderly? Don't you worry about trouble when you're out here alone?"

"I'm old, but I have weapons. I'm careful. This is way out of the ordinary."

"Freaky. At least tell somebody when you're out here, Erin admonished. "You've got that other hunting friend, or you could let Mr. Fraser know."

Major started restlessly pacing, sniffing, and stopping to look toward the woods.

A distant yowl sounded over the trees.

Mark stiffened, "What was that?"

"*Tabarnak!* Grab that big tree limb over there. It's probably the damn cougar that came through here last week."

Erin jumped up from her crouch. "We have cougars... here?" she squealed. "I was only afraid of meeting an angry bear."

The man shot her a pitying look. "The odd cat passes through, and a cougar may hunt and kill people if it's hungry or vicious enough. You can beat it off sometimes, but you must watch your neck. A bear usually goes the other way."

Erin wanted to rub a hand around her neck, but her hands were too muddy. "Thanks for that info. You said your gun's useless?"

"It's blocked solid. You'd blow yourself up when it backfired."

Major growled while continuing to gaze into the far bushes.

Mark glanced around. "First moose, maybe bears, now cougars. Are there other animals we're going to meet?"

Another yowl sounded, louder and closer. The animal seemed to be steadily approaching. Major growled again, and his hair stood up along his back. He was rigidly poised, staring directly into the woods ahead of them.

"A mountain lion will chop my head off in one bite. I'm too vulnerable." He looked from Erin to Mark. "Can you two keep a secret?"

"Only a legal one," Mark stuttered. "I'm a lawyer and already in enough trouble."

Erin gawked at the man. "Mr. Gagnon, if you have means to defend ourselves, tell us right now."

The man stared at the bushes, then back at the broken cabins. "I own other guns, have them hidden out here in case of break-ins at home. They're registered, and I keep only two cheaper models at my house in town. Go behind that crumbled cement wall over there to the old brown doorway. You have to bend down at the bushy entrance to get in; there's a cave inside. Take the old gun and bullets resting on the sawhorse table. Bring both back here."

Erin sprinted past the wall to what she guessed was an opening, dragged away the brush, and pulled the small rotting door open. A lantern sat on the floor. She grabbed and turned it on with shaking hands and flashed the light around, her body trembling and hands fumbling in haste. She bent over to crawl through and stood up in a cave, shining the light around to see assorted guns lined up in cabinets against a rock wall. The meagre light from the lantern illuminated a table. A small box lay next to a gun. She grabbed the weapon on the table and a box of ammunition before edging outside. Why was the damn gun slippery?

Mark stood frozen, a tree limb in each hand and rocks beside him, anxiously watching the bushes. Only his eyes moved.

Erin placed the gun beside Mr. Gagnon. "Can you shoot with that one injured hand? Those swollen fingers look awful."

The man's puffed-up digits made it difficult for him to close his fingers. "*Non!* Take a couple of bullets out of the box and open this lever. Now, slide one bullet into the magazine clip under where your hand is. You need a rag to wipe the barrel dry."

"Got tissues in my pocket to dry this. Why is the handle covered with oil? You're likely to drop the darn thing when hunting."

"The dampness ruins guns, and we need to keep them oiled. A few are in a cabinet, and there are humidity-absorbent packages inside with them. I keep most of the ammo at home and bring some out for the days I'm here. Put one bullet in for now. *Esti!* You're shaking and likely going to shoot one of us."

Erin frowned as another approaching yowl echoed off the surrounding trees. She dropped a bullet from her trembling fingers.

Major's fur remained on end, and his growl became a constant rumble.

Mark glanced over. "Stay, Major. Hurry, Erin. That animal... sounds... real close."

"Have either one of you ever shot a gun? *Merde!*" The man swore and looked disgusted when Erin and Mark shook their heads. "Do you weaklings want to flip a coin?"

"I handled Mr. Fraser's gun, but I don't think I could hit anything."

"You don't have to. One shot in the air, and he'll go looking for easier prey."

Erin leaned forward after closing the gun's cavity and lifted the rifle to her shoulder like she'd seen Mr. Fraser do. "There's no scope." She gazed off into the far bushes. "I won't be able to spot its movement."

"You don't need to see a thing. Cats blend into their environment anyway. He's quiet, getting closer now. Quit waving the rifle up and down."

"It's darn heavy." She balanced the gun, clutching both hands around the center. She needed to up her weight training.

A low growl echoed around them. Mark and Erin both gulped, scanning the dense bushes.

"Do you think there's more than one?"

"They often travel in pairs, but I've only spotted the one."

Major rumbled and bristled, his whole body on alert, ready to attack.

"Now, slide your left hand along the barrel—yes, that long part. Shove the base against your shoulder—the right one if you're right-handed. Aim up and toward the pine trees. No, swing the firing end away from us. Never aim directly at anyone. Over to the right—yes, there, and aim above the treeline. You don't want to hit anyone concealed in the bush. Hold still, use your index finger and squeeze on the trigger."

Erin squinted and pressed down. *Crack!* The shot blasted across the trees. Erin's body flew backwards, the rifle sailed from her hands when the gun's recoil tossed her onto the ground.

"Oops. *Pardon.* I forgot to warn you of the kick on that old rifle. Good thing you only loaded one bullet, the way you flung it around. Pick the rifle up and put the safety on—no, move your finger over. Always point the barrel down and away."

She struggled up using her one good arm. "But it's not loaded, now." She picked up the gun and took out another bullet to load again if needed. They all stared into the distance.

The ensuing silence broke on hearing a motor and hail from behind them.

Mark exhaled. "Here comes the cavalry."

Erin rubbed her shoulder with her chin, staring into the distance with the rifle aimed toward the far bushes, still on edge. Major gave a joyful bark and raced to meet Adam dismounting the quad. He jumped off, patted the dog, and began shovelling around the man, saying others would arrive soon, as he'd got stuck coming back. Hearing their bone-chilling story, he told them to keep watch for the cougar and that he'd use his gun if necessary.

Luke and Trevor arrived shortly after on an official overland vehicle. Luke shook his head at the absurd scene. Mark stood watching the bushes, legs poised apart with large tree limbs brandished in both hands, a pile of rocks at his feet. To the side, Erin looked wild, hanging onto a rifle with both hands unsteadily but now aiming it down. Lastly, there was a man's head and shoulders sticking out of the ground with Adam digging around him. Major lay down, watching as his ears twitched toward the bushes.

After evaluating the scene, the men waited for a small excavator being towed behind them on a bush tractor trailer. On arrival and working carefully, the machine dug a well around the trapped man, taking care to keep away from his body. When they stopped, the men used hand shovels next to him. Soon, a rope was tied under his freed arms and attached to the tractor that pulled him slowly out of the grasping mud.

"Hey, lady," he yelled. "Turn around. I think my pants are coming off."

"That's okay, I'm a nurse."

"I'm a bachelor," he yelled again. "*Merde*, turn around."

She complied. Luke would get mad at them again for their continual involvement and fruitless excursion, but at least they helped save a man's life.

When Mr. Gagnon lay on the ground covered with a blanket, Erin checked his breathing and as much of him as modesty allowed. "Are you going to tell the inspector about your cache?"

The man hung his head. Luke didn't think he was going to admit to murder.

"I hide my rifles here in an underground cave. I keep a collection, fully licensed, for my own use and enjoyment." He cursed again in French when they loaded him onto a stretcher, saying everything hurt, but nothing was broken. "With the gun laws threatened, I feared confiscation and always worried about robbery."

Luke shook his head. "I did miss something out here."

Mark followed Luke and opened the small door, both stooping to enter. Luke pulled out a flashlight but also used the lantern. The corners lit up an arsenal of about a dozen rifles.

"Wow!" Mark spoke first. "Wish we had these out there for that cougar. I'll have to learn to shoot if I keep chasing Erin around looking for your murderers."

Luke turned and threw him a nasty look, which was reciprocated.

85

Back at Fraser's, Adam, Erin, and Mark thanked him for lending the quads after telling their incredible story.

The trapper shook his head. "I'm not surprised Marcel hides extra guns, but I can't believe that many. You can only use a few, and only one at a time."

Mark answered. "It's an addiction. He said losing them would kill him. He's afraid the police will think he's stocking firearms. It's like the guns are his babies."

"Well, plenty of collectors are possessive, and—except for a few hunting buddies—he's been alone forever." Mr. Fraser nodded. "They're putting out a call for the MNR to check on that wild cougar. If it's that aggressive, it's likely a loner and possibly sick."

Adam apologized for the slight dent on the back of the man's trailer from the cow moose ramming into them.

"That's natural for a mother protecting her babe. But what a mess you met on the roads. The weatherman promises an end to the rain this weekend. We'll get to see the sun soon."

On the drive home with Adam and Erin, Mark spoke up. "You know, I'm sorry now that I got angry with Luke. I only understood his position when Craig badgered me about being friends with the police inspector. He said I got preferential treatment and wasn't being hounded for the murders, even without an alibi."

Adam steered around a slippery corner and glanced at Mark. "I'm glad you said that. The inspector doesn't show his feelings, but he worked extra hard on this case because of you. He wouldn't let up on our investigation."

Erin reiterated how incensed she'd become while pressed under Luke's suspicions.

"I worried that my friendship with him was over." Mark pursed his lips. "My wife would have made me see sense, only I worried she wouldn't trust me either. Now, no more of these deadly games. I'm going to hide from all the managing women around me."

"We'll get answers, Mark. Luke knows we won't quit trying. Who cares if we upset the police force—and you, too, Adam."

"Well, you'll likely get murdered along the way if you keep interfering."

Mark shuddered. "Never mind a murderer. We almost became that animal's lunch."

86

"Bill, you should have seen your sister." Luke acted out the scene. "There she stood, legs braced apart, looking around for varmints and brandishing a rifle like Annie Oakley herself."

"Annie, get your gun." Bill smirked. "I warned you. She's lethal. I wouldn't want to stand near her holding a rifle. She doesn't know which end points where."

"If you guys are finished making fun of me, I'll offer you coffee or tea. Anyway, Mark seems fed up with my company. He thinks I'm too dangerous to be around. I'm only trying to help prove his innocence."

"Dangerous? You're a disaster." Bill held both hands out in mock prayer. "Lord, please protect me from my sister's follies."

"Funny man! Wait till you beg me for help someday."

"I will rue the day that happens. Luke, can't you stop her?"

"Celine might have the powers for that, but not me."

Erin bristled at their teasing. "I'm listening guys, enough already."

Speaking with Celine later, the older woman said that she felt no undercurrents of worry over Erin's predicament. No attacking moose, no growling cats, and no cache of rifles. "Safer than you thought, *Chérie*. There were no bears."

Erin rubbed her sore shoulder. "Do you know how to shoot a gun?"

"*Oui, mais* not well. In France, during the wartime, we kept handguns ready to guard the underground passageways and to send refugees in boats to cross over into England. I knew only the basic use for the weapons, *mais* I would have shot a German soldier if *nécessaire*."

"You don't talk about your history with war often."

"Those years were cruel. Most soldiers block out their war memories. They do not want to discuss their experiences, their losses of comrades and of *amis*—all bad dreams: *méchant*."

Erin sat lost in distant thoughts for a while, then roused and glanced at her quiet friend, changing the subject. "I met the foreman who's building your apartment block when I walked the dogs. He lives around the corner and owns a Rottweiler."

"Such a *bon* man. Did you not find him so?"

"Well, yes, but not in the way you're meaning."

"*Comment...*" The woman raised her eyebrows innocently. "How do you know what I mean?"

"You get that gleam in your eyes when you start matchmaking."

"I am not getting farther up the road with you and Luke, though all the chemistry: *c'est correct.* You are both silly and stubborn."

"Stop trying to organize my love life. I have no desire to begin another relationship."

"You can have fun, *Chérie.* You do not have to get *très* involved."

"Sorry. To me, sex is not a passing fancy. I believe in full commitment—not necessarily marriage but the once-in-a-lifetime caring for each other. I believed I'd found that, but love needs two people going in the same direction, holding hands."

"*Vraiment.*" Celine sat in thought. "I forget that young building fellow's name, *mais* I remember that he is a Virgo sign."

"Good thing you remember the important stuff. His name is Dave. I forget the last name. When the twins return from England, we'll throw a Virgo party and invite you to run a séance."

Celine frowned. "*Rien!* I have never held a séance in all my long life. Why should I try to talk with dead people? *Impossible!*" She shrugged. "The twins will like him."

"Oh, really? Is that a promise or a guess?"

"Both, *je pense.*" Her eyes misted over, and she whispered.

> *The other symbols float on by,*
> *Not important to the case.*
> *Watch the ones that this sign rules*
> *Only then can you be safe.*

Erin shrugged, yelped, and grabbed her sore arm. Holding it tight against her body, she hurried home for a hot bath, envisioning the relaxing jets pulsating the ache out of her arm but not landing the harsh spray directly against her poor, bruised shoulder. Last month, she received an injury that displaced her other shoulder blade. This one was all sore muscle.

87

At work, Erin travelled down another narrow road toward a lakeshore. Her directions pointed the way to one of the numerous cottages encircling small Joe Lake. A few people dwelled there year-round. She stopped at the designated number and peered around the forested scenery before getting out and approaching the door.

When she knocked, the door swung open wide, and a burly woman grabbed her arm and hauled her into the kitchen. "My oven's smoking, and I can't get the damn door unlocked."

"Shut the dial off. Once the oven cools, the mechanism will unlock."

"There are flames inside!" The woman reached over and twisted the knob. "Well, a lot of good a self-cleaning oven is if the damn thing sets the house on fire."

"Likely too much buildup of drippings or spilt grease?"

"Well, I wouldn't run the cleaning cycle if the oven wasn't dirty, would I?"

Erin grinned, noting the smoke thinning. A fire alarm by the door began to blare. "I'm supposed to be out of my fiery Aries month," she muttered.

"What's that? Never mind." The woman pushed the reset button on the alarm and turned on the stove vent. "You must be the visiting nurse?"

"Yes. I'm Erin Rine. Are you Mrs. Harris?"

"No, that's my mom. I'm Mrs. Hancock, a widow. Come into the front and meet her."

"Will all this commotion upset her?"

"Not her. She's a war veteran. My dear mother's seen all and knows all. But she took a stroke and can barely talk." The woman smiled. "Still, she's a crotchety old bat."

"I'm supposed to check her vital signs and movement capabilities. My notes say she was discharged from the hospital on Thursday."

"That's right. She's doing better. She must be since she's cranky as hell."

Erin followed the daughter into the room, and they both ducked, narrowly dodging a small book thrown with considerable force across the tidy room.

"Now, Ma, don't act miserable. The nurse wants to make sure you can stay here with me. Please try and be good."

Erin assessed the woman from the door. "Does she have any more missiles?"

"Not likely. I bet you don't get stuff shot at you too often?"

Erin laughed. "You'd be surprised. Once, when I was in training, a young boy in the hospital hid his bowel movements and rolled his diaper excreta—uh, shit—up into little round poop balls. He yelled and pitched them at us whenever we dared to enter his room."

The woman guffawed, and the old lady smirked. "Ma, don't you be getting ideas," her daughter said, wagging a finger.

Erin sat in the chair by the woman's bed and explained about health care wanting to keep her well and in her daughter's home. The doctor's orders stressed checking on her health and making sure she was cared for.

The old woman allowed Erin to check her blood pressure and pulse. The patient kept her eyes riveted on every movement.

"My notes say that you can walk slowly using a cane?" Erin asked.

The woman nodded. Her daughter answered. "I help her to the bathroom. It's right beside her room. She's getting a lot stronger already."

"Where did she live before the stroke?"

"A small apartment in town, but we gave it up. I've been widowed three years and wanted her to move in with me. Then this stroke happened. She lost her independence and gets angry because of it."

Erin smiled at the old woman. "Think of all the summer sunshine you'll enjoy soon, sitting by the lake—if the rain ever stops."

The old woman glared at her when she left. Erin gave her a cheerful wave and a promise to be back soon and check on her.

Next, Erin travelled farther down by another small lake. The roads seemed to weave in and out with no pattern to them.

There were two small cottages with no numbers. She rapped at the door of the cottage with smoke rising from its chimney. A young woman with a toddler on her hip opened the door and looked through the outside screen. "We're not buying."

"Sorry, not selling. I'm Erin Rine, the nurse for this area. I'm looking for Mr. Faraday."

"He lives next door, but the ambulance brought him to the hospital last night. I called the medics. They think he suffered another heart attack."

"Oh, thanks for the information. I guess they haven't contacted our office yet." Erin gestured behind her. "Does this road take me back to the main highway?"

"It sure does, and quicker. Watch out for a big bear, though. The MNR set a trap by the corner, but the animal's too smart. Hopefully, when the rangers relocate it, that'll be the end of its wanderings around here."

Erin's hair raised along her arms inside her sweater. "Thanks. I heard the bears often work their way back after being released."

"That's true, but if they're caught three times, they're put to sleep permanently."

Erin left, driving at a snail's pace and eased around the winding curves. Near the exit, she spied the green metal bear tube sitting beside the road. Was her imagination in overdrive, or was the cage moving? She slowed and gaped at the huge black form whipping around inside. The shadows and movement showed through the numerous air holes patterned over the trap.

Nearly hyperventilating, Erin continued to the highway, then she stopped and dialled the MNR's number. She kept telling herself that the animal was locked in a cage. She was informed the collection unit was already on its way. When Erin turned onto the highway, the MNR truck with uniformed staff passed by. She wasn't sticking around in case the beast escaped. They would back up and hitch onto the wheeled cage and drive it to a remote area. From a safe distance, they needed to nudge and prod the animal with poles through the open gate to let it escape into the bush. If the bear became too ferocious, they would use a tranquillizer dart. The problem there was they had to wait for the animal to wake up. The bear needed to be alert enough to protect itself from other predators before they left.

88

Luke stopped by later to see Erin. Adam's truck sat next door. "Adam seems quite taken with Celine's granddaughter," Luke said.

"Her name is Janelle, and she's the same age as him."

Luke gave her a steady look. "He was infatuated with you. I know that for a fact."

"I'm not arguing with you over this nonsense again." She pointed to the kitchen chair and sat in the opposite. "He's a nice boy, too nice. He'll get disillusioned in his job."

"Why, because we deal with the seamier side of society?"

"Partially. But you suffer alongside victims, too. Some atrocities are harder to deal with than others. And some officers become corrupt dealing with decadent aspects of their jobs."

"I'm not corrupted yet, but I know what you mean." Thinking of Trevor, he added, "A few get a hard crust and shut their emotions from outside problems."

"Nurses struggle with empathy, too. Feeling too much can destroy you, but you don't want to lose your humanity either." She gazed at him. "Do you want a drink? You look like you have questions to ask. I'm not hiding anything."

Luke shifted in his chair. "No thanks. We're hosting a children's carnival on Saturday afternoon. Adam's asking Janelle to help supervise the groups since there's a petting zoo for the children. You're a nurse and a black belt, and we're short on woman supervisors."

Erin raised her eyebrows, having no intention of making it easy for him. "And?"

"Beth said if I asked you, she'd make sure I behaved and wasn't rude." He grinned. "Actually, she said, 'Hands off the nurse, there will be children present.'"

Erin laughed. "That seems safe enough. Too bad Celine's omens are shrouded and distant. She embodies the role of a real fortune teller."

Luke almost jerked. "These are children. Could you see the parents condoning a scary adult who whispered evil prophecies to them?" His voice dropped to sepulchral tones. "Smoke and shadows will envelope you. Beware!"

85

The weather co-operated for the carnival. It wasn't too sunny and warm, but a welcome respite from the demoralizing, steady rainfall.

Luke met Erin and Janelle at the gate and handed them passes and name tags. "Beth has a radar aimed at me. I don't like to mix work and pleasure, and I don't want her berating me for misconduct if I stick with you. She'll think we're an item."

"Don't worry," Erin answered firmly. "We're not."

Erin strode to the carousel. Two small girls clung to the horse's pole as the ride started, staring ahead. They looked petrified. Erin jumped onto the ride, balanced herself, and sidled between their two mounts. "What's your horse's name?" she asked the older of the two girls while resting her arm along the back of the younger one.

The girl peeked at her before quickly returning her gaze forward to ensure she remained glued to her seat and wasn't in danger of falling off. "They have no names."

"Great, then you can call your bronco whatever name you like. How about Midnight?"

"That's silly. He's white with brown spots."

"My brother has a horse with these same colours. He calls her Spirit."

The girl smiled and looked at the horse she rode while Erin patted the hard mane. Meanwhile, she held her remaining arm around the smaller girl, who seemed to relax slightly. "Why don't we name your horse, too, Curly?"

The little girl shook her blonde curls and didn't answer. Erin petted this horse, too. "Your pony is a pretty grey colour. We can call her Misty."

The younger girl looked shyly at the pony, keeping a desperate clasp on the pole.

When the ride slowed down, she said, "Whoa, horses. Slow down, Spirit and Misty. We're running out of fields now and coming up to the gate." She pretended to haul on the plastic reins. When the ride stopped, she lifted both girls off and stepped down to meet an agitated woman clutching a younger boy's hand.

"Thank you." The woman glanced at Erin's tag. "My son charged off to get on the little red train, and I needed to chase him. Were the girls scared?"

"A little, but they rode Misty and Spirit across the fields like real cowgirls."

The older girl smiled. The younger one grasped her mother's free hand tightly and muttered, "I donna like the big horsy."

Erin wandered, checking out the rides and keeping her eyes on the older children. The afternoon hours were closed to the public but open for grade school children, but some of the grade seven and eight children looked big: a few early, troubled teens.

The older group seemed to get along, with only a few of them shoving and squeezing ahead in lineups for the rides. Adam hung around them, his height deterring mischief. Only a couple of the staff wore police uniforms, one of whom was Beth, visible for the women's comfort. The other was Jackson, who had a small but wiry frame. They didn't want their afternoon outing to intimidate their guests. Other men Erin didn't know walked around, name badges prominent on their jackets. Janelle supervised a group at the scary roller coaster ride through the haunted house beside the petting zoo.

When she rounded a corner near the tilt-a-whirl, a small hand encircled her wrist. "Hello, I'm Shana. Do you remember me?" the tiny Chinese girl asked.

"Yes, and your mother brought you, I see." She smiled at the gracious woman. "Who's managing your lovely tearoom?"

The older woman smiled. "My sister helps. Shana wanted to come, but I don't like these rides. I tried one but I got queasy right away. I even get seasick on a small boat."

Shana smiled. "You have a badge, and you're working here. Are you a policewoman?"

"No, I'm a nurse, but I have a Korean black belt. I'm here helping with crowd control and monitoring the kids' behaviour."

The little girl glanced at her mom. "She's too scared to get on with me, and I want to ride the tilt-a-whirl. She'd trust you with me."

"Sure, if you won't get sick or frightened? The chairs on the ride flip around, and the forces pull hard on your neck."

"I won't get scared." The girl placed her hand in Erin's. They hurried to stand in line, her mother holding her camera ready on the side.

"You're nice. Mom said she gave you that bad picture I found under the table. She got upset that I looked at it."

"Well, the image wasn't appropriate for anyone to see."

"My dance pictures on the wall are nice, happy ones. The precious movements we step to stand for dignity, beauty, grace, and freedom."

"They are lovely. The man sitting with the two other ladies was in the picture you found, and it probably fell out of his pocket. I gave it to the police to help their investigation."

The pair shuffled into one of the chairs and buckled in. The little girl clutched the bar in front and grinned the whole time. She laughed when her small body flung against Erin as they spun. When the ride slowed on the slants, she waved at her mom, and when they went into the spirals, she grinned and clung to the bar.

The ride slowed to a halt, but their chair kept rocking sideways. While they waited for the attendant to grab the car and release the bar, Shana looked at her. "My mother said the picture seemed important to you. I didn't tell her all of it. It didn't fall out of the man's pocket. One of the women dropped it out of her purse. He wasn't there yet."

Erin held her breath. "Do you know which woman?"

"No. I was busy greeting another couple. They left before I picked up the picture. I gave it to my mom. You left soon after, too."

She smiled and thanked the petite girl. "Are you okay by yourself now?"

"Yes. That was the fastest ride I wanted to try." She took her mother's hand and waved goodbye with a sweet smile.

With the three-hour session almost over, Erin looked around, noting the workers checking families and watching the children. She spotted Luke by the Ferris Wheel and hurried over, planning to tell him about the picture, when she heard her name called. Turning, she spied Beth sitting on a stool beside one of the tents, clutching her abdomen.

Erin ran over and knelt before the sweating woman. "Did someone hurt you?"

"No. I think I'm having an appendicitis attack." She gasped and leaned farther over when another wave of pain hit her.

"We'll call an ambulance." She spotted Luke checking everyone's positions and waved to attract his attention. He jolted and broke into a lope to reach them quickly.

"Beth, you're holding the left side, not the right?" Erin asked.

"Oh-h, the spasms travel right across."

"Luke, call an ambulance. She may have a ruptured appendix."

He pulled out his cell phone and dialled.

She frowned at Beth. "Could you be pregnant?"

"No. I had a tubal a couple of years back."

"Do you know if they tied the tubes or cut and cauterized the edges?"

Beth shrugged. "I don't remember. I've got kids. This isn't like labour pains or a miscarriage."

"Maybe you have a tubal pregnancy. Sometimes, an egg gets trapped in the passageway. Your symptoms remind me of one of my co-workers with the condition. The same thing happened to her, and they diagnosed appendicitis at first."

Janelle spotted them and ran over. Luke told her to find Adam and get him to direct the ambulance over to their corner.

With the afternoon's activities over, the families trickled off the fairgrounds. The ambulance pulled in quietly, and the attendants jumped out and checked Beth over. They hoisted her on the stretcher before leaving with lights flashing but no sirens.

Luke waved the driver off, calling out. "I'll phone her husband and get him to go to the Emergency department." He went back to stand beside Erin. "Beth's in her police uniform, so she'll get instant care. We spend a lot of time hauling drunks and druggies out of their ER department, and the employees are on a first-name basis with many of our staff."

"I'll see if Janelle wants to return with me or wait for Adam." Erin started to go but turned back. "Luke, I met the girl, Shana, from the teashop."

"Yes, I saw you talking to her. She was the one you mentioned before?"

"She didn't tell her mother, but that picture of Craig and Jewel fell out of one of the women's purses, not Craig's pocket."

"And she didn't know which woman, I gather?"

"No. She couldn't tell them apart. She said the picture fell out before Craig came in, and then the place filled up."

"That's a scary thought, but they are strong women. Their involvement is a possibility we've been following. Thanks for the help this afternoon, Erin. I need to sign out the department crew. The carnival opens to the general public in ten minutes. I'll get back to you about Beth."

Luke dropped by Erin's house later after phoning. He sat at the kitchen table and petted the dogs that kept crowding each other out. "I've seen Beth at the hospital, and she's groggy. You were right. The doctors took her to surgery and removed a tubal pregnancy, and they cauterized both tubes this time. She'll be home in a few days but needs to be off work for a couple of weeks."

Erin poured herself a glass of red wine and offered one to Luke. He declined, saying he drunk two cups of decaf coffee while waiting at the hospital.

"You look tired, Luke. Are you upset with the ongoing investigation?"

"It's not ongoing; it seems stalled. We have plenty of suspicions and ideas but no proof." Luke smiled. "You look wary of sitting too close to me. I'm not hitting on you or staying long. I spotted Adam, Janelle, and Celine all looking out the window when I drove in. They're probably timing my visit."

Erin grinned. "That's a good reason to get my own apartment. I'd entertain company without Celine offering me advice."

"If you're planning on that new building that Celine is co-buying, she'll likely stay on the main floor, checking everyone who enters."

"You're right, she probably will. But I like the idea of the apartment being close enough to exercise the dogs and keep my privacy. Bill will relax with my ominous presence gone."

Luke got up. "Well, goodnight. Tomorrow's another Monday."

31

The next day, Erin returned to Mark's office after work. "Lois, has everyone left?"

"Mostly. Both lawyers are in court and may not be back. The rest of us will soon close up shop and leave. Almost quitting time. Do you want more information?"

"No. I'm like a dog gnawing on a bone. I feel I should check up on Sheila, but I've no excuse to bug her. Besides, I wouldn't get anywhere. She's hostile toward anyone she thinks is interested in her husband."

"Cathy can answer more questions if you know what to ask."

Erin walked over to see Cathy pulling on her jacket. "Hi, I'm buzzing around with enquiries. I talked to that young Melanie. She only lived with the two victims for a short while. She doesn't know anything or anybody."

Cathy shrugged. "She wouldn't know Craig or the rest of us prime suspects anyway. Craig said Jewel talked about her roommates and how that Melanie chick was a nervous twit."

Erin fumbled for more conversation to keep her there. "The girl's frightened. I said I'd help her find another place, but she's going to move into residence at the university soon. She promised to call if she got too scared, and if she did, I said I'd go out and visit."

Cathy seemed cross. "Sheila's downstairs with Craig. I must hurry; I shouldn't keep the princess waiting. You don't want to ask her more questions?"

Erin recoiled in distaste. "No thanks. She's too bitter. Other than glaring at me and making ridiculous insinuations about me and her husband, I'd only get hateful innuendoes."

"I'm really angry today. Got another damn speeding ticket." Cathy flung the violation and her license on the desk. "Look at that. I considered getting Craig to find a loophole, but I'll suck it up and pay. The problem is I'll lose more points."

Erin glanced at the licence. "You got a decent picture on yours. Mine doesn't..." She froze. "Your birthday is April 30th? You're a Taurus?"

"Sure am. Why? Who cares what sign I am?"

"I assumed, wrongly, that wearing that diamond ring made you an Aries, like me."

"I'm the bull, and if you're thinking of emeralds, I don't qualify as a suspect on those grounds. Sheila mentioned that people seemed fixated on the fact because of a cheap green ring on the first victim's finger." Cathy frowned. "Your look tells me you think the date matters."

Erin stared, almost blankly, trying to gather her thoughts. Celine's words *"check the date"* rang in her ears. She stammered. "No, I was surprised... that's all." She rubbed her fingers together while watching Cathy's baleful expression. "Celine mentioned something about too many Taurus people around now, though this is their month to shine. Well, I must go." She felt Cathy's eyes burning through her back as she hurried out the door.

Erin returned to Lois' office. Mark entered and stuffed papers into his briefcase. Lois had already left. "Mark, do you know for sure if Craig and Cathy are still an item?"

"They are close. Cathy and Craig dated, and then he met Sheila. You know all that. If they're having an affair, it wouldn't mean murder."

They left together, but Erin stopped to use the bathroom. She must be nervous. She peered out the small window. Mark and Craig were talking outside, so she decided to wait. When she came out, there was a sign on the elevator saying, "Out of order." No sweat: she was only on the third floor. She headed for the far stairwell and descended. Before reaching the main floor, the lights went out. She pulled back her hair in a nervous reaction when a sense of foreboding or whisper of sound unsettled her. A thin rope snaked around her head and arm. She swung around and grabbed with her other hand to jerk hard on the rope. The loss of pressure at the other end caused her to tumble backward down the remaining few steps. She slammed onto the floor, rolled over, and bounced to her feet to race back up the stairs. She spotted a tall, shadowy figure rush through the upper doorway. On reaching that closed door, she tried turning the knob. The action proved futile, as the door seemed wedged shut. Clutching the slim rope, she wound it over her arm while hurrying down, testing the other doors till she reached the basement entry. That door was also locked and on an alarm.

Erin wondered whose idea it was to keep her locked in. Would they return with a gun? A few minutes later, she smelled smoke and watched wisps of it seeping under the doorsill. She'd left her cell phone in the car. How stupid! Erin ran up the stairwell to the top floor. No water sprinklers in the ceiling. She looked through the custodian's supplies in the corner closet, searching for anything to use as a weapon besides her pocketknife. She found two metal rods for opening windows and a broom. Not much good against a gun or smoke.

Glancing around, she looked up at the narrow window. There was no way to reach up there and climb out, but she seized on an idea. Holding the length of metal with both hands, she swung the rod up toward the window, unbalancing herself in the process. On her third try, the rod broke through the window, and she fell down a couple of steps. The security alarm blasted her eardrums. The fire must have started at the bottom of the building, and she would do better higher up, though smoke rose. She'd rather die from smoke inhalation than burn alive.

She guessed that Celine wouldn't know where Erin went if she sensed Erin was in danger. The deafening noise clanged in her ears, making her head throb. She hoped the racket masked sirens coming to her rescue. She wouldn't be able to hear anything else. Then the fire alarm piled on, blaring with a new cadence throughout the building and shrieking its warning. If help didn't come soon, her brain might explode.

Celine gasped. "*Mais non*, I cannot be smelling smoke again with Erin—oooh, the noise." She glanced around, hands trembling, then clutched both hands over her ears. The clamour abated. This time, having kept her phone numbers handy, she called Luke's private office. When she mentioned Erin, smoke, and bells, he swore and said he got notice that the break-in and fire alarm at Mark's office had gone off. Luke promised Celine he'd check, grabbed his jacket, jumped in his truck, and sped to the office.

Celine called Gladys and stuttered in broken French and English sentences for her to tell Mark that his office was on fire.

Gladys spoke in a calm voice. "If Mark's in his car, I can reach him on his cell. I hope he's left work already. Why are you worried?"

"I smelled smoke and have the vibrations and hear bells—faint now. About Erin, I have the sense of fear. *Pas définitivement!* Luke said Mark's building alarms are ringing. He is gone there."

"She may have looked for evidence and tripped an alarm."

"*Mon Dieu*, I hope that is all there is to this affair."

After hanging up to call Mark, Gladys called back. "Mark isn't answering." She sounded anxious now, too. "Do you think they're both stuck in the building?"

"I do not know. I am *très* worried." Celine hung up and paced around the room with her cats meowing and stalking along with her. "This is a game no longer. Luke must find the answers." She sank into her chair and rocked, her mind wheeling around all the facts surrounding the murder. Craig had no guts and little flexibility in the brains department, but the two women were resourceful characters. Either one was a possible murderer, and Celine guessed that both could kill without compunction. Somehow, the two women seemed enamoured of the feckless Craig. The man attracted paramours before, but why the elaborate removals of some now?

Luke arrived and showed his badge to bypass the guards, noting the smoke-filled building. "Did someone ring the alarm? They may be stuck inside."

The fireman shouted. "The break-in alarm sounded first, and the police arrived when the fire alarm went. We'll have to climb the stairwell. One of the men is using a crowbar to pry open the seized door. The fire hasn't taken hold; it just seems like a lot of smoke right now."

Luke stepped back and glanced at the gathering crowd. Firebugs often watched their handiwork go down, but this farce seemed too connected with his murder case. He dialled Celine. There was no news from Erin, and Celine's voice vibrated with anxiety. She told him Gladys couldn't reach Mark either.

Luke paced and whirled around when a hand grabbed his arm. "Mark, you're here. Thank goodness you're not inside the building. Have you seen Erin?"

"Grandma called me. Erin and I left last. She stopped to go to the bathroom, and I got waylaid outside by Craig. I told Craig I was terminating his contract with my office and gave him a month's notice to relocate. Then Sheila, followed by Cathy arrived and decried the police department. They wanted me to represent them in a suit for bullying tactics. When I went back to check, the door was locked. I figured Erin snuck away to avoid meeting them."

"I hope we find her alive. This means you're last on the scene again."

Mark's face turned ashen, the same colour as the smoke billowing from the building. "Don't you think... she went home?"

"No, Celine's hitting the panic button, and I won't disregard that."

Mark glanced toward the building and exclaimed on seeing a fireman escorting a stumbling Erin away from the building to a waiting ambulance. Placed on the stretcher, an attendant fixed an oxygen mask over her face. Erin coughed and sputtered.

Luke flashed his badge, ran over, and spoke to her. "Is anyone else inside the building?" he asked. The firemen held Mark back.

"Don't think so... unless my attacker—" She took another deep lung full of revitalizing oxygen. "Surely she'll be gone by now."

Luke froze. "You said 'she.' Who was there?"

"Hmm, don't know." She yawned. "I had an impression of a tall woman running away."

Luke saw Erin being worn down more from the stream of questions than from the billowing smoke that had ascended the stairwell. The broken window helped clear the air alongside the prompt arrival of the fire trucks and emergency crews. Erin recovered and didn't need a trip to the hospital. He didn't act annoyed and didn't rail at her for investigating again. She stressed to him that she had needed to use the bathroom. She nearly became a lone casualty. She hadn't seen Craig and his wife come inside. She thought Cathy left ahead of her and Mark.

"But how and why did someone attack you?"

"How? Oh, a rope or cord, like a noose. I knew I'd be killed the same way." Erin looked off into the distance thinking and prattled on a bit. "And what do I know? Nothing. Didn't Mr. Fraser say Cathy and Sheila rode and roped like pros?"

Later, Erin rocked in the lounger and drank tea at Celine's. Luke listened to Celine explaining the dramatic event to Gladys over the phone. Luke and Mark sat beside each other on the couch, both looking drained from the near disaster. The older women promised they wouldn't put Erin in such peril again but declared she must be close to the answers if she was a danger to the murderer. They also reasoned that the killer might panic or begin to enjoy the act of killing.

Mark stated he was afraid to go anywhere alone. "If I'm set up for the killer role, then I always need someone with me. How many more are they planning to kill?"

"A bodyguard would be advisable." Luke pondered the mystery. "The murderer needs a scapegoat. I'm thinking they'll plan to set you up as a suicide born of guilt and remorse."

Mark bent forward, his head down with his hands in front of his face. "How can I guard myself from someone that cunning?"

"Keep your eyes open and try not to be alone," Luke advised him.

Mark almost snorted. "Lois has been practicing self-defence. I'll have to rely on my tiny, older secretary for protection."

Luke turned back to Erin, who seemed more alert. "Erin, there were photographers out there, likely with long-distance camera lenses. Your grimy looks will make the news."

She groaned. "The oxygen mask hid my face. And they have no intriguing details to make up a story about me."

Celine patted her shoulder. "I called Maggie. She would get angry if your picture came on the news and we didn't tell her."

"And my name, too." Erin frowned, thinking. Her bossy oldest sister wanted to be kept up on family news. Her other sister and her rambling brother out west managed their own lives at a distance. "I'll talk to Bill later."

Luke posed his question. "On a profound level, I think you both can guess who we're looking at. I'm talking feeling here—a woman's intuition, not ESP stuff."

Erin shook her head. "I sense it's a woman. Cathy and Sheila are too much alike physically. I can't decide which one could be the killer."

"*Mais*, Gladys and I think it is the secretary, Cathy. I know Erin thinks Sheila is *très* vicious. But that is only the presumptions from the gut, I think you say. You need evidence."

Luke didn't realize that the ominous revelation about Cathy's birth date totally slipped out of Erin's smoke-filled brain. Later, Erin would ponder that fact and realize he wouldn't have given credence to Celine's chattering anyway.

The next day Erin spent quietly following orders to rest after her ordeal but otherwise feeling fine. She soon became impatient with their lack of results pertaining to the murder. Luke felt the murderer was one of the women. What did she know about the case that provoked them to try and murder her, too? Did she see something in the offices that set off alarms? Did she give away her suspicions to anyone? What if the two women were jointly involved in this murder? Well, Craig and the two women shone as the prime suspects, but there was no evidence against them. She told Bill about the risk she faced, as well. For once, he was non-committal and left for work, shaking his head.

Erin jerked upright, placing her hand against her mouth. The date. She'd forgotten about the birthdate. She'd felt too dense and groggy last night. She let Cathy see that her birthdate held significance. The woman didn't know what Celine had said. But she could know, from Lois and through Mark, about Celine's eerie foretelling and that maybe Erin knew too much or even guessed. There was no proof. That old adage about murder getting easier each successive time fit. The act eventually became an answer to stress and an acceptable response mechanism.

Erin's phone rang. Melanie's shaking, high-pitched voice came on the line.

"Erin, I'm scared. I didn't know who to call. A person phoned telling me I have something dangerous, and that I planned to blackmail them." She choked. "But I don't, and I wouldn't. Can you pick me up and find me a place to stay now?"

"I'll be right over, Melanie. Don't go outside, and make sure everything's locked up."

Melanie gasped. "I was warned not to tell anyone, so come in alone and quiet."

"Maybe sit down and try to relax. I'll be right there."

Erin, remembering her promise to be careful, dialled Celine's number.

"*Non*! Do not go out there!"

"Celine! I haven't said hello yet, and you don't have caller ID."

"I know someone wants your *aide*." Celine's voice shook. "The phone emits shadows and foggy *photos*. All is not *bien* there."

"It's Melanie. She's scared. I'm going to pick her up to bring someplace safe."

"*Oui*, Melanie, *c'est vrai,* now that makes sense. She has dark clouds around her. I can't tell if they are her darkness or another's."

Erin's voice carried harshly. "You're wrong. That nice woman's not a danger. I'll be fine with her."

"*Mais*, we need to take the precautions. You cannot blunder into another disaster. Taurus people are abroad *ce soir*."

"Fine. Then call Gladys. She's able to see the front of their building. Tell her to keep a lookout for me. I'm going to help the woman."

"Wait, I'll call Luke, *mais* I have nothing exact to call about."

"I'm picking up Melanie because she's scared. Besides, I'll call Luke later. I need to tell him about seeing Cathy's late April birthdate. She's a Taurus. You told me to check the date. But I don't think that'll impress him, do you?"

35

eline tapped a finger on the counter while waiting for Gladys to answer the phone. "*Vraiment,* Gladys. It is Celine *ici.* I want to tell you that Erin is going to pick up Melanie, who is terrified, *mais* I am *très* worried. Can you keep an eye out the window for her?"

"I'll call Mark to come over, but he won't go anywhere alone. I need to make sure someone is with him. Do you want him to pick you up as a safeguard?"

"*Oui,* at least we will discuss the strategy at your place and worry together."

Celine hung up and dithered a bit. Then she paced, almost tumbled, and grabbed the table. "*Comment!* Is the floor shifting, or am I dizzy? No, I see ground sliding and an earthquake happening." She sat and stared down at the linoleum floor while her cats meowed and wound their bodies around her legs. "I will call Gladys back." When she answered, Celine asked, "Do you see anything, *ma vieille?*"

"Erin went in the front door of the building. She hasn't come back out. Neither has Melanie. Mark will arrive at your place soon."

Celine released her breath when Adam and Janelle drove into the yard. She begged them to go and check on Erin. When Celine picked up her coat and cane, she saw the sweater that Erin left on the chair last night. "If she is cold or full of mud, she needs to cover up." She shook her head. "I am way over the reacting this time. She cannot be in an earthquake if she is in the building across from Gladys." *If* was the big word, she thought.

After his last lecture from Luke, Adam told Celine he needed to be upfront, and he phoned and caught Luke before he left the office. Celine listened while Adam talked. "Janelle and I will keep an eye on Erin, who's checking up on Melanie. She called, scared witless, and Celine's getting bad vibes. Janelle wants us to go, too. I've Major in case there's trouble."

Luke's exclamation of annoyance could be heard over the phone by all three of them. "If Celine is that anxious, I'll get Jackson and meet you out there. Melanie hasn't lived with the other two long enough for the killer to think she knows something."

Celine hoped Melanie wasn't the murderer. She remembered Erin talking about Melanie's expertise with the ribbon dance. The girls developed great control and co-ordination and strong wrists with the practice. But what reasons would the young woman have? There was nothing to gain. Celine watched Adam and Janelle leave with Major in the truck. Five minutes later, Mark arrived to pick her up.

He held the door open for her. "You're protecting me if they're luring us into a trap. Can you be my alibi if we find more bodies?"

"*Vraiment.* I am worried it may be Erin's body we find this time."

Erin knocked at the apartment door and got no response. Nervous shivers twitched up and down her body when she tried the handle and found the door unlocked. She eased in while calling Melanie's name, flicked on the light switch in the shadows, and flicked open her jackknife. "Melanie, I'm here. It's Erin."

Staring into corners and sliding through the small rooms, she spotted a note perched on the kitchen table. The words were jumbled, and the writing was distorted. She read that Melanie heard someone scraping at the window latch and would be hiding down in the laundry room. Erin checked the bedroom window. The latch appeared pried open. She looked under the bed and inside the closets, not finding Melanie. "Guess I'm going down to the basement."

Back at the entry, she located the laundry room door and flicked on the basement light. She didn't meet any other tenants. Where did they all go? They would be wary, seeing her with a knife. Erin held the weapon tight against her side and crept down the stairs, trying not to think about how a monster could reach out and snag her leg with each leery step taken like in old horror movies. All seemed quiet. Too quiet. "Melanie? It's Erin. You can come out now. You're safe." Looking behind the stairs, Erin spotted a basement door ajar. She must have run. Erin closed her knife and eased the door open to slide through the narrow opening, finding herself behind the building facing the overgrown trail to the river. "Darn, I don't have my bear spray with me, but I can't waste time getting back to the car. Her life might be in danger."

The evening held enough light. Erin peered around and wandered down the overgrown pathway till she came to a fork in the lanes. On the ground, to the left, she recognized Melanie's ornate hair clip, picked it up, and started down that path. She tried to walk on the grassy edge to quiet her footsteps, becoming nervous about startling a lurking animal. She centred herself in the path, away from the bushes. "I think this takes me to the opposite side of the river from Mr. Fraser's cottage."

Erin's thoughts were scrambled, and she hesitated a moment. Should she make noise to keep the bears away or stay silent to help Melanie? She opted to stay quiet, but with her hands shaking slightly, she cleared her throat, a subtle noise. She scanned the bushes before snapping her jackknife open again.

Luke arrived to see Mark climbing the stairs of the Manor and followed to check if Celine heard anything else. Celine sat with Gladys, who spoke to her grandson. "Mark, tell Adam there's another way out through the laundry room in the basement."

Celine's hand went to her head. "*Pardon*. Erin is not in there. She is in the bush and in danger. You must find her."

Mark glanced at Luke. "Celine has us all in a panic. What if Adam guards the front with Major, and I go around the back with Janelle beside me? You're the investigator. You go in."

Luke nodded and hurried with Jackson behind him. When he passed the open door of the apartment, he skulked through the rooms with his gun drawn. There was nobody there. He spotted the open bedroom window and read the crumpled note. The two men hurried down to the laundry room and spotted the open doorway. There, they ran back outside and determined the elderly women couldn't see anything from that angle. He scooted to the front, checking the perimeter, before conferring with Adam.

Celine came out and met him at the entrance. "Luke, she will need this sweater when she is cold and full of mud."

Luke regarded her quizzically, barring himself from asking why Erin would be muddy. She would be. It made sense, right?

After listening, Adam hurried over and took the sweater from Celine. "I have a better idea, sir. Track, Major." The dog sniffed Erin's sweater, woofed, and crossed before waiting at the entry to the apartment building. He sniffed a trail through the hall to the unlocked apartment door and moved quickly ahead of Luke and Adam. Major sniffed through the rooms and backpedalled before moving down the basement stairs. They trailed the snuffling dog to the ajar rear door. Luke and Adam followed the dog outside to meet with Mark and Janelle, who had circled the building. The dog raised his head and, smelling something in the air, woofed and veered over to the sheds and garages. The others followed, stopping when the dog sniffed and howled at a tarp on the ground.

Mark groaned. "Oh, no, not again." The men pulled off the tarps. A dark-haired girl lay prone on the ground, unconscious.

"It's Melanie." Luke checked her. "She's still breathing; it looks like blood from a head wound." He pulled out his cell and called for an ambulance and immediate police backup—no flashing lights or sirens. Then he covered her with Erin's sweater for warmth. "Jackson: you, Mark, and Janelle stay with her. Adam and I will follow Major down the trail. The dog, sniffing again at the sweater, put his nose to the ground, circling.

Starting off, Luke phoned Mr. Fraser, quickly rattled off the situation, and asked him to try and spot Erin from his side of the river. He didn't know if the old fellow could make his way to the top of the hill. If his friend was there drinking coffee, he could help Fraser set up. Maybe he could spot something in his rifle's scope before it became too dark.

38

Erin slid down the rocks near the river, skidding to a stop a few yards away from the rigid woman. Erin eyed the threatening rifle aimed at her and tried to act nonchalant.

"Hello, Cathy. What have you done with Melanie?"

"I wore a mask and made her call you, then knocked her out. She didn't see me, so I'm safe. I didn't need to kill the twit. I needed a ruse to get you out here. I dropped her hair comb to entice you down the right path."

"Why, Cathy?" Erin waved her free arm. "Why all this? What did you hope to gain by killing all these people? No one would care about Craig's affairs."

"Sheila would, especially with me involved. She always wanted to be one up on me and gloated over stealing him from me. I let her think she won. I kept the peace."

"But, why all these murders?" Erin kept her voice from shaking. "And why trap me?"

"I sensed that my birthdate told you something, and the way Mark talked about your elderly psychic friend caused me plenty of worry. My grandmother had native blood and knew things: she had visions. She was as bizarre as people said—maybe I am, too."

"What did these people know that proved dangerous enough for you to commit murder?"

"I can tell you. Jewel came to the office late one day without warning and caught Craig and I in a compromising situation— literally caught us with our pants down. She reacted in such anger and threatened to tell Sheila about us. I wasn't letting that happen." She tossed her head back and sneered. "I'm on the fringes of the elite as it is. Sheila would cut me and Craig off if she found out. We've both become too accustomed to the rich side of life and her bounty to change now. I know we Taurus people like to keep what we have, and we're resourceful enough to resort to emergency tactics."

Erin felt her only chance was to keep the woman talking. "But why not tell Jewel to go ahead, that his wife wouldn't care."

"No way. Sheila wouldn't like the repercussions in her circle. Jewel kept screaming that she would tell his wife that he screwed his secretary and her, that the two of us carried on and laughed behind her back."

"And Sheila would hate that. Did you not try reasoning with her?"

"Sure. Such a silly bitch: unworldly. And dumb Craig stood there with his mouth and fly open, trying to zip up his pants."

"But then you let her go. I suppose Craig wouldn't help you get rid of her."

"I may love the guy, but I know what a weakling he is. I convinced the idiot woman there was money in it for her to keep quiet. Told her she'd be telling on herself. She knew he was married. That Jewel whined, saying that he told her it was a marriage of convenience."

"She was young and insecure, Cathy."

"She was stupid. She came out with me to the lodge, later. I told her Craig wanted to see her and make plans. I killed her there and planned to bury the body, but the ground around the lodge was too hard. I threw her ID in a hole I dug. Then I wrapped the body in plastic and drove to that loose, mucky place across from Fraser's."

"Won't Craig get suspicious of you always clearing the way for him?"

"Even if he did, so what?" Cathy shrugged. "His mind would deny implications and block unpleasant thoughts. He avoids thinking. He's frozen in his narrow quest for sexual gratification."

"How did you trick Kelly? I thought you must have waited with her unconscious body till you lined up Mark to play the role of fall guy."

"You screwed up that plan. Now it's payback time. That Kelly wasn't nervous being with a woman. And that lowlife Lester was no problem either.

Erin slid a foot forward again. "But three murders, Cathy?"

"Four, with you. Those women and the lowlife were no loss. The creep snapped a picture, a photocopy I lost." Cathy smiled. "Enough nonsense. I dug this hole out of the soft mud to make you a grave. They won't think to look for you here. I'll bury you deep."

"But no one has evidence to prove you guilty of the murders." Erin tried to keep the woman boasting to buy more time. "You proved too smart and were home free except for the dog's interference." Erin took another sliding step toward the woman.

"Stay there." Cathy aimed the gun at her. "I know all about your dangerous arms and legs. And that knife you're hiding is useless. You're not getting near me, and I'm a crack shot. Buried my best .22 repeater after that damn dog took a bullet. This 12-gauge shotgun will blast you apart, not pepper you. I'm using a double 0 load of buckshot, but you're not savvy about guns. I'll toss in your body parts when I've blown you away."

Erin peered to the trees at the side. What if she somersaulted down and hid? How many shots would Cathy have available?

"Don't bother to run. My finger is faster than your jump, and I can track you."

Erin glanced up at a slight movement on the slope far above Cathy. Her hands clenched while her heart fluttered and seemed to stop. She found that abject fear can escalate. A huge black bear stood and sniffed the air above them. She almost shrieked. "Use your first shot for that bear standing right above you on the hill, Cathy."

"You don't expect me to fall for that old gag. I know you fear bears, but I've lived in these woods for years and hunted."

"Cathy, I'm serious." Erin, with a trembling running up her legs, began sliding backwards toward some trees. A dog barked in the distance.

"That damn dog is a cripple like Fraser. No help for you there. I won't have to waste more shots on him, and your body won't be found."

BETTY GUENETTE

"You're wrong. A dog can track the scent. Luke will find out that it's you unless you're planning on casting the blame on Craig."

"I have a much better idea. I'm arranging for dear, sweet Sheila to be arrested. Our profiles are the same. I only need to add a few touches to push her into the investigation's limelight. What a coup for all the years she's wronged me. Then Craig gets control of her money, and I get control of Craig. Like your friend hung up on astrology knows, we Taurus people crave money and the security it brings."

Erin took deep breaths to relax her vibrating limbs while watching the bear and Cathy. She slid her feet back more. "How did Kelly and Lester get involved?"

"You're stalling for time and help, but I'll tell you anyway. I want to brag about my cunning. Each one believed themselves the smartest and finally threatened and blackmailed Craig. I came in late, heard this Kelly on my office phone, and Craig did intend to meet her. I drugged his coffee and met her myself and clubbed her over the head when we reached my car. She wasn't worried about a woman being a killer. I took Mark's ring from his desk, only you followed too close and backed him up. No time to frame him for murder, even when they found the ring as evidence clutched in the woman's hand."

"But didn't Craig know you killed Kelly?" She slid another foot back in the wet mud.

"He supposed it was his good luck. That Lester guy was dumb enough to leave a message on the private line, which I got, of course. Then he dropped off a note. The creep trailed Jewel a couple of times hoping for money, and he shadowed Kelly, too."

A shot rang out across the river, impacting the ground beside the bear, spraying dirt and pebbles, and setting off a mudslide above Cathy and the newly dug grave.

100

Luke and Adam sighed in exasperation at coming to the divided fork in the trail. Major kept sniffing, circling a way down each side, before giving a soft woof and starting down the left branch. "We can't break up, Adam. There may be other split trails. We have to trust your dog."

They hurried forward, following Major, slipping and sliding on the shifting ground but always descending closer to the river. Adam flopped backwards onto his butt twice and jumped right back up, not bothering to swipe the mud off his pants. Major ignored him, still sniffing and tracking along the side of the narrow path. Occasionally, he stopped and zigzagged to sniff the center of the path and then barked, refocused, and carried on. The lower they descended the path, the stronger the smell of water became. They were startled when they heard a rifle shot and a fearsome rumble. The two men hurried after the agile dog to climb over the rocks and slide over the mud in the thickening shadows. Luke pulled out his gun. Major started to bark.

101

The bear roared and jumped, careening down along with the mud over the perilous slope. The bear rode toward and over Cathy, and the woman glanced up too late as she screamed and dropped the gun before toppling sideways into the open grave. Mud and rocks filled the hole with the woman buried beneath the mudslide. The bear slid further on its rump, bawling and leaping all the way to the bottom of the hill till only a few rocks clattered.

Edging backwards, Erin heard the bear coming down, squealing. She turned and raced away from the bear and the cascade of rock and mud. She dropped her knife when she grabbed the branch of a large tree and hauled herself up while the edge of the mucky flow banged against her shoes and slid beneath and past the base of the tree, bending the trunk forward before the landslide finished its cascade.

Another roar from the angry, injured bear sent her adrenaline soaring. She climbed higher, grabbing a few more branches to haul herself up. The stealthy movement of the animal alarmed her as it ambled awkwardly back up the hill toward her perched position in the tree. Her skin ran icy cold from the top of her head to the tips of her toes, and her body seemed to shut down. She shook herself, trying to wake her numb brain, make herself think, and be a survivor. "Yikes! Bill said bears climb trees, and I think this one blames me for its misfortune, and its coming after me now." Erin cried out in dismay when she realized she had dropped her knife in the muck.

BETTY GUENETTE

The bear drew near, stopping numerous times to lick a paw, then shuffled closer on three legs. It sniffed the air and roared again. When the massive beast reached her tree, it clawed the bark with its good paw. Then, the animal growled and tried to climb but licked the sore paw before getting a good foothold and heaving its bulky body upward after her.

She climbed higher again. Her reach would only take her up a few more branches. She tried to stop hyperventilating, knowing she'd grow faint and land at the bear's feet. "If I hadn't dropped my knife, I'd need to turn upside down to use it. Then I'd likely get another slice off my face." She hoped she wasn't delirious. She glanced away from the bear's horrid, thick head and beady eyes and tried to yell and shout, making ominous tones to try and scare it away. Her resulting gasps sounded more like moans. Then, she remembered the whistle attached to her pouch. The noise could frighten the bear away. She fumbled for it with one free hand and raised the muddy whistle to her lips to blow.

Pfft! The damn thing was blocked. She shook the whistle, trying to dislodge the mud encased inside. No go. She spat into it and rubbed it against her muddy clothes. *Pfft!* This thing was a total loss unless she threw the useless thing at the bugger.

Erin clung to the tree, realizing she couldn't go any higher. She could use one foot to kick the bear on the snout. No, the jaws would clamp down on her foot and drag her off her perilous perch. Her body quaked with dread, and she felt her bladder let go. How embarrassing if they found her soggy body later. Her mind was flitting around in spirals. Did she think that spraying urine on its head would disturb the beast?

She glanced back down, sorry she had. The animal licked its paw, grumbled, and climbed higher. She eyed the shortening space between herself and the bear. The bear flicked its head around to gaze off in the distance. Then, Erin heard it. The sound of barking getting louder and closer. The bear turned, crawled backwards, and leapt down, running away with a limp on all four legs into the far bushes. She stared toward the trail. That bark sounded like Major. The German shepherd burst out of the trees and pranced over the slippery, oozing mud, approaching her with an exultant bark. She spotted Adam and Luke coming down the hill, trying to stay upright as they slid and sidestepped past branches and marked debris on their way down the muddy pathway.

102

Erin called out, turned sideways, then descended to the lower branches, dangling her feet till she tested each sturdy limb. She found the way down more difficult than the upward climb. Well, the bear was chasing her, and her adrenaline was surging then. Edging onto the last branch, her muddy boot slipped, and she toppled sideways to roll and splatter face down in the muck. She pushed her arms in the guck, found traction, and held up her upper body to better breathe. Major licked her ear, not her mud-encrusted face, gave a soft woof, and tilted his head, seeming to ask if he found the right person. She managed to move and sit by sloshing and tumbling onto a log and hugged Major before Luke and Adam reached her. "Luke, the murderer must be dead under that mudslide."

"Cathy or Sheila?"

"Cathy. I only guessed because Celine emphasized the date being important. When I read that she was an April Taurus, I gave my suspicions away to her. I had suspected Sheila."

"That subtle information's a little abnormal. We can discuss it later." Both tired men stood, slightly bent, a short distance from mud-encrusted Erin sitting on a rotting log before them, not that their clothes weren't mud-spattered, too.

"I found Melanie's hair brooch... on the trail... Cathy said she didn't kill her?"

"Major found Melanie knocked out under a tarp. She's hurt but should be okay. Cathy must have used her as a lure to catch you unawares. You mentioned helping her out."

Luke assessed the area and asked Erin for the location of the grave.

"Right below where that big boulder fell." Erin pointed and shuddered. "She dug the hole for my body. The bear and mudslide flung her into it. Maybe because of that gunshot I heard."

Luke looked over at Adam petting his dog, proud as a new parent. "I saw the bear climb down, and then you fell out of the tree. Did you hurt yourself?"

"Only my dignity." With all this mud, they wouldn't know she'd peed herself when the bear climbed the tree after her. "I'm cold, wet and need a bath."

"Celine sensed that and sent you a sweater, but I put it over Melanie. The dog tracked you from the smell on it. I'll find a blanket when we get back—if you're up to the trek. I can help you." He glanced at the equally muddy, younger policeman. "Adam, hurry back up the path. When you get within range, try your cell. Tell them Erin's okay and we're on our way back. Also, call in for an excavator and crew." He waved. "I see Jackson coming down, he must have followed us."

Erin peered around, noting the forest's growing shadows but no other animals. "Keep Major with us in case that bear's hanging around. It's in one foul mood. Damn, I lost my jackknife too." She looked up at Luke. "Do you know who shot at us?"

"Must have been Mr. Fraser. I don't think he could see either of you from that angle. We asked him to keep a lookout from his hill if he could."

"The bear was high on that rock, though. He probably gave it a warning shot, thinking it was stalking us. His action saved my life and killed Cathy."

"I'd say that was a good trade-off. The old fellow will feel bad, though, since he spent time with the girl when she grew up here."

At the top of the rise, the ambulance loaded Melanie while the police sifted the area for evidence. Jackson had followed Luke and Adam at a distance. Once the other police cars arrived, Luke instructed him to lead the others to the burial site.

When Adam returned, he filled in Mark and Janelle, and they went inside to sit with the elderly women to ease their minds. Adam said he was too dirty and stayed outside waiting for Luke, Erin, and Major. When they returned, Erin told the whole story before going home. She wrapped the blanket from one of the ambulances tight around her body and stood inside the Manor's door. "At least I'm only caked in mud and not dripping wet."

They spotted Mr. Cresswell wandering around, watching the events with avid curiosity. Mrs. Billings peeped out her window. Many curtains and windows throughout the Manor were opened, with faces peering out. They didn't plan on missing out on anything. Mr. Cresswell approached Adam to say he spotted a van parked down the trail behind the manor. Checking the license plate and make of the car, Adam recognized the vehicle as Cathy's. He frowned when the press began pulling into the lot behind the other vehicles and went over to warn Luke.

Luke glanced around. "Lucky the media hasn't found us here. The elders are having a field day. I'll leave Jackson with the backup crew to get started, bring the ladies home, get the info from Erin, and then come back and check on our progress with the excavator." He hurried Erin and Celine to the car as the first camera flashes went off.

Mark stayed the night with his grandmother to discuss the murder. He figured the other residents might be along to gossip with them soon. He didn't want her to tire herself out with all the commotion.

Luke asked Adam and Janelle to check up on Mr. Fraser and let him know the evening's results. He told them to make sure the trapper got safely back inside his cabin. He didn't want to worry that the elderly man fell outside while watching and shooting at an angry bear, one still on the loose. He also checked with Jackson about arrangements for the excavator and equipment to dig up Cathy's body. There wasn't a chance she would be found alive under that slide, but they had to make the effort. The group set up lights as dusk settled in. He warned Jackson to keep his gun handy, keep an eye out for the injured bear, and make sure the workers were protected.

At least they avoided talking to the press. Luke, Erin, and Celine sat quietly on the drive home, all immersed in their own thoughts. Erin shivered occasionally. Her mind didn't shut down. She wasn't sure how she'd retrieve her car, though it was a stupid thing to worry about now; she was incapable of driving herself tonight.

Luke glanced over. "I turned the heater on."

"I'm not really cold. It's a delayed adrenaline reaction, I guess." She roused herself and told them as much as she remembered about her confrontation with Cathy. "She was besotted with that man, and being a typical Taurus, she didn't want the game plan to change. Do you think Craig and Sheila's marriage will last, Celine?"

"With no trial, *peut-être*. There will be much news reporting. *Je ne sais pas*. Craig won't change, *mais* he may become more guarded with his affairs. The Taurus sign doesn't like to correct their lifestyle, good or bad. He'll need to get a new office, likely on his own with all the gossip and Mark kicking him out."

"It seems futile, unnecessary to use murder as such a dramatic solution. I was horrified that Cathy was intent to keep on killing."

Celine leaned forward from the back. "The bad ones get a taste for it, *je pense*. You would have become more frightened when the bear *arrive*, *Chérie*, than fear being shot."

"I was. Cathy intended to kill me, and I couldn't have prevented her. But a shot is a fast death compared to a bear ripping you apart and chewing you while you're alive. I get nightmares from my childhood, and I'll likely get more now." Erin sighed. "I'm lucky she wanted to brag about how she fooled everyone. She planned on incriminating Sheila next."

When they arrived at the house, Luke got out, went around, and helped Celine out first. Erin had already opened her door, stepped out, and leaned on it.

Celine hurried home with a wink at Erin, bidding them, "*Au revoir*."

Luke offered his arm to help Erin to the stairs.

"I'm not hurt, Luke: only filthy, shaken, and a bit scratched up."

"My offer as a great back washer stands. I need a shower, too."

Erin shook her head. "I told you that I'm not into one-night stands."

"Oh, I think we'd have more than one night. You're addictive, and I know you're not immune to our sexual attraction." Luke grinned at her with heated eyes. "You vibrate like a coiled spring when I'm with you. I want to make sure I'm around when that spring releases." He sighed. "However, I need to get back to the crime scene. When we do finally spend quality time together, I want the whole night to savour your company."

Erin stopped inside the door and gave him a cross look. "You're being difficult and unreasonable again, Luke."

"Again? I'm only stating the obvious about our mutual attraction. I can take a rain check on our inevitable pursuits. With your penchant for finding bodies and attracting their murderers, I think we'll clash, and sparks will fly soon. *Bonne nuit,* Erin."

ACKNOWLEDGEMENTS

Story set in early millennium around the Greater Sudbury district. Positive or negative response, the astrology signs are simply fun.

Thanks to my daughter, Karen Guenette, and her husband, Pierre Bradley, for some basic knowledge of Chinese culture, touched on when they travelled to China and adopted a delightful, ten-month-old baby girl, Arielle Shan, now attending Laurentian University. Special thanks to the Chinese community for benevolent acceptance of our family into their sphere and for our attendance at their various gatherings, especially Karen Chen and Joan Hum.

Thanks to my nephew, Mark Henry, for his knowledge of rifles, ammunition, and hunting lore, plus his take on the elements of fur trapping and his pelt retrieval information.

A blessing for my sisters, Gail Payne, Gloria March, and Janice Henry for reading my first endeavors and for always being there when needed.

I value our Sudbury Writers' Guild's continuing support and input. The group knows I'm quiet, but a not-so-subtle warning—I sop up information and write.

Thanks to my medical workers and friends for assistance over the 45 years of my nursing career.

Thanks to my husband Norm, children, Lori, Karl, Karen and Paul, plus seven grandchildren-Jade, Rane and Reena Gibbs, Arielle and Sophie Bradley, and Xavier and Felix Guenette.

To Renaissance Press always; I appreciate and thank you.

Betty Biggs Guenette, BScN., Métis.

If you enjoyed this book, please consider leaving a review where you bought it.

You may also enjoy these other Renaissance titles